HUNTER ON THE SLY

Hunter on the Sly

Donna J. Evans

This novel's story and characters are fictitious. Certain long-standing institutions, agencies, and public offices are mentioned, but the characters involved are wholly imaginary. Some actual place names exist; however, details ascribed to them are fiction. For example, Steamboat Lake and Columbine Store exist, while the bandstand and Columbine Campground are the author's creations. Some events, such as the fire at the sawdust pile, are drawn from the author's memory.

To my husband and our nine children, the loves
of my life.

Prologue

The elk was not shot but the decision was made. Today was the hunter's last day to stalk his game. He possessed a coveted cow elk license, but he had been unable to get close to his prey. Ordinarily he would enjoy the company of a hunting party made up of friends and business associates, out for the annual respite from the real world. This year was different. There was no holiday atmosphere.

Earlier in the afternoon, he had glimpsed another solitary hunter but avoided contact. He had no desire to share hunting stories. He camped alone, cooked alone, drank alone, and slept alone. He had needed solitude to think and to plan his course of action. Now he knew what he must do, and he sought satisfaction in besting his quarry.

A movement caught the hunter's eye. Below, by the stream, stood a cow elk. She was sleek and fat, ready for the cold winter about to engulf her. She lowered her head to the water to quench her thirst after a long day of rest, preparing to graze under cover of night. The hunter removed the safety on his Sako .300 Magnum rifle, pressed the stock to his shoulder, and aimed through the telescopic sight. Slowly he squeezed the cold, hard trigger, carefully aiming at the elk's heart.

A shot rang out and echoed around the forested hills. The elk abruptly raised her head and fled as the bundled figure above on the hill collapsed, dying, in the gathering darkness and cold. His rifle clattered raucously down the slope.

1

Jean Branning woke Sunday morning to the aroma of fresh coffee, crackling bacon, and warm maple syrup. She felt before she saw the rising sun's glow peeking over the curtains into her bedroom. Jean opened her eyes. Come to think of it, this wasn't home. She was in a tiny room at one end of her camp trailer.

Jean snuggled into the warmth of the comforter while she listened to her family come to life.

"Dad, what's the altitude here?" Matt asked, his voice skipping an octave as he studied the topographic map's legend. Thirteen-year-old Matt was always asking about elevations, distances, and all the things that his father knew by heart.

Jean heard the sound of a metal spatula scraping the bottom of the cast iron skillet. Chad must be cooking breakfast. She smelled pancakes and bacon, and heard grease crackling as it was moved around in a pan. Chad is good at flipping pancakes without breaking them, Jean mused, and he can fry bacon to crispy perfection, between chewy and scorched.

"We're at about 7000 feet, far enough north that winter weather can be severe," Chad replied. "You should see how deep some of the drifts get in winter. Later we'll go find one and pack some snow into a cooler to keep the pop cold."

"You mean there's no clean ice?" Josie said, disgust written on her face. Jean knew how much Josie loved to chew ice and that she was probably thinking about water without ice, tea without ice, a summer without ice. Not to mention the absence of friends and the family telephone, a landline. While cell phones were gaining popularity, Jean's family had just purchased one for the summer, but the cost of roaming was too high. More important, there was no cell service at the campground. The office had a phone inside, restricted to official campground business. That meant the payphone near the office was the only means for Josie to communicate with friends in the outside world.

Jean commiserated with her daughter in that this was the summer before Josie's senior year in high school. Her daughter seethed with indignation and resentment at being torn away from the familiar in this last carefree school break, though she hid it most of the time. Next year, work and college would commandeer her time.

"Yes, we'll have ice," Chad said, turning another pancake. "We can buy it from the Columbine store. But snow is here for the taking. We might as well use it in the extra cooler to keep pop and beer cold."

"What are we going to do today?" Matt asked, sunshine streaming in through the window behind him, outlining his silhouette.

"Mom's the boss—she'll tell us what to do," Chad said. "Since we've never been campground hosts before, and this is a new campground, we need to organize and prepare for campers to arrive."

Jean, dressed in jeans and a sweatshirt, opened the bedroom door, and slipped onto the closest end of the u-shaped bench. She sat next to Kelsie, her youngest, avoiding getting in Chad's way. Matt and Josie sat against the window wall, and Ty was opposite Jean, sitting in his dad's spot. Glasses, plates, and tableware surrounded a pitcher of orange juice.

"I'd love to hike by Whiskey Creek," Jean mused. "But I think we'll have to wait until we set up camp."

His back to the table, Chad said, "I'm glad we had a chance yesterday afternoon to take a good look around the campground. There isn't much to do right now. You and the kids should have some free time this week to explore."

"It's nice here, isn't it?" commented Jean. "I wonder how much publicity has gone out about today's opening. I can't imagine it filling right away, but by the Fourth of July, I hope it'll be packed."

The U.S. Forest Service had built the new campground near Hahn's Peak because so many people were crossing the Continental Divide from the crowded east side of Colorado for outdoor recreation. The Forest Service decided the time had come to provide services. Officials hoped to limit RV and trailer camping, and some tent camping, to developed sites where clean water, sanitation, and garbage service would make the campers' stays more pleasant as well as minimize environmental damage. No more soggy mattresses, rancid garbage, and odd pieces of clothing and shoes left behind as Jean had seen in the past, she hoped. Or exposed piles of toilet paper and human waste. The little town of Columbine, consisting of one lone store, provided the perfect anchor for the first site, and Jean was the first host at Columbine Campground.

Jean took mental stock of the facility. The shower houses and restrooms would be easy to clean—they were finished with durable materials. The firewood shed was stocked with bundles. All she and her family needed to do was put brochures in the pockets of the information board and at the registration window.

Jean gazed out the window beyond her children at the framed panorama. A varied palette of green spread out before her—lush tall grasses, majestic Ponderosa pines, and pale aspen leaves fluttering against the clean blue sky. Flowers—blue and white columbines, white yarrow, lavender tansies, and more—spattered pops of color across the verdant canvas like those of a Monet painting, but sharper and brighter.

"Can you believe this view?" Jean asked, waving her hand toward the window. "We'll have enough shade from the trees in the afternoon to keep us cool, and just look at the scenery—it's gorgeous!"

This was exactly what Jean had envisioned when she applied for the job, the area where she'd spent week-long camping vacations with her parents as a child and young teen. Blue skies, high mountains, the rock spire of Hahn's Peak, and tall trees. A meadow carpeted with flowers, butterflies floating above them and bees skipping from blossom to blossom. Outside the trailer, a lark sang from the top of a small blue spruce set against denser forest. The constant ache she'd felt in her neck and shoulders over the past few months began to subside.

"Mom, can we go fishing?" asked eleven-year-old Ty. He had one eye on the stove, eager to get breakfast out of the way so he could go into the meadow and practice dribbling, and bounced a soccer ball off his knee.

"How about early tomorrow morning? Dawn and dusk are good times to test the water. Maybe we'll catch some brook trout for breakfast." Jean said, leaning on the table, tilting her head to make eye contact with her younger son. "And be careful where that ball bounces."

"Sure," Ty muttered, not looking at Jean.

"I want to play in the stream," said Kelsie, ten years old and always eager to get into the water. She had joined swim team last summer and earned a series of blue ribbons for personal best times. But the closest swimming pool was in Steamboat, too far away to take her to regular practices and too expensive for the Brannings' current circumstances.

Jean put her left arm around her daughter. "Kelsie, it's too cold. We'll have to wait for a warm afternoon. There'll be plenty of opportunities."

Kelsie shrugged.

Chad set platters of steaming pancakes and golden-brown bacon on the table and stepped back. Jean read pride and satisfaction on his face. She knew that Chad savored the prospect of spending the summer here with family. Their children's voices receded into the background as she reflected on what had brought them here.

Last fall, Chad had accepted a temporary position in Steamboat Springs as an engineering consultant. The phenomenon of the 90s, downsizing, was reemerging in the new millennium as rightsizing, catching him in its talons for the second time. From Jean's perspective, there was nothing right about this: not the pay, not the time he had already spent away from family, not the potential relocation of her family away from extended family and friends, not the assault on professional identities. Downsizing compelled current and former employees to ponder career changes, learn how employment insurance works, consider cashing in retirement accounts, and accept help from friends and neighbors in order to get by until a new job was secured. The irony, though, was that few existing or new jobs would provide security, not in the sense that her father's generation had known it.

Although Chad's current pay wasn't as good as it had been at the food processing plant, Jean was grateful that it was enough to provide for their family until something more permanent came along. They could pay the mortgage and other essential bills, and they could buy food and gas.

For a few short months, this small trailer would be home, and Chad wouldn't have to make the grueling drive over the Rockies to their actual home in Loveland every weekend. Their family would be together at the campground, just thirty miles from Chad's job in Steamboat Springs.

"Chow's on—let's eat!" Chad announced, signaling Ty to scoot over, and sat down across from Jean.

For now, Jean thought, they had food on the table and a safe place to sleep. They had each other. What more did they really need?

§

Jean assigned jobs to each of the kids, and the work went fast. Josie supplied the bathrooms with paper towels and tissue, then wiped the sinks and mirrors until they sparkled. Since the toilets had not yet been used, she checked to be sure that deodorizers were in each, finishing by sweeping a light layer of dust and a few dead insects from the floors. Matt made rounds through the 30-unit campground, lining all the garbage cans with trash bags. He returned to his family's campsite and strung clothesline between two tree trunks, wrapping the cord around branch stubs. Ty tested water hydrants to make sure they worked and filled a bucket to keep beside the Brannings' fire pit, getting drenched in the process. Kelsie helped Jean and Chad unpack the van, carrying and depositing items where she was told. She soon tired of this, though, and wandered off after butterflies and wildflowers.

"Remember not to pick the flowers, Kelsie," warned Jean. "It's against the law in a national forest."

"Why?" asked Ty, as he eyed a bunch of blue and white Colorado columbines.

"If everyone who comes into the public forest picks flowers, takes rocks, and digs up young trees, soon we wouldn't have any forests left. 'Take only pictures, leave only footprints.' It's a good motto for all of us," replied Jean.

The sound of a diesel engine chugging up the hill drew their attention to the road. Dust drifted through the trees and sunlight glinted off the chrome trim of a large RV as it ambled around the last bend leading to the campground. Jean looked at her watch, happy that the first campers were arriving. It was just past noon. The campground was officially open.

Jean walked to the office at the entrance of the campground, about a hundred feet away from her camper. She opened the window for her first customer and waited. A man in his late sixties slid down from his seat in the RV and approached the small log building.

"I need a campsite for a week for my wife and myself. Do you have a space off by itself?" the man asked, his manner brusque.

The man's cool tone wasn't what Jean expected. She turned the site map 90 degrees to point out the camp's layout.

"You're our first campers, so you have your pick of sites on the lower loop," said Jean, looking up with a welcoming smile.

"I said I want a space by itself. Just tell me where to park," said the man.

Jean's smile faded. She touched a spot on the map. "I recommend #10, although you'll be farther from the shower houses than if you choose some of the others."

"I don't care about that. How much is it?" he said.

"Fifteen dollars per day," said Jean.

The man grunted and reached into his back pocket for his wallet. The man didn't want to talk, so Jean handed him a clipboard that held a pen and registration form. He scribbled the required information, pausing to walk to the front of his RV and copy his license plate number. Returning the clipboard to the counter, along with payment for seven days, he turned his back and walked away.

"Thank you!" Jean called after him. "Have a good stay!" The man climbed into his RV without another word. With a deep knock, the diesel engine sputtered to life and carried the couple to their campsite.

Jean, taken aback by the man's churlishness, watched the RV until it was out of sight. She remembered the campgrounds of her youth as places to meet interesting people and make long-term friends, people you would enjoy camping with the next time you vacationed. Once, on her parents' wedding anniversary, a woman they had met the previous summer in the same campground baked them a cake to celebrate. But the last thing this man seemed to want was to engage in idle conversation, make new friends, or be neighborly.

Jean learned from the registration form that her first guests were Henry and Joyce Gowen, and they lived in Denver. These were no snowbirds migrating north for the summer. The Western Slope and Steamboat area were in their backyard. Jean wasn't surprised they had made this campground their destination, though. While it took time to get here, travel was easy once outside the metro area. But she was disappointed that she might not be able to get to know them. Jean liked people and was curious about their lives.

With a sigh, Jean turned around and surveyed the spartan office. She labeled some shelves for forms and other papers, and looked around for a place to stow the cash box. The shelf to the right and below the window would work for it, far enough out of reach that it wouldn't tempt some unscrupulous passerby but close enough to be convenient for her. Twenty minutes later, Jean had imparted a semblance of habitation and order.

A dense dust cloud floated up the hill as a bright yellow 60s era VW Bug churned its way to the office. Jean watched as two young men in their late teens or early twenties unfolded from its opened doors. The driver, over six feet tall, had auburn hair pulled back into a ponytail, his mustache and goatee more orange than red. He wore jeans and a t-shirt bearing the name "Sugarloaf," a classic rock band from the 70s, with his feet clad in good quality hiking boots. A few inches shorter than the driver, the passenger wore his medium brown hair shorn to stubble, and a silver stud flashed from his left ear lobe. His oversized white muscle shirt and baggy denim shorts hung from his brawny body, and he wore similar boots.

Stretching their long arms and legs, the pair smiled as they approached Jean. The passenger licked his lips and something silver winked from his tongue.

"Hello! Do you have a tent space?" the driver asked as he approached the office.

"I do! You can pick your spot—all the tent spaces are open," Jean replied.

"Jim and I have a week until our summer jobs start, and we're here to do some serious fishing. We heard that the rainbows and browns are waiting for a hook to sail past them...and zap! There's supper!" He imitated casting a dry fly over a stream and snagging a fish as he spoke, then grinned.

The young man's enthusiasm was infectious. Jean remembered her dad making similar claims. Fishermen are incredible optimists—and inveterate yarn spinners.

Jean leaned against the counter, smiling. "I don't know whether the fish are biting since I just arrived yesterday, but I do have tent spaces at the top of the upper loop." Speculating that these guys would want the ultimate camping spot, Jean was reluctant to make the selection for them.

"If you like, you can fill out the registration form and pay now, then come back and tell me where you pitched your tent," said Jean.

"Yeah, dude, let's take a look for ourselves," Jim said. "Maybe we'll find a real cool view from one of them."

Jim looked up the hill, trying to glimpse what lay to the north, but he wasn't having much luck. Trees blocked his view.

The driver picked up the pen and began filling out the form.

"Yo, bud. How about getting our tag number?" Con asked. He kept scribbling their registration information while Jim walked toward the car, stooping to look at the license plate.

As Jim returned, the driver opened his wallet and took out two twenties, a five, and three one dollar bills.

"OK, time to shell out. There's my half," said the driver.

Jim reached into his back pocket, pulled out his wallet, hunching over it to count out his share. Turning his back to the office, he raised his right hand in farewell. Con started to follow Jim but paused.

"Jim, I left our copy of the registration on the counter," the young man said, raising his voice. "Go on to the car; I'll be there in a sec." Jim continued on while Con retraced his steps toward Jean.

"Jim isn't as weird as he likes to make people think," said the driver. "Actually, he's my cousin and my best friend, so I know him pretty well."

Jean asked, "Are the two of you in college?"

"Yeah, we go to the University of Wyoming in Laramie," said the driver.

"My daughter will go to college a year from this fall," said Jean. "Laramie is close to home, and she's been thinking about applying."

"Cool," the driver said.

"What are you majoring in?" Jean asked.

"Jim's in business. I'm a journalism major," said the driver. "This year I'll be co-editor of the school newspaper, and that will keep me pretty busy. In the fall, the studs come out of Jim's ear and tongue, and he plays first string quarterback on the football team."

"This camping trip must be a welcome break," Jean commented.

"Yeah, it's great to get out into nature for a while," the young man said. "But we have to work, too. Jim and I got summer jobs with a friend of our uncle in Steamboat. By the way, my name is Conner—call me Con."

"I'm Jean. What kind of work will you do?" she asked. With Josie approaching her first year in college, Jean wanted to know how other students managed time and money.

"We'll be working for a friend of our uncle's doing lots of things—in his car dealership, motorbike shop, real estate office, some sort of bank...you name it," said Con, grinning and shrugging.

Con looked down and fell silent, kicking his toe at a rock before continuing. "Actually," Con said, raising his eyes to Jean's, "our boss this summer was our Uncle Brian's business partner till our uncle disappeared hunting last fall."

"Your uncle disappeared? How awful!" exclaimed Jean.

Con again looked down at his feet, then toward the north. Jim, who sat in the passenger's seat of the VW, had fixed his gaze on some distant point in that direction as well.

"Jim and I are really here to look for him…I mean, try to find his body." Con swallowed and looked down.

Jean shuddered to think that her kids might stumble across a body as they roamed the woods.

"Uncle Brian didn't come back from elk hunting last fall," said Con. "He went out alone, which was dumb. I mean, he taught us that no one should hunt alone."

Con kicked at the rock some more, lost in his own thoughts. Jean waited.

"And a huge blizzard blew in the last night of his trip," said Con.

Jean recalled hearing about this on the news. The sheriff's office looked for him, but the weather got so bad they couldn't get an air search going for three days. By then, the snow had drifted to over seven feet deep on back roads, so even the ground search had to be called off. After a week, they gave up.

"They figure he died of exposure," said Con.

"Do you know where to look?" asked Jean. "I mean, where will you start?"

Jean worried that these young college students were going out into the woods to find a dead man and might become lost themselves. Nighttime temperatures were low, even in the summer. It would help to have some idea where to send a rescue party if they didn't show up in camp one night. And while she empathized with Con and Jim, she wanted to keep her kids far from the area where they thought their uncle might be found.

"We know where he camped," said Con. "It was over by Whiskey Creek, just downstream from where the main road goes over the culvert. Jim and I've fished this area before, so we know the terrain pretty well. Our plan is to start there, where Uncle Brian camped, and hike game trails in a radius of about five miles."

"I hope you find him, Con. It must be hard not to have been able to say goodbye," Jean said, glancing at Jim, who was sitting in the VW, beating the top of the car with his open hand, in sync with the deep bass of Sugarloaf's *Green-Eyed Ladies* issuing from the sound system.

"Yeah," said Con.

"Let me know if there's anything I can do," said Jean. "And please, leave a note in the office with the general area you're searching every day."

"Thanks," Con replied, his eyelids blinking as he turned away.

Picking up his pace as he strode toward the VW, Con yelled, "Yo, man! I'm coming! Let's go drive a few stakes!"

Jean watched the little car claw its way up the hill. She thought about Con's and Jim's uncle, probably lying dead nearby.

A cold finger traced her spine.

2

A procession of campers, the whine of their rigs' transmissions rising and falling in synchrony with the road's path through the forest, rumbled their way to Columbine Campground. Jean kept busy helping guests complete forms, collecting their fees, informing them about amenities, and directing them to the loops where available campsites were located. She sent Matt and Josie to open the firewood concession, while Ty and Kelsie went off with Chad to investigate what appeared to be a hummingbird's nest hanging from a bush downhill by the stream. She was just organizing completed registration forms by date of planned departure when a Forest Service-green pickup pulled up and a ranger stepped out.

"Hello, ma'am. I'm Ranger Bob Duncan—call me Bob," the man said.

Bob appeared to be in his late forties and fit. He wore the traditional Smokey Bear hat with his uniform, a khaki green long-sleeved shirt and dark green pants. Jean noticed that he also carried a holstered gun.

"Three other rangers and I oversee this sector of the White River National Forest," said Bob. "I came to introduce myself and to let you know that we're here to help with anything you and the campground may need this summer."

"I'm Jean Branning. Thanks for coming by," Jean responded.

"Nice to meet you, ma'am," said Bob. "How's it going? Is the campground filling up? We've been advising people who try to set up camp along the roads and in off-road areas to come your way," Bob said. He gazed down the road toward the woodshed and the campsites beyond, where metal and glass reflected the afternoon sun, indicating there were RVs, vehicles, and camp trailers nestled in the woods.

"So that's why we've had such a good turnout our first afternoon. Thanks!" Jean said, doing a quick mental tally of registrations. "We have eighteen spots taken, and Sunday is considered a weeknight. I didn't think we would fill the grounds until the Fourth, but at this rate, I won't be surprised if we reach capacity by Friday night."

"Neither will I," replied the ranger. "We've had a tremendous increase over the past few years in the number of people swarming the hills looking for a place to be alone. This new campground may help save a lot of pristine forest land from overuse and abuse."

"I remember when I was growing up that my dad would move our campsite a little farther up the hill every year to get away from other campers," said Jean. "We used to camp by King Solomon Creek, but I've heard that spot has been closed."

"The trees in this forest are getting old," replied Bob. "A lot of them around King Solomon were falling, and we had to pull down quite a few more so that no one would get hurt."

Jean said, "My parents were in the last bunch of campers to use the area. A tree crashed down in the middle of the night, smashing their camper shell and pickup bed. What they said felt like a major earthquake jolted them awake. Fortunately, they were sleeping in the small trailer attached to the truck hitch."

"They were lucky, alright," said the ranger.

Bob took a handkerchief out of his pocket with one hand, grabbed his hat by the brim with the other to remove it, and mopped his forehead with the cloth.

"And that old sawmill site over there," Bob flapped his hat at the view Jean had from her reception window, "gave us a real scare about ten, fifteen years ago when some brainless camper lit fireworks on the Fourth, right over the hill of wood shavings. We were lucky then, too. Everyone in the area pitched in and formed a bucket brigade to put it out."

"I remember," Jean said. "I was here when it happened."

Jean noticed Josie reading in a chair near the picnic table and called her over to the office.

"Josie, will you take care of the registration booth for a few minutes, please?" Jean asked. "I want to walk with the ranger for a few minutes."

"Sure, Mom," Josie said. She closed her book and stood to walk toward the two adults.

"Josie, this is Ranger Bob Duncan. Bob, Josie is my oldest daughter," Jean said.

"Hello!" said Bob. "Glad to meet you. I hope you have a good time out here this summer."

Josie looked to the side in doubt, but didn't give a full eye-roll. She met the ranger's eyes to respond.

"Thanks! I hope so, too," Josie replied.

"We'll be gone just a few minutes, Josie," said Jean. "Thanks for helping out."

"No problem, Mom," Josie said.

Jean opened the office door, letting Josie in as she went out. Rounding the small building, she joined Bob.

"Come with me, Bob, and I'll show you the layout."

"I'd enjoy a tour," said Bob.

They headed into the campground, passing a couple of RV sites on the main trunk of the road before it branched into upper and lower loops. Turning uphill toward the tent camping sites, Jean and Bob continued their conversation about the fire.

"My family was coming back from jeeping in the woods north of King Solomon Creek," said Jean, "and we saw thin whiffs of smoke rising from the sawdust pile. The fire was smoldering at that point, but within minutes, flames broke out and cinders popped, sparking new little fires. Then the flames grew higher and the fire spread so fast!"

Jean recounted how people shouted and ran from their campsites carrying buckets and bowls of water, axes and shovels. Some brought blankets and towels to smother the fire. But as the fire expanded, doubts arose about whether they could succeed against the hot flames.

"We needed help," Jean continued, "so I drove out to find a telephone and call for help. But I had to go all the way to the highway. I broke a sidewall on a rock as I drove too fast around a curve on the way back and had to change the tire. Then I raced here to help with the fire." She sighed.

"It took me almost two hours to get back, and the fire had spread much farther," Jean said. "But by then, other campers nearby had seen the smoke and come to help. The way everyone cooperated—it made all the difference."

"It was past dark when the local ranger got here several hours later, and the fire was pretty much out," said Jean. "He set up a watch crew made up of campers in case it flared during the night, and the ranger stayed with them. The rest of us went back to camp. We had a very late supper and dropped exhausted into our sleeping bags. Talk about hard work!"

Bob nodded. "Yes, firefighting is hard work. You folks did well to get that fire under control and save this forest."

"You appear to know the area well," Bob said. "You'll be able to give the campers some pointers about camp etiquette."

"I suppose I will," Jean replied, "but the handouts printed by the Forest Service say it all pretty well." She pulled a folded copy of a brochure displaying area maps and campground rules out of her pocket and handed it to Bob. She had placed a small stack of these near the office window earlier that morning.

Bob scanned the brochure as they continued their hike.

Jean gestured toward Bob's holstered gun. "I don't remember seeing a forest ranger carrying a gun before."

"I don't much like it," Bob said, grimacing. "But there's been an increase in the number of strange characters spending time in the forests. Since our service interacts with poachers and other people breaking laws that govern public lands, we have to carry these for our own protection." Bob unhooked his canteen from his belt, on the opposite side from the gun, and took a long drink.

"A couple of years ago, a ranger was shot and killed in western Idaho while he was doing his rounds alone," Bob said. "Every once in a while, you'll hear of another incident or shooting involving a ranger. I hope I never have to use it."

As the pair approached the tent site loop, Jean's uneasiness about Jim's and Con's plans to search for their uncle's body welled up again. She didn't know much about the missing hunter except what she had learned from Con and the little she remembered from the news broadcasts last fall.

"Bob, two young men on a personal mission checked in this afternoon," she said, gesturing at their tent, which seemed vacant at the moment. "They told me that their uncle disappeared while he was hunting near here last fall. Do you know anything about it?" Jean waited as Bob doffed his hat to smooth his damp hair back again, considered his answer, then donned the hat.

"Yeah, I helped with the search," said Bob. "It seems that he hunted alone for the first ten days of elk season. He was reported to know the area and was an experienced outdoorsman. The day after he was supposed to return home, we got a call from his wife asking us to check his camp and see if he needed help."

Jean gestured to a clear path dropping through the trees to the lower loop, and Bob paused his story, lost in his thoughts, as they negotiated rougher ground. Jean waited.

"We'd had a big storm blow in the night before the hunter was scheduled to have broken camp," said Bob, "and even with four-wheel drive, the roads were impassable. A couple of rangers went in on snow machines and found his campsite by Whiskey Creek. His truck and camper were there, and the camp was tidy and undisturbed, as though he had gone off for the day and hadn't returned. Snow was still coming down and wind was blowing, making visibility bad, but we got the sheriff's rescue team to come up and do some scouting. The drifts were so deep that the search dogs were plunging into snow over their heads." Bob pulled out the handkerchief again and turned to blow his nose. "The ground search had to be delayed—heck, we all knew that we wouldn't find him."

"When the storm cleared, the Civil Air Patrol hunted for him from the air, but all they saw was snow, trees, and some deer and elk. After ten days, when a new storm was approaching, we abandoned the search. With wind-chill below zero, there was little hope that the guy could have survived exposure away from camp."

Bob pulled sunglasses from his pocket and lifted them onto his face. "We didn't find any trace of him, but the plan is to search for his body as soon as most of the snow has melted. That should be soon."

The ranger turned north, the same direction Con had stared, and appeared lost in thought. Then he shook his head.

"Something feels wrong about his disappearance," said Bob, frowning. "He knew how to handle himself in the forest. We were told that he had arctic survival training and would be prepared to hole up in a blizzard. His wife verified that he wore hunting clothes, a thoughtful assortment of warm layers. Those were not in the camper. His rifle, a Sako .300 magnum with a scope, was missing, which indicated to us that he had gone out hunting that day.

"But the blizzard didn't start till well into the night, about eleven o'clock. So, unless he was injured or had trouble packing game out, there was no reason for a hunter familiar with these mountains to be out in the forest that much past sundown. And if he had dug a snow cave to sit out the blizzard, he should have been able to find his way back or signal to the air searchers before the search was called off." Bob sighed, the muscles in his jaw tightening and wrinkles across his forehead deepening. "I think something happened to him before the blizzard."

"Where was he from?" Jean asked, checking her footing as they stepped onto the lower loop road. "His nephews say they're working for his partner in Steamboat this summer."

Jean couldn't help thinking about the sadness and grief that Con and Jim were experiencing and how they would react if they didn't or —maybe worse— did find their uncle.

"Brian Gowen was from Grand Junction," said Bob, "but he had recently moved to Steamboat Springs. From what I heard, he had businesses all over the Western Slope and over into Utah. He seemed to be respected in the community and a good family man. This has been hard on them, I'm sure. I've heard that the family may have a memorial service up here this summer, but I don't know when."

They had completed their walk through the campground and returned to the office. Bob removed his hat again, what Jean surmised to be a tic, and used his free hand to smooth back his hair. Standing up straighter, he put the hat back into place.

"It would be a good idea to keep track of those boys if you can," said Bob. "I'd hate to have to go searching for them, too. Let me know if you think I might be of any help to them." Bob handed Jean his business card. "I'm sorry about their uncle."

Looking down at the card in her hands, Jean sighed. "I don't know whether anyone or anything can help them, but I'll contact you if they raise any concerns."

"I drive by here at least once a day. I'll check in with you when I do," the ranger said.

"I'll be around most afternoons, but I hope to be out fishing and hiking with my kids most mornings. If you have any messages for me, either leave them on the answering machine or slip them into the registration slot." Jean indicated the brass mail opening on the front of the kiosk.

"Glad to have you aboard, Mrs. Branning." Bob tipped his broad hat down to hide his eyes and started walking toward his truck, turning back to wave at Josie, still in the office.

"Call me Jean," she said to his retreating figure.

Over his shoulder, the ranger called, "Right, Jean. Have a good day, ma'am."

Jean, chilled again by the suspected proximity of death, watched as Bob turned the truck around. It drifted down the hill in a plume of dust.

3

Supper that first night on the job was a traditional camp meal—roasted hot dogs, canned baked beans, potato chips, and toasted marshmallows. Matt lit the fire, and Chad found the old metal roasting forks that had belonged to Jean's grandparents in the camper's underbed storage. Kelsie carried the plates, cups, and silverware out of the camper and placed them on a checkered plastic tablecloth covering the picnic table. She went back for marshmallows as Josie emerged from the camper carrying a tray loaded with ketchup, mustard, potato chips, dill pickles, and a plastic storage container of watermelon chunks. Jean poured milk for everyone, then sat down in one of the camp chairs arranged around the fire.

Ty, carrying hot dogs and buns as he bounced down the steps, sang, "Oh! I wish I was an Oscar Mayer wiener!" and began opening the packages.

In unison, Josie and Matt groaned, "Aargh!"

"This feels like home," sighed Jean, smiling as she threaded a hot dog across the double-tined roasting fork.

"It feels so good to be sitting here on a Sunday evening with all of you instead of driving hundreds of miles across the mountains alone," said Chad. "I am so glad to be here together." Chad's contented gaze fell on each face in the circle.

"Dad taught Kelsie and me how to skip stones on the water today," Ty announced. "You have to pick real flat rocks, and when you throw them, you have to kind of spin them from the side instead of pitching 'em like a baseball." He tried to demonstrate, but the half-eaten hot dog in one hand and the dill pickle in the other prevented him from doing more than raising his shoulders and pointing elbows.

"It's so much fun!" Kelsie said. "Ty got one of his stones to skip three times before it sank!"

"Cool," said Matt, who was busy watching his second hot dog sizzle over the coals. "I did a little experimenting today. I'm trying to catalog landmarks so I can figure out locations with my compass in case I get lost. If I know where something is supposed to be, I should be able to find it just like pilots who fly using instruments."

"That's true to a certain extent, Matt, but they use radio signals and triangulate their positions using vectors," Chad said, reaching for his milk and drinking some before continuing. "You can use a compass and map to find your way around, but be careful not to get out of sight of any visual landmarks."

"Which reminds me," inserted Jean, with a stern look at each of her offspring. "I brought metal whistles on cords for each of you." A collective moan rose from her kids. "And I expect you to have them around your necks each and every time you leave the campsite. We'll each have a code so if we hear someone whistling, we'll know who it is. I'll use three long blasts, and if you hear that sound, you are to come to me as quick as possible. Josie, you have two short blasts; Matt has one long and one short; Ty, three short; and Kelsie, two long blasts. Count to fifty, then repeat the blast until someone comes for you. And remember, stay put if you get lost! It's easier for others to find you."

"Geez! You sound like Captain von Trapp from *The Sound of Music*," protested Matt, who didn't think his parents would ever believe he could take care of himself.

"While I was at the woodshed," Josie said, ignoring Matt as she rotated her long fork, toasting her marshmallows to an even golden tan, "a couple of guys from Laramie came to buy a bundle of firewood. We started talking about college and stuff, and they asked if I'd like to get together sometime to hike or something." Her face remained expressionless as she continued rotating the fork. She removed it from the coals and inspected the swollen golden puff as it began to sag away from the handle. Josie pulled it from the hot tines and bit in. The crusty outside covering collapsed and sticky white crème threatened to ooze down her chin. She stuffed the rest of the marshmallow into her mouth and sat back in her chair.

"Why don't you invite them to have supper with us tomorrow night?" suggested Jean. "I talked to them for a little while when they checked in. They seem like nice young men."

"Did they tell you why they're here?" inquired Josie, as she ran her forefinger around the edges of her lips, mopping up residue from the sticky dessert.

"Con told me that they're trying to find their uncle, lost in a storm last fall," Jean said, shooting a look at Chad to see if he was listening.

"I want to help them," Josie said, her determined tone challenging her mother.

Jean knew that Josie felt it was time that she was allowed to make some decisions for herself. She was seventeen and almost an adult; she would leave home for college in just over a year.

"Josie, do you understand what they're looking for, what they may find?" asked Chad.

"Yes, Dad. I know the man is dead," said Josie, choosing her next words with care. "These guys seem pretty responsible, as far as I can tell. They work, go to school, and are involved in respectable campus groups." She again paused. "They need to find their uncle. He was like a dad to them. Con and Jim were related to him through their moms. Both sets of parents are divorced. Oh, they have stepfathers now, but their Uncle Brian was the one who taught them to fish and hunt. He went to Jim's football games whenever he could. He gave Con a computer in high school so he could write. He was the one who went to their graduations."

Josie took a deep breath and looked down at her hands, fighting her emotions but keeping her composure.

"You and Mom have always taught me to have compassion and do what I can to help others," said Josie. "This is something I feel I should do."

"Let's have them to supper," said Jean. "I need your help tomorrow, but Tuesday you can go, if your dad agrees." Jean glanced at Chad, who thus far had said nothing. One of the problems with having been apart almost a year was that Chad hadn't wanted to come home on weekends and be the heavy. Discipline and authority had become somewhat anathema for him, but Jean hoped that he would relieve her of some of the parental responsibility and decision-making while they were together this summer.

Chad looked up and met Jean's eyes, then turned to Josie. "I agree with your mom. I'd like to meet these guys tomorrow, and if you still feel comfortable with the idea of searching with them, you can go Tuesday."

Josie looked in turn at her father and her mother, relief and surprise radiating from her face. "Thanks, Mom and Dad," she said.

Josie, in big sister mode, stood up then and started issuing orders. "Okay, kids. Pick up whatever you brought out. Then take the dirty dishes inside. I'll be the kitchen slave tonight."

The kids scrambled to get everything done so they could bring a board game out to play on the picnic table while Josie washed dishes. Jean and Chad exchanged meaningful glances. The kids were growing up. They were growing up well.

§

Jean returned to the office after supper to finish paperwork. As she listed the names of all the registered campers on the daily log, she noticed something odd. Wasn't the missing man's last name Gowen? The elderly couple in #10 was named Gowen. Another Gowen was in #23, a woman alone from Grand Junction. Could she be the dead man's wife? People from Steamboat Springs occupied six spaces. Did they know each other?

Jean tried to shake fatigue away as she stood up and secured the log and the cash box in the small safe hidden in the back half of the file drawer. The campers were strangers to her. So what if they had planned to meet here? It was natural to re-member someone who died by holding a memorial service or a celebration of life. But if that was why they were here, why hadn't anyone told her?

She turned off the light and locked the door, leaving all the newness and turmoil of the day behind it. The one thing left on her mind was the welcoming comfort of a bed at the back of the small trailer, warmed by the man she loved.

4

Birds began chirping long before the alarm clock buzzed the next morning. Why was it that chilly morning air combined with sunlight so that Jean felt fresh and ready to start a new day after only a few hours of sleep? That sure wasn't the case back at home.

Chad lay next to her, an arm thrown over his eyes to block bright morning rays from interrupting his sleep. Jean slipped out of bed, trying not to wake Chad, grabbed a towel and a bag of personal items, and headed toward the private bathroom attached to the back of the office. She was pleased with the architect's foresight in providing this space. A whole summer of showering over a toilet in a tiny trailer cubicle held little appeal for her, especially since all six members of her family would have shared its use. Keeping that room clean and dry would have been a nightmare.

The bathroom had solar heat, so yesterday's sunshine provided enough warmth to take off the chill. Steam rose above her as she let strands of spray and clean-smelling shampoo wash pine smoke from her curly, shoulder-length, dark-blonde hair. She savored the comfort and solitude until she heard insistent knocking on the door.

"Mom, aren't we going fishing this morning?" Ty's sleepy voice reminded her of yesterday's promise. She dried herself with a fluffy white bath sheet and hurried as she dressed in jeans, sneakers, and a t-shirt. Then she slipped the sweatshirt her kids had given her over her head, smiling as she read its words backwards from the mirror: "Don't Mess With Me! I'm a Mom!" After hanging the towel to dry and gathering her belongings, she met Ty at the door. Her wet hair caused her to shiver in the crisp mountain air.

"Is anyone else up yet?" Jean asked, as Ty slipped past into the bathroom. He was already dressed much as she was, except he was wearing a plain navy hooded sweatshirt and a black baseball cap.

"No, they're still sleeping," Ty answered. He closed the door, and Jean walked back to their camp. She picked up a canvas creel sporting an assortment of flies, tiny brass hooks tied with a variety of feathers, fur, and threads. In the pocket was a pair of needle-nosed pliers for removing hooks from fish and tightening weights on fishing line, a large pocketknife for cleaning fish, a bottle of insect repellent, and a small plastic case with spare leaders and weights. She opened the zipper compartment and picked some fresh grass, being careful not to pull up the roots, and placed it in the bottom. This would cradle the fish, if they caught any, and help keep them cool. Without making much noise, Jean approached the trailer, reached underneath, and slid two fly rods out. She inspected both to be sure the reels were securely fastened, and propped them against the picnic table. She was just about to go to the van to get a pen and notepad when the camper door opened and her husband emerged.

"Goin' fishin'?" Chad drawled with a smile. Jean knew that Chad would never enjoy the sport the way she did. He had not grown up in a family where the main form of rest and recreation was a trip to the hills with rod and reel in tow. His family had traveled a lot, making long, fast trips by car, and eating out of cans, whenever time allowed. During the twenty-odd years since their marriage, there had been some attempts to blend their styles, but most of their vacations had kept them moving, preventing Jean from doing much campfire cooking or fishing.

In fact, the last time Jean had wet her line in a stream had been that trip to this area when the fire broke out. She wasn't sure she remembered how to go about it. Not only that, but her father wasn't here to remind her of his little tricks—how to keep from snapping off a fly when casting, finding a promising hole where trout would be waiting to jump for her fly—or to help clean the fish. She had never maintained her own reel, so she hoped that neither hers nor Ty's would jam up their first time out. In a sense, being here with the kids and teaching them what their grandfather had taught her was a kind of pilgrimage, passing on the traditions of her own family to the next generation.

"We should be back in about an hour. You don't have to leave until 7:30, do you?" Jean queried.

"That should work." Chad walked to Jean, put his arms around her, and kissed her. "I'll have the frying pan ready to cook your catch."

Jean looked at his warm cornflower-blue eyes and thinning brown hair, raised her eyebrows, and grinned. "Optimistic, aren't we?"

"I have a backup plan," he responded, wearing a smug grin.

"Mom, are you ready yet?" called Ty, already walking down the hill to the bend in the creek.

"Wait right there! If you're going to fish, you have to carry your own pole." Jean flashed her hazel eyes at Chad and hurried toward their son.

Jean and Ty made their way to the rippling stream and chose a spot near a boulder, where the huge rock cast its shadow over a deep eddy and the bank was free of trees in which to snag a line. This seemed a good place to try their luck, Jean mused.

"What we need to do is stand upstream of this boulder and be careful that our shadows don't get too close to the area where we want to cast the fly," said Jean. "We'll do what is called wet fly fishing. First, we have to choose a fly. Do you see any insects around us?"

They watched for few moments and saw a trout rise out of the water to snatch a caddis fly, a small moth-like insect, for its breakfast. Jean selected a fly from the creel that was close to the size and color of the caddis fly they saw and secured it to Ty's thin nylon leader.

"Pull out a length of the bright yellow fly line from your reel with your left hand, like this," Jean said, going through the motions as she spoke. "With your right hand, extend your index finger like a pointer along the cork handle of the rod, with your second and third fingers straddling the reel mount. See?" Jean pulled line from her reel until it was about three times longer than the length of her pole.

"Take your left hand and pull the line back toward you through the eyes of the pole and out to your side. Bring the tip of the pole behind you, keeping the fly out of the bushes." Jean concentrated as she looked over her shoulder for bushes and positioned the pole's tip opposite the spot she wanted to cast the fly.

"Now watch my arm," said Jean. With a rhythm remembered despite years of disuse, she directed the fly-tipped line over her head to the edge of the current. Glittering diamond ripples carried the fly downstream toward the smooth dark pool near them, where big, fat trout might be lurking out of sight.

"See how my left hand is cradling the line?" Jean asked. The line lay across her open hand with her left index finger serving as a sensor, testing the line for the slightest tug. Without warning, she flicked the tip of the rod up to a 10 o'clock position and held it there. A small brook trout dimpled the surface then dove for safety.

There wasn't any movement on the line before Jean set the hook, but Ty watched as she turned the handle on her reel, bringing the fish in, stopping every so often as the creature fought to escape.

"You have to be careful not to yank so hard you pull the hook out of the fish's mouth," Jean said. "Sometimes it will catch in the lip and be secure, but other times the fish might have brushed past the fly and hooked its gill." Jean swung the tip of her pole to the right while pulling the line toward her body through the tip with her left hand, at the same time winding the extra line onto her reel. "The worst for me is when they swallow it. I hate having to remove it. In fly fishing, though, that doesn't happen as often as in bait fishing. Fly hooks are smaller, so if a section of the river is only open to catch-and-release fishing, the rules require lures or flies."

The fish tired as Jean reeled in line, dragging it to the edge of the stream. After swinging the brookie far enough onto the grassy bank that it couldn't flop back into the water, Jean squatted beside it. Reaching into the creel, she found pliers. With the line snug, she grasped the fish under its gills with one hand and removed the hook with the pliers. She dropped the fish into her grass-lined pouch and stood.

"Okay, Ty—your turn," said Jean.

Jean observed as Ty eyed his rod and got into position. Having never done this before, there was a lot for him to remember. He repeated his mother's moves, but when he flicked his wrist to cast, the fly dug into a rotting branch lying on the ground behind him. He sagged with discouragement.

"This is harder than I thought it would be," said Ty, frowning.

Jean strode to the branch and released the snag. "Don't feel bad, Ty," she counseled. "Casting takes practice. I was lucky that my first cast went where I wanted it to. Try again." She watched her son as he prepared to cast again. This time the fly sailed over his head and into the water, though it fell short of its target.

"Nice cast!" Jean said. "Leave it there. See if a fish hits it."

Jean watched as Ty stood still as the nearby boulder. Without warning he brought his whole right arm up, tightening his line, and Jean saw a disturbance at the surface of the water. Ty cranked the handle of the reel, taking his time, and was rewarded by the silver flash of fish scales.

"You've got one!" Jean cried. How many hours had she stood by a stream before she caught her first fish? She grinned.

Jean helped lift the fish out of the water. It was a little larger than Jean's and a bit feistier. Mother and son worked together removing the hook and bagging the fish.

Ty's eyes gleamed with pride as he surveyed his trophy. Ty himself was hooked—on fishing.

"I'm going to move upstream a little way," Jean said. "Let's see if we have any more luck."

The pair continued to fish and each caught one more trout large enough to keep. They moved up away from the stream's bank, cleaned the fish, and buried the entrails. Then they took their catch back to the water for rinsing.

Just as Jean and Ty were ready to trudge back uphill to camp, Con's little yellow bug putted northward up the road. Jean raised her hand and waved as Con stuck a long arm out his window in salute. Some of the bright pleasure of the morning evaporated as she contemplated Con's and Jim's quest. Somewhere nearby lies a dead man, their uncle. Would they find him?

5

Except for the trout, Chad had cooked breakfast and was ready to serve when Jean and Ty returned to camp. Jean rinsed the fish again, this time with water from the tap. Then she coated them in corn meal and arranged them in hot bacon grease at the bottom of a cast iron skillet. She sprinkled the trout with a little salt and pepper, and fried them to a crispy golden brown. Drawn by the warm, savory scent, the family assembled at the picnic table.

"Guess what, Dad! I caught two fish!" Ty was more excited than he had been since making his very first soccer goal.

"Good job, Ty," Chad said. His plate boasted one of his son's catches. After removing fins and skin, he lifted a fork full of flaky meat from the bone into his mouth. "Ummm. Am I imagining things, or do fish taste better in the mountains?"

"I've always thought so," Jean said, smiling.

Jean and Ty each took one of the small fish, and the Ty's three siblings split the remaining large one, still waking up as they dug into the food on their plates.

Jean considered her plans for the day. "Shall we go for a hike before doing all the chores? There aren't any big jobs to do yet, so this might be a good time to become familiar with the terrain near camp."

"Sure, Mom," Matt said, tipping his head back to drain orange juice from his glass. "I'd like to map some trails."

Chad wiped his mouth with a paper towel and stood. "It's time for me to go to work," he said. "Have fun today!" He leaned down to kiss Jean goodbye, ruffled Kelsie's already messy hair, then walked to his little white Geo Metro.

Jean turned to her brood, clapped her hands together, and said, "Let's get the dishes done and go explore."

§

Morning soon passed as the Brannings followed well-worn deer trails winding through the trees above the campground. Sun-warmed air filtered through the tall pines, and every so often, a cool finger of shade brushed along Jean's cheek and arm. In the meadows, bees and butterflies almost sparkled as droplets of light splashed off their delicate wings. Jean and the four kids crested their mountain, and Hahn's Peak came into view. Its pointy summit, stark gray and naked except for where deep creases of snow lingered in shadowed crevasses, was dressed in a respectable skirt of forest below timberline.

All too soon, Jean and the kids had to return to camp for lunch and to prepare for arriving campers. As they walked through the tent area, Jean noted that the VW was still absent.

"Did you have a chance to talk to Jim and Con about eating with us tonight, Josie?" asked Jean.

"Yes! I saw them as they were leaving this morning," said Josie, "and they thought it was great that we asked. I told them we'd eat around 7 o'clock. They said they'd come."

Josie flicked Ty's cap off his head and held it behind her back, out of his reach.

Ty got in front of her, yelling "Stop it, Josie!" He lunged from side to side as he tried to retrieve it, finally giving up and pleading, "Mom! Josie won't give my hat back to me! Make her stop!"

Josie grinned, slapping the hat back on his head.

Jean stifled a smile, realizing that before long, Ty would be too big for Josie to tease like this. This banter between kids would either end or transform into something altogether different. She hoped it would continue to be good-natured.

"Then will you please make a salad and a cake for supper, Josie?" asked Jean. "I need to update the camp registry and be available for new check-ins. We can have pork chops and baked potatoes, too. Does that sound good?" Jean knew that Josie loved to be alone in the kitchen and that her daughter sometimes dreamed of becoming a great chef. Jean started toward the camper to get lunchmeat and bread for sandwiches.

"Sure, Mom," Josie called, raising her voice a little. "What are our chores for this afternoon?"

"I was just thinking about that," said Jean, leaning out of the camper's door. "I'd like you and Matt to drive the garden tractor and trailer around and collect all the garbage, then take the trash to the dumpsters over by the RV dump station. Be sure to put new bags in the cans. Then we'll all pitch in and clean the shower houses. It shouldn't take too long. I'll be in the office if you need me."

§

After sorting through paperwork, and with the kids finished with their chores, Jean decided to walk the loops to check registrations against occupied spaces. Leaving Josie to attend to new campers, Jean set off uphill to the tent sites. Few sounds, other than birds and insects, broke the stillness since most of the campers were out fishing, hiking or four-wheeling. She had seen at least two Suzuki trail bikes, but she didn't hear the annoying high-pitched chatter of their two-stroke engines nearby. Instead of following the road, she cut through the upper loop lengthwise, walking behind and between tents, then descended the hill to the far end of the lower loop reserved for RVs and trailers. As she approached #14, she saw a couple of women sitting under trees in lawn chairs and talking. Jean stopped to speak to them.

"Hi! Isn't this a gorgeous day?" Jean said, greeting the women with a warm, comfortable smile.

"It's beautiful! And so quiet. I haven't heard a car for hours," said the petite brunette. "Would you like to join us?" she asked, gesturing to a third chair, folded and leaning against a tree.

Jean tilted her head and considered her schedule. A few minutes wouldn't hurt.

"Thanks!" Jean said, smiling as she picked up the chair and opened it. "I'm Jean Branning, the campground host. I was just walking through camp to see if my registration list is correct. So far, so good." She glanced down at her clipboard. "This is my first year—actually, my first week—as host, so I'm trying to develop some sort of system."

"New jobs are always like that, aren't they, Marni?" The brunette shot a glance at the other woman, a blonde wearing shimmering silver earrings etched with kachinas that danced an inch from her shoulders. She was a little taller than the first woman, but Jean could see a resemblance between the two. They both had warm brown eyes and small dimples in their chins. The woman called Marni had a fresh, healthy appearance, making her appear younger than she probably was. The smaller woman had a pale complexion and looked fragile. Marni responded with a nod, and the other woman continued talking.

"This is my sister Marni Cole, and I'm Kristi Weller," Kristi said.

"Welcome to the campground," said Jean. "Have you been to this area before?"

"Yes! We used to come here camping with our family when we were younger," said Kristi. "When we heard this campground had been built, we decided to come and check it out."

"That's great!" said Jean. "I hope you have a nice time. Like I said, this is my first time as a campground host, so I'm learning the ropes of my new job. If there's anything you need..."

"We need new jobs, too," Marni laughed, "even though we thought we'd never have to go job hunting again." She raised an eyebrow and squeezed out a half-smile. "Oh! But we don't mean we're looking for jobs here," Marni said, exhaling an embarrassed titter.

Kristi pursed her lips, frown lines appearing on her forehead.

Ignoring Marni, Kristi's demeanor turned serious, and she said, "We were both working for our brother in Steamboat

Springs. But he disappeared last fall, and his partner decided not to keep us."

Seeming unsure again about how much to say, Kristi continued. "Marni did the accounting for all of Brian's Steamboat businesses, and I was in marketing—you know, ad campaigns, selling ideas, finding clients. Brian had a lot of business interests on the Western Slope, and working for him kept us busy."

"Steamboat Springs isn't that big, though," said Kristi. "It's been hard finding other work in this town," she continued, sighing.

Jean looked first at Marni, then at Kristi, seeing resemblances between them and Con and Jim. "There are two college students staying in a tent up the hill. Do you know them?" Jean's mind connected little bits of information as she waited, but she was sure she knew the answer.

"Jim is my son," replied Kristi. "We saw him and Con, Marni's son, drive down the hill this morning. We didn't know they would be here, and I don't think they've noticed us yet. I'm guessing the boys are here for the same reason we are." Kristi glanced at Marni, who nodded in agreement.

Pausing, the lines in Kristi's face deepened, indicating what Jean surmised as accumulated stress and grief from recent months. A quick glance at Marni's expression confirmed that it was also grave.

"Marni and I came to look for our brother Brian's body. He must be dead. He's lying out there somewhere, exposed to the weather and animals, and we want to find him and give him a proper burial." Kristi, distracted, wrung her hands and stared into the forest. "Mom and Dad are taking his disappearance hard. They need the agony of not knowing where he is to end. So do we."

"Are your parents Henry and Joyce Gowen?" asked Jean.

"How do you know their names?" Kristi asked. "Did you read about Brian's disappearance in the newspaper?" Agitated, she shifted forward in her chair.

This was beginning to look like an unplanned family re-union. Jean wondered how so many close relatives could be unaware of such serious plans.

Jean answered, "They're staying at #10. I wondered about them last night after I talked to a forest ranger. He told me about your brother. Didn't you know your parents or sons were coming here?" she asked.

Kristi hopped out of her chair and walked to the center of the road. When she was able to see the end, she stopped and stared at the familiar rig sitting. She walked quickly back to Jean and asked, "Did they tow an old red Willys Jeep behind them?" She looked worried.

"Yes, they did," Jean said. "They were the first people to check in, and I remember the man pretty well." Jean paused, deciding not to say that she had thought of him as gruff and unfriendly. That wouldn't reflect well on me or the campground, she thought. "I didn't see his wife, but her name is on the registration form."

"Oh, no!" said Kristi. "They're probably here looking for Brian, too. And they really shouldn't be. This altitude isn't good for Dad's heart. He's had health problems since last winter." Shaking her head, Kristi added, "He's so upset."

Kristi looked at Marni with anguish. "What should we do?"

It was becoming clear to Jean that the sisters were close, but up to this point, Marni had been quiet and, thus, an enigma.

"There isn't much we can do," Marni said, shrugging. "You know that, Kristi. Dad is the most stubborn man I've ever known, and no one has ever been able to keep him from doing something he's decided to do." One corner of Marni's mouth lifted into a half-smile as she shook her head. "Not even Mom."

"Then we'd better find them and tell them we're here. We should talk to Con and Jim, too. If we're all here for the same purpose, then we might as well try to work together. We could cover a larger area that way," Kristi said. "At least we know where Mom and Dad are. If they need us, we'll be nearby."

"Yes, but I'm not looking forward to the moment when Dad finds out *we're* here," Marni said. "He probably thinks of this as his responsibility." Marni leaned back in her chair and closed her eyes. "I just hope that Dad doesn't get sick this far from a hospital."

Jean stood. "We have an emergency telephone at the office. Don't hesitate to ask to use it if you need to," she said.

Jean felt the sadness of the whole situation seep through her as a small puffy cloud drifted over the treetops.

"Thanks for stopping by," said Marni. "We're sorry if our problems have distressed you." Marni rose, seeming to gather strength from movement.

"No, don't apologize. Your family has suffered a lot," Jean said. "I hope you find your brother."

Jean remembered her own father's death while he and her mom were with Jean's family on a fishing and camping trip to Flathead Lake. The day her parents left home to meet her and her family, Jean had spiked a high fever, which turned out to be a viral flu. Both of her parents had caught it, as had three of her kids, but her dad's heart hadn't been strong enough to withstand the resulting pneumonia. Jean felt responsible for his death.

Although Jean knew she couldn't have prevented exposing her dad to the virus—she had tried to call her parents as soon as she started feeling ill, but they had already left home—her grieving for him was unfinished. She suspected that it had to do with her father having been cremated rather than buried. His ashes were still in an urn on her mother's chest of drawers, waiting to be mixed with her mom's after she died, then scattered. All of her grandparents' remains were located in a cemetery, and she remembered their funerals and burials, and visiting their graves each Memorial Day when she was young. Her dad's funeral had helped, but lacking a place to go and remember him, Jean felt unsettled and rootless.

"Con and Jim are having supper with my family tonight," Jean said. "Shall I tell them that you and their grandparents are here?"

"Sure," said Marni. "Tell the boys we'd like to talk to them tonight before they go to bed. And thank you." Marni squared her shoulders with feet planted firmly, having emerged from her silence to show herself a thinker and decision maker. "It doesn't surprise me they came. They loved their uncle a lot."

"I got that impression from Con." Jean started walking, turning to say, "Keep me posted on how things go."

"Sure," replied Kristi. "This week is going to be hard, especially with Mom and Dad here, but I'm glad you told us."

"Take care!" called Jean as she hurried back to the office. She wondered if there were other people coming to join in the search. And why.

6

By the time Josie finished grilling the pork chops, Jean had put up the "Campground Full" sign at the entrance. Newlyweds from California, some German exchange students who were biking across the Rockies, and a small troop of Boy Scouts were all pitching tents on the hill. Three older couples, traveling in a Good Sam caravan from Arizona on their way north to Alaska, gathered in comfortable chairs near one of the RV's, enjoying their own mobile community. Other campers had come here to fish, their poles prepared for the next day's expedition. A nervous-looking man arriving alone had requested #2, even though he didn't need the pull-thru for his 4-wheel drive pickup and low camper shell. Two families were vacationing together, yelling instructions and asking each other for help, their children tasked with running things back and forth. Ty and Kelsie watched the action, sizing up the new kids as potential companions.

Con and Jim came down the hill to join the Branning family a little before suppertime. Con carried a hardshell guitar case over his shoulder, and Jim placed kindling and small pieces of pine he'd picked up along the way in the concrete fire pit, lighting it with one match.

"I was a Boy Scout," Jim said, grinning.

"Yeah, but you never learned to tie a decent knot," Con teased. "Remember what happened the last time we went back-packing? You used a rope to pull our food up between some trees to keep it away from bears?"

Con continued to poke fun at his cousin. "That big 'whump' woke us up. Then something squealed as it ran off into the woods, scaring us half to death. It didn't sound low-pitched enough to be a bear, but we decided to climb a tree just in case."

"How was I to know that a raccoon was going to come along and start scratching at the knot?" Jim said, scowling.

Wow!" said Matt, his eyes seeming as big as pine cones. "That must have been pretty scary!"

Eyeing the surrounding forest, Con nodded and continued. "We stayed way up in the branches till the next morning," Con said. "Man, was it cold!"

"That was your brainy idea," razzed Jim. "When we looked at the tracks the next morning, we realized we had been robbed by a pair of raccoons, and we felt pretty stupid about spending the night in the tree."

"Those critters are pretty persistent," remarked Chad, who had returned to camp just before the boys' arrival. "Raccoons can get into things you wouldn't expect an animal of that size to be able to manage, plus they have toes that are as long, and almost as functional, as fingers; they also have prehensile front paws, allowing them to grasp things." Chad walked over to the cooler, bent to open it, and took out a beer for himself; he of-fered soda pop to everyone else, selecting one for Jean. "Raccoons can be vicious, as well. You were wise to not investigate till morning."

Jean called, "Supper's on! Come and eat!" The young men and the family converged on the picnic table, already laid out with food, plates, and eating utensils.

Devouring the hot dinner with impeccable manners, Con and Jim seemed to relax a little. With everyone finished eating, Josie and Jean made quick work of storing leftovers, and the younger kids cleaned the table and washed up. Tidy at last, everyone retired to the fire ring.

"Thanks for dinner!" said Con.

Jim chimed in, "It was great! Thank you!"

"You're welcome," Jean said, smiling and adding, "Josie prepared it."

Con and Jim grinned and gave thumbs up signs to Josie.

Josie's blush was almost hidden by approaching darkness. The sun had disappeared over the mountains, and stars were beginning to pierce the evening sky.

"Are you going to play your guitar?" Kelsie asked Con.

"Sure," Con grinned. He removed his guitar from the case and strummed soft, pleasant sounds. He turned the tuning pins, making minor adjustments, then began playing sweet, drifting chords and humming the melody to *Where Have All the Flowers Gone?* The gentle melancholy of the folk song floated among the trees, a lullaby to war in the gathering darkness. After a while, Con stopped, propped the guitar against his chair, and stretched.

"We started looking for our uncle this morning," Con said, then fell silent for a long moment.

"It's as if Uncle Brian was never here," Con mused. "Last fall, when he didn't come back, the searchers packed up his camp and delivered it to his wife, Cathy. The grass and flowers are straight and tall where they told us he made camp, as if no one had ever set foot on that spot."

Con picked up the branch the Brannings had placed next to the fire pit as a stirring stick. He jabbed at the dirt, leaving pockmarks in the dry soil.

Chad said, "This is a difficult time for you and Jim."

Sighing, Con said, "I feel like this is a bad dream."

"Yeah," said Jim, as he stretched his legs out and inspected his hiking boots. His muscular shoulders pressed back against the canvas director's chair, which seemed too delicate to contain such brawn. He began speaking, his voice soft despite his size and usual brusqueness.

"When Uncle Brian was getting ready to go hunting last year," Jim said, "he was acting strange. Most of the time he talked and laughed when we were together. And he loved being out in the woods with his hunting buddies."

"But when he came to my football game against Colorado State the weekend before elk season opened, he was preoccupied," Jim continued. "I asked him why he was going out hunting alone, and he said he needed to think about some business problems. I reminded him that he had always warned Con and me not to go into the woods alone. He laughed and said that he had been to this particular area so many times that he knew the trees on a first-name basis. He told me not to worry, that he would make some decisions while he was alone, and everything would be fine." Jim's voice rose as he choked back his grief. "I believed him."

"Uncle Brian knew these mountains," Con confirmed. "He knew how to take care of himself outdoors in any weather. He wasn't being macho by coming alone. He was competent to handle it."

Jim frowned. "Some people are saying that maybe he committed suicide, but Uncle Brian wouldn't do that," Jim said, with growing emphasis. "He loved being alive. He loved Aunt Cathy, and he cared a lot about you and me. That's who our uncle was." Jim shot a look at Con, then Chad, quit talking, and stared at the fire.

"The insurance company told Aunt Cathy that they can't pay out on Uncle Brian's life insurance policy until his body is found or until he is legally declared dead," said Con. "That could take years. They've insinuated that he might have just decided to disappear, and unless he's dead, they are not required to make the payment."

Con sat up straighter in his chair. "In the meantime, our uncle's partner, Stan Cline, is making all the decisions regarding their joint business," said Con. "He told Aunt Cathy not to worry, she has enough to think about already. But Cathy told me a while back that her share of profits has gone down a lot since Uncle Brian went missing. The economy in Colorado has been pretty good, so she doesn't understand why the business isn't doing as well as last year."

"Not for engineers," said Jean, looking to Chad, who didn't react.

"Aunt Cathy is worried about being able to keep her house," said Con. "With no insurance money, she may need to find a job, and that would be hard for her. She's been a community volunteer for years since she and Uncle Brian didn't have any kids. She doesn't want to give that up, but she may have to.

"The thing is," Con said, letting out a deep sigh, "until Uncle Brian's body is found, we're all having trouble, even more than just missing him." Con leaned forward, propping his bony forearms on his thighs. "Jim's mom and mine worked for Stan and Uncle Brian for years, but about two months ago, Stan told both of them that he was going to have to reorganize the company. He said that he was combining some of the operations, especially accounting and marketing, and he had to reduce the number of employees in those areas." Con jabbed at the fire with the stirring stick, and sparks exploded. "What seems strange to my mom and to me is that her job already involved doing the books for all of their Steamboat businesses. Someone else had to pick that up and combine it with the Grand Junction accounts, but she would have been in a better position to do it than anyone else."

"Does anyone want to roast marshmallows?" Matt asked. "I'll get them out."

"Yay!" said Ty and Kelsie together, scrambling to the table to grab roasting forks. They handed the forks to Matt, and he pushed soft white orbs onto the tines of each fork. Everyone settled back in their chairs with their dessert floating over coals at the edge of the fire.

"I haven't thought to mention to you yet that I met your mothers this afternoon," Jean said.

Both young men looked at her in astonishment, faces growing pale in the firelight.

"What?" Jim asked in surprise.

"How?" Con asked. "Are they here?"

Jean nodded affirmation. "Actually, so are your grandparents." Jean knew that Con and Jim hadn't been back to the campground long enough for their mothers to find them. "Your mothers would like to talk to you tonight before you go to bed. They're down the hill from you in #14 and #15." She paused. "They came to look for your uncle, too."

"What?" sputtered Jim.

Con was quiet, staring into the fire. Then he said, "Jim and I didn't tell them we were coming here because we didn't want to upset them. We figured that if we looked for...Uncle Brian...and didn't find him, it would be better for them not to have to go through the torment of waiting. I don't know why we didn't think that they would want to help." He sighed, his head bowing. "None of us have talked much to each other since last fall.

Josie had been silent for a long time. Now she looked across the fire at Con and said, "A lot of people want to help, Con. Tomorrow morning, I'd like to go with you and Jim."

"Have you talked to your folks about it?" Con asked Josie. He turned toward Chad. "I realize you don't know us well, but I promise that we will watch out for Josie if she comes with us. Another set of eyes would be a big help."

"It's Josie's decision," Chad said. "I think she's already made up her mind." Chad tipped his head toward his daughter. Josie nodded.

"I have, Dad," Josie said, adding, "I'm going."

"Thanks, Josie. We'll pick you up at about 6 a.m.," Con said. "Be ready for a long day." Con gave her an awkward smile as he began packing his guitar in the case.

Rising from his chair, Con said, "Jim, let's go. We have another visit to make, and it's getting late."

Jim rose and circled the dying fire to where Jean and Chad sat. Extending his hand, he said, "Thanks for the dinner. The food was great."

Chad stood and shook hands. When Jim held out his hand to Jean, she hesitated, then put her arms around him for a quick hug. With a slight blush, but smiling his thanks, he turned to leave. Jean walked over to Con, giving him the same treatment.

The young men turned away from the Brannings and their fire, and Con followed Jim up the hill into the darkness.

§

Jean lay awake next to Chad for a long time after turning off the light. She admitted to herself that she was becoming emotionally involved in this tragedy. She smiled to herself as she realized that this was a reverse case of "like mother, like daughter." Still, she was glad to see the compassion motivating Josie in volunteering for what might be a grisly task. Or maybe it was an emerging crush...on which boy?

Chad snored, and Jean dozed off at last, dreaming of something dark and cold reaching out for her from the forest as sunlight retreated.

7

When the alarm buzzed Tuesday morning, Jean pulled her pillow tight over her head. Chad reached over her and hit the snooze button to silence it. But the chill mountain air and intensifying sunlight streamed through their window, rousing them both. Sensing warmth from her husband, still by her side, Jean heard the trailer door's latch click and sat up, startled, before remembering that Josie was joining her new friends for the day in their search for their uncle. Josie must be leaving, she thought.

Chad swung his long legs out of the bed and leaned sideways to kiss Jean. "You've missed out on the good fishing this morning, sleepyhead. I'd better go earn some money because there aren't going to be enough fish to keep us fed at this rate."

Just then they heard rustling out by the picnic table. Chad stepped into the main room of the trailer as the outer door was tugged open. Ty stuck his head inside the trailer and yelled, "Mom! The fish must have been really hungry or something. Come and see!"

Jean, drawing a robe around herself, joined her exhilarated young son. Ty opened the damp creel and pulled out a large rainbow trout—a silvery fish with a pink stripe on each side.

Peering into the pouch, Jean could see four smaller fish, brookies comparable in size to yesterday's catch. All had been gutted and were ready to be cooked.

"Hey, Chad! Maybe you won't have to work so hard after all," Jean said. "We seem to have a natural-born fisherman in the family." Ty beamed as his mother gave his shoulders a one-armed hug and then knocked his hat askew.

"I could get used to this," said Chad. "Ty, I like fresh fish for breakfast." Chad gave Ty a high-five. "But what's your trick? I could never catch anything."

"I don't have any tricks, Dad," Ty answered. "At least not yet. I'm just doing what Mom taught me."

"Well, some people have the knack, and some don't. You must have inherited it from your grandfather," said Chad.

"What do you mean, Chad? Jean stiffened, indignant at Chad for ignoring her part in the effort. "I showed him how to fish!" said Jean, hands on her hips.

"I meant you must have inherited it from your mom, Ty!" Chad said, covering his slip.

Jean was proud that Ty had gone fishing that morning on his own initiative. He knew that fishing was more than luck. It was a lot of observation and patience, as well as skill. And the stream was small and Ty could swim, so she didn't have to worry about the water posing much risk. She was a touch concerned that neither she nor Chad had noticed his exit from the trailer early that morning, though. She'd have to try to be more aware of what was going on around her.

Jean took the bag from Ty and said, "We're having trout and hashbrowns for breakfast. Why don't you two get cleaned up?"

Matt and Kelsie came outside to eat with the rest of the family. Matt was looking pretty tired this morning. He had stayed up late the night before to stargaze. The Milky Way had received most of his attention. Since the city lights on the Front Range often obscured all but the brightest stars, the dense band of the milky white galaxy intrigued him. But Kelsie was bouncing with energy as she ate, and Jean and Chad talked about the coming weekend.

"Mom, may I go down and talk to the kids camping in the bottom loop? Please?" Kelsie asked. "There's a girl about my age, and I think there are a couple of boys that might be the same ages as Matt and Ty." Kelsie waited while Jean swallowed her coffee.

"We'll do the chores first thing this morning, since the campground is full," said Jean. "Then you can go. Just be sure to tell me where you'll be," Jean cautioned.

Jean knew that being away from home for a whole summer meant that her children would scout for new friends as they came and went. She understood, though. Jean was already missing a couple of the close friends she had come to rely on since Chad had begun working away from home. She now needed friends to talk to, while in the past, she had confided in Chad.

Something had changed between herself and Chad since he lost his job. Jean now needed friends—other women—to talk to.

Anyway, it would be nice to talk over the problem of the missing man and his family with other women just to relieve her uneasiness. Some people could ignore intuition. Why couldn't she? Jean thought. Life might be easier.

As Jean watched Chad drive away, she thought how awful it would be if her own husband disappeared. She shivered.

§

Early in the afternoon, Jean worked in the office sorting through a burgeoning pile of paperwork. Since several campers had checked out earlier, she was listing available campsites when the phone rang.

"Columbine Campground, Jean speaking," she said. Leaning her head toward her left shoulder to hold the receiver in place, she continued scanning her records.

"Hello," said the woman caller. "Are you taking reservations? We plan to arrive tonight and stay for several days, but I wanted to be sure that there's space available."

"Yes, I am. What kind of site do you need?" Jean saw that she had one tent, three pull-thru, and a half-dozen RV sites. No problem.

"I'd like a pull-thru, if you have one," said the woman. "I'm towing a small camp trailer with my pickup. I'm not very experienced with backing it up. Neither is my husband." She laughed.

"Sure, I'll reserve #8 for you. If you arrive after the office is closed, just leave your registration in the letter-drop by the window. May I have your name?" Jean picked up her pen and began writing on a sticky-note. In a few moments, she had the information she needed and confirmed the reservation.

As Jean hung up the phone, she noticed the Forest Service pickup coming up the hill. There were two people in the cab.

Bob Duncan, the forest ranger she had met Sunday, was driving. She left the office and walked to Bob's window to greet them.

"Hello, Bob. I must have missed you yesterday." Jean waited for an introduction.

"Jean, this is Deputy Travis Jordan. Travis, meet Jean Branning, the campground host." Bob's speech was formal, except for the use of first names. They chatted about the area and the weather, with both men staying seated in the pickup cab. Then Bob asked Jean, "How are things going?"

"Well, we filled all the spaces the second night. We have just a few open tonight, and I have one reservation yet to arrive." Jean leaned down to swat a persistent horsefly that kept attacking her calf. Straightening up, she asked, "Are you finding fewer people camping out of boundaries? Can you tell yet whether opening the campground has helped to keep campers in check?"

Bob nodded, "Yes, the campground does seem to be taking some pressure off of undeveloped areas. It's a bit soon to tell for sure, but it would be nice if this helps mitigate the impact people are having on the forest."

Pausing, Bob glanced at the deputy, then continued. "Jean, the deputy and I are here on business. Yesterday, I noticed quite a few people over in the Whiskey Creek area looking for something. I remembered what you said about the two college students coming here to look for their missing uncle, and I suspected the rest of those people were out there searching as well. I talked to the sheriff this morning, and he decided to reopen the search for Brian Gowen. He was about to do it anyway.

Deputy Jordan led the search last fall, and he's in charge now. I brought him over to meet you and explain his plan."

Jean looked past Bob to the deputy, who wore a tan uniform with a trooper's hat shaped like Bob's, and nodded. Deputy Jordan was in his early fifties with graying sideburns. He was a bit husky but looked strong. His expressionless face transformed to purposeful as he met Jean's gaze.

"You're aware that a man was lost up here last fall, aren't you, ma'am?" the deputy asked.

Deputy Jordan's question seemed odd to Jean. Of course she knew, and he must know that she knew if for no other reason than because of her conversation with Bob.

Jean responded, "Yes, I've heard about Brian Gowen not returning from an elk hunting trip." She waited for the deputy to continue.

"Bob called yesterday to say that people were out searching the area around Gowen's campsite," said Deputy Jordan, repeating what Bob had just told Jean. "He was surprised to see so many. He was also concerned that if they wandered too far out into the woods, someone else might get lost. Bob asked if we had any plans to search this summer for the missing man, and if so, when. Sheriff Ramirez reopened the search this morning and put me in charge."

Jean shifted forward, leaning her forearms on the pickup door, listening with full attention.

"I'll get a couple of trained dogs and their handlers up here tomorrow to scour the area adjacent to the original campsite," said Deputy Jordan. "We have about a week available to do an official search, and we'll cover as much ground as possible in that time."

"With so many people already combing Whiskey Creek," the deputy continued, "I've decided to enlist their help as volunteers. Most likely, they would go out searching anyway, but if they're part of an organized group, my men can keep track of them."

Jean nodded in agreement. "Yes, that's a good idea," she said.

Deputy Jordan pulled a sheet of paper from a folder lying on the seat. "Here's a flyer to post on the camp bulletin board, announcing the search and informing those interested to meet at the bridge over Whiskey Creek tomorrow at 8 a.m. There, we'll divide into groups and assign grids for each to search." Deputy Jordan shifted his weight in the passenger seat. "I don't want to have to start another search for someone left behind in the woods, so I would appreciate your help in keeping an eye on your guests to make sure they all come back to camp."

"Sure," Jean responded as she took the flyer. "I can do that. I'll have my family make rounds just after dark and see if everyone has returned. If anyone seems to be missing, we can watch for them here at the entrance and report their absence, say, at 8 p.m. Does that sound good to you?"

Deputy Jordan nodded his head to affirm. "That would be a big help, ma'am," he said. "With any luck, this search won't take too long now that the snow is almost gone. It's melted much faster than we expected, causing flooding that blocked roads. I wish we could have done it before all these people came, though. There might have been clues buried under the snow as to which direction he went, and we might have found them right after they were exposed. By now, evidence may be trampled."

"Do you know that the missing man's parents, sisters, and nephews, and maybe his wife, are staying here at Columbine?" Jean asked, realizing that Deputy Jordan had only mentioned the boys, Con and Jim. She didn't know whether this information was important to the deputy but thought she should tell him. "His nephews have been out looking today, and I suspect the other family members have been, as well."

"I thought it likely that they're the people seen in the area near where Gowen camped," Deputy Jordan sighed. "I hope that a stranger discovers his body. Better yet, one of my deputies."

"Now that I've met much of the family," said Jean, "I'm curious about something. How did they react when they were notified of Brian Gowen's disappearance last fall?" Since Jean was being drawn into the search, she felt justified in asking a few questions. After all, she was going to be checking on their safety every night.

"What's your interest in this, ma'am?" said the deputy.

"I'm trying to understand whether I need to be concerned for my family, especially my oldest daughter, Josie, interacting with the Gowens," said Jean. "They've gathered here without telling each other, and Josie's helping the nephews search. Is there any reason to suspect any of them being involved in the disappearance?"

"Well, as I recall, they seemed shocked," Deputy Jordan replied. "They couldn't understand how such a capable outdoorsman could disappear." Staring at the floorboards, he added, "The man made his biggest mistake in hunting alone. If a search could have been called earlier, we might have found him before exposure did its work."

The deputy looked up from the floor to Jean. "Every year we have people hunting for elk or deer all over these mountains," he said. "Some of them are here to enjoy being outside and know how to cope with its capricious nature. Others come here more for the macho image of being a great hunter. Still others are here for the social scene. Some of the parties end up in drunken brawls. It's amazing there aren't more accidental—and intentional—shootings related to drinking."

"I know," said Jean. "My dad told stories about hunting parties he encountered."

Shaking his head, the deputy continued. "Brian Gowen doesn't fit the profile of most missing hunters. He had a habit of being well prepared."

"Well, I hope the search is successful," Jean said. She wondered what would happen if it wasn't. Would there be people out there searching on their own all summer?

"Thank you for your cooperation, Mrs. Branning," said Deputy Jordan. "Don't be reluctant to call if anyone is late returning to camp." He touched the tips of his fingers to the brim of his hat in farewell as the ranger turned the key in the ignition.

Bob nodded his goodbye to Jean. "I'll be back later. Let me know if you need any help explaining the search to your guests."

Lifting her hand in a solemn farewell, Jean backed away from the truck and gave a stiff smile, grim as she imagined a faceless man lying in the forest.

§

Con and Jim returned Josie to the Branning's camp just before dusk. Barely lifting her feet as she walked away from the little yellow car, she joined her family by the campfire, sagging onto a chair and staring into the fire.

"No luck, I take it," Chad said. Jean watched him survey their tired daughter from head to toe as he let his comment sit unanswered. Jean noticed that her husband was learning the art of avoiding addressing direct questions to their teenage daughter whenever possible.

Jean filled a plate for Josie. As she handed the food and a glass of milk to her daughter, she restrained herself from smoothing Josie's shimmering copper-red hair. Josie was approaching adulthood, and she often interpreted her parent's interest and gestures as them treating her like a child, and she told them so. Of course, that is not what Jean and Chad intended, but they were trying to give their daughter some space. They were allowing her to make decisions on her own, especially since more responsibility had fallen on her to help at home since Chad began commuting.

"We must have walked ten miles today!" Josie's voice was quiet, frustration evident. She slumped in the chair as she picked at her salad with a fork, reflecting the defeat she was feeling. "There wasn't any trace of Con's and Jim's uncle. We couldn't even tell where he had camped, except there were some ruts where he must have gotten stuck when he backed up to park."

"After an entire winter, it would be difficult to find any signs," Chad said.

Josie sighed and sat up straighter. Setting her fork on the plate and reaching for her hamburger, she looked at her dad and said, "We're going to search again tomorrow." Taking a big bite, she leaned back and chewed.

"Your mom said the sheriff's office has decided to reopen the search," said Chad. "They are asking anyone interested to meet at the bridge over Whiskey Creek tomorrow morning at eight. I think it would be a good idea if you and your friends joined that effort. You can cover a lot more ground with a larger group." Chad didn't add that he would be less worried about their safety as well.

Josie lifted her glass of milk and drank enough to wash the burger down. Then she said, "That's a good idea. There are so many places to look!" she said. "We searched all sorts of nooks and crannies around rocks and logs, and we couldn't even get to gullies and cliffs within view. The ground was too rough and inaccessible."

Josie shook her head, appearing frustrated. She fell silent and continued to eat.

Jean, worry etching her face, looked at Josie. She could see how much Josie cared about her new friends' predicament. Jean cared, too, about Con's and Jim's suffering, and her daughter's involvement with them. And she hoped that someone would find the body. Jean just hoped that someone wasn't Josie.

8

The fourth morning dawned clear and crisp. The Branning family was settling into a comfortable routine, and Jean was beginning to get a handle on being campground host. Ty went fishing at dawn, but he didn't catch anything. Matt and Kelsie were up and dressed, and Kelsie was already clamoring to visit the kids down the hill. Josie went to tell Con and Jim about the official search, while Jean and Chad hurried to finish their coffee.

"If I can arrange for the kids to spend the morning with their new friends, I think I'll go for a hike." Jean took Chad's mug and set it with the breakfast dishes waiting to be taken inside.

"Are you going to join the search?" inquired Chad, reaching into his pocket and pulling out his car keys.

"No, I want to get away from the crowd." Jean was feeling a bit overwhelmed by the immediate success of the campground. The paperwork and maintenance were going well, but talking with so many strangers the evening before had made her realize that she was somewhat responsible for a nomadic town of thirty units. "I was thinking about driving east to a place I went years ago. The mountain was clear-cut, and I'm curious to see how well the forest has reestablished itself. I'll be back by noon. I just need a little break."

Chad hugged his wife and lingered on a soft kiss. "Be careful, and enjoy yourself," he said. "With another quick kiss, he said, "See you tonight!"

Releasing Jean, Chad strode to his car and left for the day.

Jean cleared away the debris of another meal and followed her children's path to their newfound friends.

§

To get to the logging road Jean remembered from her childhood, she first steered the big family van north over King Solomon Creek, uphill and around several switchbacks. Sunlight filtered through the treetops and flickered over rippling water in small streams. As she swung around a curve, Jean looked up the hill away from the road and saw a doe staring down at her before it bounded out of sight.

Descending into the next valley, she approached Whiskey Creek. On the west side of the road were two improvised parking lots, one on each side of the glistening creek. She counted three sheriff's vehicles, all four-wheel drive, and a dozen other assorted vehicles surrounded Con's yellow VW. Two officers followed leashed German shepherds along the stream banks. People fanned out to begin the search, and Jean spotted Josie's familiar coppery head in the throng. Jean felt comfort in knowing that today's search would be supervised by the sheriff's department.

Continuing down the road, Jean pondered the magnitude of the search. Time and terrain were determined enemies against which the sole weapon was perseverance. Brian Gowen's family was persevering, Jean thought, questions flooding her mind. But why hadn't the Gowens planned this search together? Didn't they routinely talk to each other? After all, there was such a thing as a telephone. Why hadn't the daughters discussed their intentions with their parents, or for that matter, the sons with their mothers? There could be some strain between the elderly Gowen's and their daughter-in-law, Brian's wife, but it astounded Jean that each set of campers had arrived totally ignorant of their relatives' plans.

Jean didn't have the answers. Shaking her head, she didn't understand how a family could become so fragmented. She hoped that her own family would keep close ties as the years passed, though she knew that might not happen. It seemed to her that more and more of her friends were wrestling with major problems. Several couples she knew, who appeared deeply committed to each other, had recently divorced. Teenagers who had been bright, energetic and good-natured children just a short time ago struggled now with rebellion, drugs, and alcohol. Kids in her neighborhood, who she watched grow up in caring homes, stole from families and neighbors to buy their drugs, or sneaked prescriptions from their parents' and grandparents' medicine chests. Employers were downsizing—usually middle-aged workers like her husband—compelling families to uproot from homes, extended families, schools, and communities. The same middle-aged workers were sandwiched as caretakers between their children and their aging parents. Sometimes, since Chad lost his job and started commuting, Jean felt that everything around her was in chaos and what she knew and valued was being sucked into a vortex. Although she and Chad remained married, in his absence, she sometimes felt like a single mother. Jean struggled to center herself and her family in a solid support system, since most seemed to be disintegrating.

It didn't take long for Jean to find the familiar logging road. One July day long ago, her parents and some of their friends had piled into an old Woodie, a wood-paneled Chevrolet station wagon, and driven to this spot. The road had been passable then for a two-wheel drive vehicle. She hoped her van would be capable of climbing it now.

Jean touched the brakes, shifting down to second gear to make the left turn onto the dirt road. As she started the ascent, trees crowded the narrow trail. The roadbed was dry, but a rivulet of water snaked its way down one side, eroding a narrow gully. The pines seemed darker green in this place where the mountain blocked the sunlight.

Driving slowly up the hill, Jean observed small patches of snow packed under fallen tree trunks and occasional rock ledges. A wide curve brought her back into bright light, and the beauty of a young forest surrounded her. Grass and wildflowers covered the deep loamy floor with soft shades of green, punctuated by blue prairie flax, yellow tansy, red Indian paintbrush, and purple lupines. Butterflies floated across the velvety surface, using camouflage to hide themselves as they drank sweet nectar. Bees buzzed around lazily, pollen clinging to their legs. Fallen trees nestled into the hillside, providing anchors for rich soil and fragile plant life.

A mature stand of quaking aspens clung to the edges of the open meadow. The gray-white trunks had thickened over the years since the hill was logged, the aspens having pioneered the chain of reforestation, cloning underground as the largest organism on Earth. Their leaves flickered in a breeze so slight it was otherwise imperceptible to Jean. She could imagine the majestic colors they would display in the fall, when frost triggered green leaves to change to yellow, gold, and red.

Beyond the aspens were young ponderosa pines. After a quarter of a century, they had grown to a respectable height of thirty feet. Scattered in uneven stands and appearing healthy, the pines had been sewn by nature. Jean could not pick out uniform rows, which were obvious in many forests that had been harvested and replanted in the Southeast. But all around the bases of the pines was debris from long-ago clear-cutting. Stumps squatted like toadstools, but grasses and wildflowers hid their nakedness. Rotting logs lay here and there, some of them left behind to prevent erosion and to enrich the soil.

As Jean penetrated the young stand of timber, towering trees again curtained the ground, casting shade that cooled the air around her, different from the pleasant warmth of the sunlit meadow. She continued to skirt the mountain, being careful to avoid deep ruts formed by spring runoff.

Just past a large boulder, Jean's path was blocked. A fallen tree, too big to move without a chainsaw, extended across the narrow dirt track. Bringing the van to a stop, she shifted into reverse, turned the engine off, and set the parking brake. This was a good place to begin her solitary hike. She could drive no farther.

Stepping down from the van with her small daypack, Jean thought how much nicer it would be if she had an old Willys

Jeep like her father had owned and the elder Gowen's had towed into camp. Granted, it always seemed to have something that needed to be tinkered with, but it had crawled over trails where newer four-wheel drive vehicles feared to tread. There was something about the dull-red beaten exterior of the Willys that said it belonged in the woods. With the windshield folded forward onto the hood and fishing poles tied on, "Hemorrhoid Hannah," as her father had christened it, had taken them almost everywhere they wanted to go. Of course, they had often been stuck up to the axles in muck, or the engine had vapor-locked while climbing a steep hill, or some other calamity had turned an outing intended for leisure into a backbreaking afternoon in the boondocks. Jean smiled. Even the hassles held charm in retrospect.

Jean walked up the road, stepping over the fallen trunk and noticing that the tree hadn't been blown over by the wind as she first thought. A smooth cut severed it at the base from its stump. The tree had been cut down and left across the road. Looking closer at the tree, she saw that its branches still bore green needles, although they were yellowing in death. Jean estimated that the tree had not been lying there for very long. She was probably the first person to drive to this point this summer, or the tree already would have been cut into sections and stacked alongside the road.

The logging trail was a comfortable walking path, which enticed her to trudge on for about a half mile. Finding another open meadow facing southwest, she left the road and climbed the hill to a rocky outcropping. Wiping her dusty hands on her jeans, she stretched her arms high over her head and surveyed the view. Off in the distance, she saw the stony top of Hahn's Peak standing sentinel over the forests. Tall pines softened the profiles of many of the other mountains, but the trees thinned out at the lower flanks where mountains blended with valleys and creeks. Shadow and light danced over the vista as fluffy white clouds drifted east, perhaps to drop their moisture on the other side of the Continental Divide in late afternoon.

A sudden movement at the fringe of the trees brought Jean's gaze earthward, where she saw from a distance the sleek tan coat of a doe. Almost too small to be seen among the vegetation were twin fawns, still bearing spots that helped hide them from predators. The doe held her head still, nostrils flaring as she sniffed the air for danger. Satisfied that there was no imminent threat, she led her offspring a short way from the trees, allowing them to bask in warm sunshine and munch on abundant grass.

Jean luxuriated in the pastoral scene. She felt like no other human had ever been there. Of course, she knew it was not so. After all, the hill had been logged, and the road still meandered below as a reminder of others' passage. She closed her eyes, basking in the meadow's peace, feeling warmth on her face from the sun, hearing the gentle hum of insects.

One of those insects wasn't so gentle. Jean felt the sting of a horsefly on the back of her hand. She swatted at it and missed, feeling the shape of her watch under her fingers. She was reluctant to look at it, guessing that it was time to leave this haven if she wanted to get back to camp by noon. She still had chores to do, and new campers would be arriving.

Jean stood, brushed dirt and grass off the back of her pants, and began picking her way down the hill toward the road. Keeping her eyes on the ground, she noticed tiny flowers she wouldn't have been able to see from a distance. Jean remembered the small lavender orchid-like jack-in-the-pulpits her brother had once pointed out to her, and she wondered if there might be some blooming now in the shade. Angling over to the edge of the woods, she made her way parallel to and just above the guiding road.

Jean could tell that the doe, still as a statue, was watching her; her ears angled Jean's way, and her tail stood straight up from its rump. When Jean began to veer toward the doe, it sniffed the air, turned tail, and led her scampering fawns deep into the sheltering trees. Jean watched them go, wishing that her children could have seen the fawns. As she shifted her line of vision down the hill to the point where she intended to enter the woods, she saw a quick dagger of reflected light near where the deer had grazed. Altering her course, she went to investigate, thinking it was an old bottle or some other piece of trash she would pack out.

As Jean approached the place where she had seen the reflection, she noticed that a small bush had broken off near the ground. That seemed odd. She looked at the dirt beside the bush and saw a fuzzy wool glove covered with grime. A hunter had probably lost it, she thought as she picked it up. That would make sense. And the glint she had seen might be a beer can. The log was just a few yards uphill. Skirting a chest-high bush, Jean swept the ground with her eyes for other abandoned bits.

Jean froze. The sparkle that had drawn her to this spot wasn't a can or foil wrapper at all. A pair of eyeglasses lay at her feet. One lens and a temple were missing, but the other lens was shining in the sun. Wedged under the big log was something bright orange covered with dirt and dried brown mud. Between the log and the glasses lay what looked like a decomposing human head.

Jean dropped the glove she had picked up as trash, and gasped in horror, covering her mouth with both hands to stifle a rising scream. She thought fleetingly of Josie; she was glad Josie was miles away from here. She stood for a long time staring at the grim scene, details imprinting themselves in her mind as her body remained rigid with shock.

Small branches were piled against the full length of the log. It looked deliberate, not random. The hunter's orange cloth was so bright it couldn't be completely camouflaged. Jean skirted the trunk. On the uphill side, she saw what appeared to be the trigger of a gun protruding from the dirt. She returned to her starting point and scanned the site again. Squatting down, she looked at the skull, lying on its left front side, but she could see that bone stopped at the nose, leaving a gaping space. Leaning closer, she saw a smaller hole in the back of the skull, partly hidden by matted black hair clinging in patches.

This person was shot, thought Jean.

Jean had never seen the body of a person who had died from violence. She'd been with her own father when he died in a hospital, but natural death hadn't prepared her for this gruesome scene. Even so, she had read enough mysteries to have a good idea that her assumption was correct. Backing away, glad that she had not stepped too close to the log or the body, she turned around and walked briskly down the tunnel formed by the road and trees, now gloomy and menacing, the peace shattered.

Jean dropped her keys as she fumbled opening the door of her van, then tossed them on the dash as she climbed in. She sat gripping the van's steering wheel while she took deep, cleansing breaths to calm herself. As her shaking subsided, she inserted the key into the ignition, started the van, and turned it around.

Striking with the speed of a lightning bolt, Jean realized she knew that the dead person couldn't have hidden under that log after being shot. She knew someone else had put the body there.

Jean knew that the man had been murdered, and the man was Brian Gowen.

9

Jean shifted to a lower gear as the van picked up speed, and the transmission whined, slowing her descent. Dust billowed from behind, blocking the view in her rear-view mirror.

How could this be? Here Jean was, alone, miles away from the search team that was looking for a man lost and presumed killed in a blizzard. They were looking for a dead man, a body. She didn't think that two men could have died here in the recent past without someone having said something about it, which meant that Jean had good reason to believe that she had found Brian Gowen's body. And he hadn't died in the blizzard.

The time it took to travel fifteen miles down the logging road from the body to Whiskey Creek seemed interminable, and Jean's mind raced. How was the Gowen family going to take this? Accidental death was one thing, but murder—well, answers had to be found. Why would anyone have wanted to kill this man? Why here? The damaged skull and face. Who shot him? And if it wasn't murder, why hide the body under a log?

Jean was relieved to know there were sheriff's deputies in the area. When she arrived at Whiskey Creek, she would tell them what she had found and let them handle the whole thing.

Then she would go back to camp and forget the ghastly open grave she had happened upon. She wanted to gather her children together and shut out the horror.

Jean thought of the doe she had seen earlier, fleeing danger with her fawns. That's what Jean wanted to do, to flee. The thought startled her. Her family was not in danger, was it?

Brian Gowen died months ago, thought Jean. Surely the murderer was long gone.

§

When Jean got to the Whiskey Creek bridge, she pulled the van off the road. The cars belonging to the searchers were still there, but she didn't see any people. Then she noticed that the driver's door on one of the sheriff's SUVs was open. A uniformed man sat inside studying a map.

Jean stepped down from her van and strode toward the deputy.

"Excuse me," Jean croaked, startled by the sound coming from her throat. "I think I found Brian Gowen...Brian Gowen's body."

The officer jumped out of his vehicle and approached Jean. "You weren't out here with the others earlier, were you?" the deputy asked.

"No, I wasn't," said Jean. "He's—the body is—east of here under a log. And I'm pretty sure he was shot." Delivering this news had made it real to her. With her message spoken aloud, Jean began to shake and her knees to give way, succumbing to shock because of what she had seen.

The deputy moved to Jean's side and helped seat her in the backseat of his car. He found an unopened bottle of water, and after getting her to take a few sips and quiet herself, the deputy began to question her.

"I'm Deputy Andy Bailey. What's your name, ma'am?" The deputy pulled a small pad of paper and a pen from his shirt pocket and prepared to take notes.

"I'm Jean Branning," she said. "I'm the campground host at the new Columbine Campground." Jean felt calmer, and her voice grew steadier as she spoke.

"I've heard about you from Bob Duncan," said Deputy Bailey. "Tell me what you saw, ma'am." The deputy listened as Jean described the body stuffed under the log, the skull rolled away from its hiding place, and what she believed to be a bullet hole in the back of the skull.

"Can you show me on the map where you found the body?" the deputy asked, reaching for the topographical map on the front seat of his car. Grids were marked off with yellow highlighter, indicating the methodical plan for searching large areas of difficult terrain.

"This is where we are now," Deputy Bailey said, pointing to a mark on Whiskey Creek.

Jean rose from the car and took the map from the officer. Studying the map, she walked to the front of the car and placed it on the hood. Jean used her forefinger to trace the route she had taken to the logging road.

"There's a tree across the logging road about two and a half miles from the main road turnoff," Jean said. "Right about here," she said, pointing to the map. "I parked the van and walked on the road, probably another half mile. The body is on the left side of a clearing, above the road."

The deputy straightened and leaned into the front of his car for a shortwave radio. He extended the antenna, switched the unit on, and instructed his search teams to return to base. After receiving responses affirming that all searchers had received his order and were complying, he called sheriff's headquarters, requesting that dispatch send the medical examiner, coroner's van, and an evidence team to the scene.

Placing the radio on its hook, Bailey turned to Jean. "It would be best if you ride with me back to the spot you found the body," he said. "I'm sorry to have to ask you to do this, but it will be much quicker for us. We'll also need to have you show us exactly where you walked and what you touched. If your impression of the scene seems correct, we'll begin a murder investigation. We will need to be able to sort evidence and eliminate anything you may have disturbed."

Jean crossed her arms over her abdomen and shivered, but agreed with a shake of her head. "My daughter is among the searchers coming back in. I need to tell her to go back to camp and take care of business and the younger kids this afternoon. Then I can go with you."

"We'll wait to leave until a couple of the other deputies return," said Bailey. "I'll need to put one in charge here and have another follow us to help secure the scene." Bailey became pensive, then said, "There are so many of Gowen's relatives out here this morning that it's going to be some feat to keep them from swarming up there. It'll be over an hour before backup arrives."

Jean scanned the tree line to the west and noticed a group of four searchers emerge from the shadows. She saw Josie, Con, and Jim, along with a uniformed deputy. They were moving fast, and Jean could see the taught, anxious expressions on the young people's faces.

Turning to Deputy Bailey, Jean said, "These kids will be your biggest challenge. The boys are Brian Gowen's nephews. It's going to be difficult to keep them away. The girl is my daughter, Josie."

Bailey waited till the group arrived, then pulled the other deputy aside. Jean couldn't hear what was being said because she was besieged by questions from her daughter.

"Why are you here, Mom?" Josie asked. "Has something happened back at camp?"

Con and Jim stood silent behind Josie, anxiety making them appear older than their years.

"Everything at camp is fine, Josie," said Jean. "I can't explain just yet. Let's wait till the officers finish talking, then they will explain."

"Then something has happened, hasn't it?" Josie persisted.

Jean saw from the corner of her eye that the two deputies were approaching. She turned toward them and waited.

"This is Deputy Cutter. I'm leaving him in charge here," said Deputy Bailey, turning to face Josie, Con, and Jim. "Mrs. Branning may have found a body. She's agreed to go with me to the site. I know you young men are anxious to know if this is your uncle, but I can't let you get near the scene until we've investigated and retrieved any important information that might be left behind."

Con blurted out, "When will that be?" Beside him, Jim scuffed the dirt like a bull ready to charge.

Bailey continued. "However, I'm more concerned about other people trying to approach the area," he said, "and I could use your help keeping them at a distance. What do you say? Can I count on your cooperation?"

Jean watched as Con and Jim struggled with their emotions regarding this proposition. On one hand, Jean knew, it would allow them to get close to the scene sooner. On the other hand, could they control their emotions and resist getting in the way?

At last, Con spoke, saying, "You can count on us."

Jean turned to Josie. "I know you'd like to come with us, Josie, but it's important that you return to camp. There will be campers arriving to check in, there might be people curious about what's going on here, and the younger kids can't be left on their own all afternoon."

Josie looked at the ground. After a few moments, she looked up at her mother. "I understand, Mom," said Josie. "I'll take care of things."

Jean stepped forward and hugged her daughter, then handed Josie the van keys. "Be careful on the way back," cautioned Jean. "You haven't driven much on these roads." A strained smile accompanied the admonition.

"I'll be careful, Mom. Don't worry," Josie said.

She's growing up so fast, thought Jean. Too fast.

§

Bailey, Jean, Con, and Jim got into the deputy's Jeep Cherokee and pulled onto the road. Jim, who was quiet and tense before, was mute now as his big eyes stared out of a pale face. The stud in his tongue flashed as he licked dry lips. Con shook his head, as if to free himself from a cloud of mosquitoes, and began to ask questions.

"Do you think the body found is our uncle's?" Con asked, his voice shaking.

"I don't know," Deputy Bailey said. "Mrs. Branning found the body, and I haven't seen it yet. According to her, the person was wearing something made of hunter's orange. We can't be sure it's Brian Gowen, but there haven't been any other hunters lost up here for a very long time."

"Why is he so far away from his campsite?" Con asked. "His truck was parked here at his camp," Con gestured back toward Whiskey Creek, "where we started looking for him. He wouldn't have hiked all that way, not while hunting." Con stopped speaking, his lips pursed, poised to explode with sound.

Jean turned around in the front seat so she could see Con. "I don't know how he got there, Con," she said. "But you need to remember that if it's your uncle, he's been out here a long time. We have to wait for more information from the sheriff's office." Swallowing hard as her mind jumped to the scene they were approaching, she turned to face forward. Jean worried that these two young men were going to have trouble coping with what she'd found.

Bailey was matter-of-fact on what needed to be done. "When we arrive, I want Jim and Con to stay at the fallen tree to direct other authorities to the site. I'll leave a handheld radio with you, and if anyone other than sheriff's department or recovery team shows up, signal me, and I'll get back there right away to keep them out. If your relatives arrive, stop them.

We need to conduct a thorough investigation in the area, and I don't want anyone walking around that hillside destroying the scene."

"What are you saying?" asked Con.

Jim turned to face his cousin. "He's saying that maybe Uncle Brian didn't freeze to death."

The young men stared at each other.

10

Jean led Deputy Bailey up the road past the fallen tree, and along the edge of the clearing back to the spot where the deer had stood. She pointed to the rotting log, then let her arm fall to her side; her shoulders drooped.

"Did you touch anything," asked Bailey.

"No," Jean said. "Uh, yes. I picked a glove up over there," she said, pointing to the broken bush. "I dropped it...when I saw the body...," she trailed off. "There it is," she added, shifting the direction she was pointing.

Bailey nodded, acknowledging that he could see the glove.

"Stay here while I take a look," said Bailey. He strode across the hillside as Jean, exhausted, found a stump to sit on and wait.

So, Jean thought, the body of a man—maybe Brian Gowen—was hidden under that log. It was miles away from where his truck and campsite had been found last fall, and if Jean was correct, there was a bullet hole in the back of his skull. Someone didn't want the body found. Jean shuddered. That someone was almost certainly not a careless hunter but a murderer. Why else hide the body?

Jean watched Bailey circle the log much as she had, not touching anything, but inspecting the skull lying below the log, pausing above the broken glasses. He stopped and scrutinized the exposed portion of the rifle hidden on the uphill side of the log. After a few minutes, he rejoined Jean.

"He was murdered," Jean stated.

"Looks like it," said Bailey, sighing. "This is going to be even tougher on Gowen's family, if it is him, than an accident. We need to get a positive identification before we inform them that we've found his body. But I don't see how it could be anyone but Gowen. We haven't had anyone else reported missing anywhere near these woods for years."

§

Jean and Deputy Bailey descended the hill toward the fallen tree, where they had left Con and Jim. From a distance, the lights on the top of the Cherokee flashed blue and red, casting bruised hues across the young men's pale faces. Lost in conversation with each other, the young men's voices floated up the hill to Jean and Bailey.

"Do you suppose he shot himself?" Con asked his cousin, as he stared without seeing down the empty road.

"Uncle Brian? Never." Jim's response was adamant. "He was happy with his life. You know that."

"Yeah, but he was upset about something those last few weeks. Remember how quiet he was? What if he was depressed and we didn't know it?" Con was agitated.

"Nah, he wasn't depressed. There was something bothering him, but it had to be something going on around him, not in him." The set of Jim's arms across his chest and his solid stance defied any claim that his uncle might have committed suicide. "Remember what he told me when he came to that last game?" Jim asked. "He needed to be alone to make decisions. He was coming back."

"Decisions about what? Aunt Cathy?" Con couldn't stand still any longer. He began pacing beside the tree. Passing back and forth between sunshine and shadow, he stared at the ground.

"Come off it, Con! You know better than to think that there were any problems between Aunt Cathy and Uncle Brian. They loved each other. And he would never hurt her—or us—by killing himself," Jim said angrily. "Besides, he wouldn't walk all the way over here to do it. He would have driven!"

Jean saw Con stop in his tracks. He leaned down and reached for something under the dying pine tree but drew back and stood. He turned to Jim.

"It's a metal button from a coat," Jean heard Con say.

The rumble of vehicles brought their attention back to the road. A white panel van approached, followed by a white Ford Explorer. Jim caught a glimpse of the sign on the side of the van reading "Channel 4 News."

"Dang!" Jim exclaimed, then went for the radio, looking up the hill toward the deputy and Jean. "Deputy Bailey, a TV crew is here."

"Hold them back. I'm almost there," replied Bailey through the handset. Bailey left Jean's side and began dodging bushes and rocks, and slip-sliding down the hillside. Jean hung back, still able to hear and survey the commotion below.

Jim and Con jogged down the road past the sheriff's vehicle to where the van was parked. Two men hopped from the front of the van and opened side and back doors to retrieve equipment. Standing by the Explorer's driver's side door, a woman dressed in gray slacks, white shell, and a red summer weight jacket peered into the side mirror, touching up her lipstick and plucking at a few strands of wayward blonde hair. Dropping the lipstick into a small gray purse, she approached Jim and Con.

"Hello. I'm Ginger Waverly from Channel 4 News—here's my card." She thrust it into Jim's hand. "We heard over the police scanner that a body had been found. This may be a follow-up on last fall's missing hunter, and we're here to gather information." The news reporter waited and watched Jim's and Con's stony faces. After a long silence, she asked, "Is the sheriff here?"

"Not yet," replied Con. "But Deputy Bailey is. He'll be back soon."

"Oh, then the body can't be too far from here," said the reporter. She surveyed her surroundings before signaling the two newsmen to follow her. She moved abreast Jim, intending to circle him and approach the tree. "Is it the hunter who went missing last year?"

Jim didn't respond. Instead, he simulated a football play and moved at an angle to block her path. "Sorry," he said, "but no one is allowed past this point."

Without slowing her stride, Ms. Waverly replied, "We're the press. We're going in."

Scrambling over the trunk, Jim planted himself nose-to-nose with the woman, bringing her to a dead stop. "You're waiting here."

Ginger Waverly stood her ground, the muscular young man blocking her path. Relaxing her body and taking a step back, Waverly said in a slow, even voice, "All right. We'll wait for the deputy."

Jim stayed where he was with Con, but Ms. Waverly joined her crew. The sound of footsteps on the road behind them alerted Jim to Deputy Bailey's return.

The deputy nodded at Jim, then Con, as though to say "Well done." He circled the tree trunk before speaking to the news team.

"Hello, Ms. Waverly," said Bailey. "I see you beat my people to the scene." Bailey's expression was inscrutable.

"We're just doing our job, Deputy Bailey. And the public knows me by my first name, Ginger." The newswoman got right to the point. "What's going on?"

"All I can tell you is that we've found a body," said Bailey. "Any other information will be released at the appropriate time by the sheriff. I'm waiting for the forensics team to arrive. No one is allowed at the scene until I or the officer in charge say so," he said with authority.

"Forensics team? Does that mean there was foul play?" Ginger's eyes glittered as she riveted them on the officer's face.

"A body has been found," Bailey said. "It is in an isolated area. Since this person did not die at home in bed, we must determine the circumstances surrounding the death. I have no more information at this time." Bailey turned his back on Ginger and walked to his Cherokee, where Jean stood watching Ginger follow on Bailey's heels.

"When can we go in?" Ginger persisted.

"When we say so. Wait by your vehicles, folks." As Bailey watched Ginger retreat to the Explorer, he reached for the radio in his car and inquired when the investigative team would arrive. Assured that support was just a few minutes away, the officer straightened and turned to Jean, Con, and Jim.

"Boys, after my support team arrives, I want you to wait here while they do their work," said Bailey. Glancing at the news crew, he lowered his voice. "It looks like the body was moved from another location. The coroner will have to determine identity, but I can tell you that it appears to be a man wearing hunting clothes."

"So, it's probably our uncle," said Jim. His face was still pale but his voice was steady as he met the deputy's eyes. Con stood at his side, staring vacantly at the ground.

"I don't know for sure, but it's likely," said Bailey. "Let's keep it from Ms. Waverly for now." Bailey lifted his eyebrows and tilted his head toward Ginger and her crew, who were setting up for a live satellite blurb to use as a tickler for the evening news.

The faint rumble of engines floated up through the trees. Jim turned his face toward the sound and squinted his eyes at the flash of sun on metal. He beckoned Jean and Bailey to the fallen tree.

"I don't know if this means anything, but do you see that button? Down there?" Jim spread the dying branches apart to give Bailey a better view.

"Let's move the barricade a little farther down the road," Bailey said. "We need to take a look around here."

Just then another sheriff's department Jeep came into view. Behind it was the coroner's van and a patrol car. After passing the news crew, the vehicles stopped below Bailey's Cherokee, billowing dust catching up with and showering everyone. Sheriff Ramirez opened the driver's door and stepped out, taking in the tree, people, and situation in one sweeping glance. He coughed.

"How long has Waverly been here?" The sheriff jerked his head towards the TV crew as he spoke.

"About twenty minutes," Bailey answered. "So far, she doesn't know anything except there's a body. It looks like we have a murder on our hands, Sheriff."

"Have Johnson keep her out." Ramirez turned and spoke to a different man gathering equipment from the van. "Mac, make sure you have a camera and plenty of film."

"The area around this tree needs to be searched and photographed," Bailey said, with a flip of his hand. "The tree didn't fall on its own—it was cut down—and there's a button partially hidden under the branches."

"Document this site first, Mac, so we can clear the road for the coroner's van. Look for tire tracks and shoe prints before any traffic moves past the tree." The sheriff waved the second man from the patrol car over to his side. "Get the chain saw and move this tree out of here as soon as Mac is finished snapping pictures."

Ignoring the news cameras, Sheriff Ramirez turned to the coroner and the detective, and gestured to move uphill. "Let's take care of business," he said.

11

That night, Jean was quiet and stared into the campfire, her mind fixed on the daylight images of the mountainside miles away, caught in deep thoughts that resisted returning to the present. Chad sat with her.

Taking a sip of the brandy Chad had placed in her hand, Jean shifted in her chair and sighed.

"I didn't even know the dead man," said Jean, "but I feel angry that someone would shoot him like that, then dump him under a log. It's so brutal, so disrespectful of human life. How could anyone do that?"

"We're not talking about the average, responsible citizen here, Jean. Not everyone goes around murdering people," said Chad. "Killers aren't thinking about the value of life or human dignity."

The dry sarcasm in Chad's voice snapped Jean out of the lethargic state she had sunk into when she returned to camp, and her mind raced.

"I'm not naïve, Chad," said Jean. "Whoever did this didn't want Brian's body to be found. I don't see how that could make a difference once he was dead."

"Oh, there could be a lot of reasons," Chad replied. "Maybe it was an accident and the shooter panicked. The killer could have thought that the blizzard would be blamed for his death."

"I don't think it was an accident," said Jean. "I don't know much about forensics, but that bullet entered high on the back of his skull and blew off the side of his face. The killer must have been behind him, maybe above, on the side of a hill."

"Hmm," muttered Chad. "That would mean that the killer should have had a clear view of what he was shooting at." Chad sipped his whiskey and gazed into the fire. He yawned.

Jean stood and poked the fire with a sturdy stick. "The poor man had his hunter's orange vest on," she said. "It's pretty hard to mistake that color for deer or elk." Pounding embers off a glowing pine log, she was forced to back away from the surging heat and smoke.

Chad picked up another log and tossed it into the fire. "What difference could it make to the killer whether it took some time for the body to be found?" he said. "Why would he hide it?"

"Brian Gowen's—Cathy—is in financial trouble because his life insurance won't pay until he's declared dead. She needs to know for sure whether her husband is alive or dead," said Jean.

"And now the insurance will hold out until the murderer is found," said Chad.

"Or at least till Cathy is cleared." Jean shook her head. "No, she needs to know what happened for both her financial and emotional well-being. Whoever killed Brian Gowen wanted it to look like he was lost in the blizzard. If his body wasn't found, then no one would ever suspect he was murdered. People might have whispered about suicide, but that wouldn't have been a threat to the murderer."

"Well, I'm sure the sheriff's department will do its best," Chad said. "At least we won't have to worry for the rest of the summer about the kids stumbling across a dead body. Maybe we can get back to the business of running the campground and being a family."

Chad stood and stretched. "I'm going to bed," said Chad. "Are you coming? The kids went in over an hour ago."

But Jean was lost in thought, the distance between them growing in the darkness. She didn't respond.

Chad walked away.

§

Jean awoke the next morning to the smell of frying fish. Grabbing a robe, she moved into the small living area of the trailer to find Josie at the stove and the boys at the table.

"Where did you learn how to fry fish?" Jean took in the bowl of cornmeal and spices, the waiting platter lined with paper towels, and the second skillet with sizzling hash brown potatoes.

"Oh, I had a good teacher," Josie grinned. "You. I've been watching you for a long time, Mom. I decided this was a good morning to practice."

Josie flipped the fish over to fry on the other side and lifted the hash browns to peer at their color. Not satisfied with color just yet, she settled them back in the pan.

"Ty and Matt went out fishing early this morning," Josie continued, "and Dad said to let you sleep as long as you wanted. He said he had an early meeting. When Ty and Matt came back with fish—which, incidentally, they cleaned themselves—I just did what you do."

"They look great! And guys, you did a fabulous job fishing," Jean said. She moved to the table, put one arm around each boy's shoulders, and gave them a swift hug.

"Fishing is awesome, Mom," Ty said. "And Matt is starting to like it, too."

"Yeah. Ty and I made a deal that if he would stargaze with me some nights, I would go fishing with him. That way we can both do what we want and have a buddy to make it more fun."

"Good plan, Matt." Jean felt a warm contentment. "You know what, kids? You're awesome. And I love you so much."

Kelsie returned from the shower and smothered her mom with a bear hug as Josie began to serve breakfast.

§

Jean had just finished cleaning up the breakfast dishes when she heard the first RV of the day drive past. Looking out the window, she saw the older Gowens make their way down the hill. How sad, she thought. They had come to find their lost son's body and discovered that he had been murdered. What agony it must be to lose a child, even a grown child.

By noon, all of Brian's family except Jim and Con had packed up and left Columbine Campground. Josie had gone up the hill to see her friends and learned that they planned to stay till Saturday night. Jim and Con were going out hiking and fishing today. Josie told her mother that she thought it was best to leave them alone to sort things out. They needed time to process what had happened to their uncle.

Maintenance for the day had already been taken care of, but Jean had records to keep, so she went to the office and started sorting through registrations. She suspected that she had more spaces than her records indicated. Some of the Gowen family had paid ahead for the week but hadn't told her they were leaving early. With a sigh, she made a list of campsites available, then a second list of those she would have to confirm were unoccupied since the Gowen family's exodus. Her bookkeeping showed that the cash she had taken in balanced against registrations, but she needed to go to the bank and make a deposit.

As the afternoon wore on, a few campers checked in. But this was a Thursday, so she didn't expect the campground to fill. Matt was at the firewood concession, and Ty and Kelsie were playing soccer out in the meadow. Josie was lying on a folding chaise lounge in a filtered patch of sunlight reading a book.

Looking out on the forest and meadow, Jean wondered how everything could seem so right and peaceful when something evil had brushed so close. But was it gone?

12

The next morning, Friday, dawned bright and sunny. After Chad left for work, Jean and the kids hurried through morning tasks so they could go to Steamboat Springs. They planned to visit the library, get some food at the grocery store deli, and meet their dad at a park for lunch.

Stopping at the office to grab the bank deposit, Jean saw the answering machine's blinking light and pushed the play button: "This is Sheriff Ramirez calling for Jean Branning. I would like to talk to you, today if possible." Jean jotted down the sheriff's office and cell phone numbers and hurried out to the van, considering how she was going to fit a meeting with the sheriff in on top of everything else already planned.

As they passed Steamboat Lake, Josie said, "Mom, I forgot to tell you that Con and Jim asked me to come the community dance at the lake tomorrow night. I guess they've gone there before, and it's supposed to be a lot of fun. It isn't just for teenagers, either. It's more like the old-fashioned dances where dads dance with daughters. They play the polka, swing, big band…you know."

Jean glanced at Josie, who rode shotgun, and smiled. She did know. "You mean like the wedding dances I used to go to when

I was a little girl? I loved them!" said Jean. "How would you feel about it if the rest of the family shows up?"

Josie didn't respond right away. Jean could almost see the arguments against having her family at the dance flash through her daughter's head.

Raising her shoulder and turning toward the window, Josie answered. "No big deal. I'm just going with friends. It's not like it's a date or something."

"Thanks, Josie," said Jean. "I'll ask your dad what he thinks about going when we have lunch. I'd love to do something fun."

They were at the edge of town, passing small businesses interspersed here and there with old farmhouses, remnants of agricultural properties sold off as the city encroached. On the left, a Honda dealership displayed ATVs and motorbikes on the lot, while snow machines gleamed in the show room window. As she drove deeper into town, Jean saw a grocery store on the left and made a mental note of its location for shopping later that day.

Downtown Steamboat featured small stores with a distinct western flavor packed together, wall-to-wall. Baskets overflowing with red, white, and purple petunias adorned many of the storefronts. Traffic was heavy, as tourist season was underway, and pedestrians meandered along the sidewalks. Occasionally, someone darted across the street, but most people used the crosswalks.

Jean noticed that most of the houses had metal roofs, ranging from aged, rusted ungalvanized steel to fresh, new peacock blue and barn red. The architecture was a mix of old and new, in part because the successful ski area attracted an influx of winter vacationers and their money. Condominiums had popped up near the slopes and along the highway, boosting the economy and real estate prices.

Jean found the library in an older section of town. She parked the van and went inside with her children to help them apply for library cards. With the paperwork out of the way, she left Josie in charge of the younger kids and went to meet with the sheriff. Jean could feel four pairs of eyes following her movement to the door. She turned to give the kids a reassuring smile and waved.

The sheriff's department occupied a newish building with smooth gray concrete walls and narrow windows in front and on one side. She walked up the steps and opened the large glass door into the main lobby. A small, neatly dressed woman with short brown hair sat at a computer near the reception desk.

"May I help you?" The receptionist's alert eyes fixed on Jean's face.

"Yes. I'm Jean Branning. Sheriff Ramirez is expecting me."

The woman glanced at the phone on her desk. "The sheriff is on a phone call right now, but if you'll take a seat, I'll let him know you're here as soon as he's finished." She gestured to a waiting area with sparse décor, dark blue vinyl stackable chairs, and a magazine rack.

"Thank you," Jean responded, as she seated herself in one of the cushioned chairs. She looked around the office, taking in the skiing trophies, a framed ski poster, and a photograph of Rabbit Ears Pass. Those rocks really do look like rabbit ears, she mused to herself. She picked up the nearest magazine, which featured a skiing competition in Steamboat Springs from the previous winter. It was pretty obvious what the main winter recreation was in this town.

Jean heard the receiver click as the receptionist placed her phone in its cradle. The sound of footsteps came down the hall-way, and Jean looked up to see the sheriff. He approached her with a self-assured, commanding air, extending his hand. Jean took it in her own and rose from her chair, slinging her purse over her shoulder.

"Thanks for coming this morning, Mrs. Branning. Let's go to my office," Ramirez said, extending his arm and gesturing toward the hall. "It's right this way."

Ramirez turned and led the way down the hall, entering the first doorway on the right. An engraved brass sign announced the office as belonging to Routt County. A smaller nameplate gave the full name of the present occupant: Sheriff Jaime D. Ramirez.

As Jean entered the office, she was struck by its orderliness. The desk was clear of papers except one file centered in front of the desk chair. A computer desk, placed at a ninety-degree angle to the main desk, held a monitor, scanner, and printer. Several file cabinets lined one wall. Fluorescent overhead fix-tures lit the room, but there were no windows. Jean realized she hadn't seen any windows since the reception area.

"Please have a seat," the sheriff said, gesturing to one of the two guest chairs facing the desk, then strode to his desk chair on the other side. Jean sat down and waited for the sheriff to speak.

Leaning back, Ramirez said, "We've made positive ID on the body. It is Brian Gowen. But as you had already guessed, it looks as though someone shot him. There is no possibility of having sustained that type of injury from a self-inflicted gunshot."

"Then suicide has been ruled out?" Jean asked.

"Yes, although we won't release that information to the media just yet. I'd like to get some statements before the whole community knows he was murdered. In fact, that is why I asked you to come here today. I want to know everything you can remember about finding the body, as well as the family members you've met in the campground. I'd like to record our conversation and have it transcribed later. Is that agreeable to you?" The sheriff held two fingers over buttons on a cassette recorder, waiting for Jean's reply.

"Sure, I don't see any problem with that." Jean breathed in and sat back to think.

The sheriff pressed the play and record buttons, then stated the date, time, location, and Jean's name as well as his own.

"Most of the Gowen family left yesterday morning," Jean began. "None of them stopped to ask for refunds, even though several had prepaid fees for an entire week. I suppose they were pretty upset."

"Start at the beginning, Mrs. Branning. When did they arrive?" The sheriff's tone was patient and unhurried.

"They each came separately, except for married couples. In fact, they didn't seem to know that there were other family members planning to do the same thing as they were—search for Brian Gowen's body. Except, maybe, the sisters. And the nephews came together. The parents, Henry and Joyce Gowen, were the first to arrive. They weren't very talkative. I really don't know anything about them."

"Then Jim and Con arrived," Jean continued. "Jim Sheets is a business major and quarterback at the University of Wyoming. Conner Jenkins is a student in Laramie, too, and he's studying journalism. They are—were—Brian's nephews. Their mothers were his siblings. The boys are supposed to work here in Steamboat this summer for their uncle's partner.

"They were very close to their uncle," said Jean. "Both of them have divorced parents, and their mothers remarried. Brian was their father figure for a long time. He was helping to put them through school." Jean, saddened by their loss, shook her head and continued. "Jim and Con are worried about Brian's wife, Cathy, because she's been having financial trouble. And the boys' mothers have lost their jobs. They had been working for Brian."

"Were the boys' mothers at the campground?" Ramirez quizzed.

"Yes. I talked to them one afternoon. They're Brian's sisters. Marni Cole is Con's mother, and Kristi Weller is Jim's. Marni was in accounting, and Kristi worked in marketing for their brother." Jean paused again to gather her thoughts.

"Cathy Gowen was camping at Columbine, too," said Jean, "but I never spoke to her. In fact, I never saw her. She dropped her registration in the box while I was out of the office."

Searching her memory again, Jean relaxed. "I think that's it. I don't remember any other relatives."

"Were any of Gowen's friends registered?"

"I don't know," replied Jean. "It was almost as though everyone was keeping their plans secret until they ran into each other at the campground." She shook her head. "I can remember thinking that it was a shame they didn't seem to communicate much with each other."

"Any idea why not?" asked Ramirez.

Jean shrugged. "Not really. I suppose that they have just gone different directions over the years, or maybe, since Brian disappeared. He might have been holding his family together."

"All right. Tell me about finding the body," said the sheriff.

Jean stared at the wall past the sheriff's shoulder and replayed the drive up the mountain in her head. She told the sheriff why she chose that road, what she saw. When she was finished, she again focused on Ramirez.

"Do you know if there will be a funeral?" Jean asked.

"Yes, I believe Mrs. Gowen—the victim's wife—said it will be Monday. I don't know what is planned beyond that."

"I'd like to be there," said Jean. "I feel like I have known him through his nephews."

The sheriff rose from his chair, signaling the end of the interview. As he walked around the desk to open the door for Jean, his face became sterner and more serious.

"Remember that someone shot Brian Gowen and moved his body, Mrs. Branning," said Sheriff Ramirez. "Whoever did it is free right now and probably frantic to remain incognito. The person could be a family member or a friend. Don't get involved."

Jean met the sheriff's eyes and answered, "I don't intend to."

But she had a niggling suspicion she was going to be.

13

When Chad arrived at the park, the younger Brannings were ravenously devouring their lunch. Fried chicken, cole slaw, grapes, and pop disappeared as though sucked into a black hole. Then the kids were off to play frisbee, leaving Jean and Chad alone at the picnic table. The sky above the Brannings was clear and blue, with just a few feathery cirrus clouds drifting eastward. Tall Colorado blue spruce trees muted the brightness of the midday sun and provided welcome shade.

Jean told Chad about her visit with Sheriff Ramirez. "I'm curious about why the different groups from Brian's family didn't plan together to look for his body," she said. "The way the Gowens arrived at the campground seemed almost clandestine. Con and Jim were the only ones who were open about their purpose." Jean's finger moved over the stitching of the quilt that covered the picnic table. "I think that most families would have organized a hunt for him together if the authorities weren't already conducting an official search."

Chad sat next to Jean, his back against the edge of the table and long legs stretching out from the bench onto the grass. "We can't presume to know," said Chad. "The Gowens are the only people who can answer that question."

"Have you met any of Brian Gowen's family while you've been living in Steamboat Springs?" asked Jean.

"I've run into one or two," replied Chad, "but I haven't spent any time with them. I've met Brian's partner, Stan Cline. He has been in my office to check on a project we're doing for him on a proposed vacation condominium development. Almost everything new built in this area requires an environmental study, so we've been getting a lot of business. Anyway, he's planning to break ground by fall on a cluster of condos to be built at the foot of the ski area. They will be nice units, but not luxury class. Everything is in order for him to proceed; he just needs to submit our analysis to get county zoning to approve the permit."

A frisbee flew in low and bumped Chad's foot. He picked it up, gave it a long, backhanded swing, and let fly toward Matt at the far end of the grass, who raced to catch it.

Wondering whether Brian had been involved from the beginning of the project, Jean asked, "Were the condo plans begun before Brian was killed?"

"Sure. It takes quite a while to get all the permits in place. I think they made their initial proposal about a year and a half ago. From what I heard, Brian was doing most of the pushing and prodding up front, but Stan had to take over last fall when Brian disappeared. There haven't been any real problems with the project, although some environmental watchdogs lodged protests at the initial permit hearings."

"What were their objections?" Jean asked. In the back of her mind, she wondered whether someone outside the sphere of Brian's family and friends might have been angry about the project, maybe angry enough to kill him. But why not kill Stan as well?

"Oh, the usual," said Chad. "Habitat for native species of plants and animals would be destroyed, further stressing their ability to thrive. Concerns about one project leading to another were raised. They even tried to say that increasing the number of people using the ski area might threaten endangered species, such as the lynx."

"Are there any lynx in this area?" Jean asked in wonder.

"I don't know. I guess they're shy creatures," said Chad. "They've always been pretty rare in Colorado, but they live in remote forests above 8000 feet. They're much more common in Canada and Alaska. The last one seen in this state was illegally trapped near Vail in 1973. Remember when some ecoterrorists burned buildings and damaged lifts at the Vail ski area because they were trying to stop expansion? Their motivation—or excuse—was the lynx."

"Have they made any threats here?" asked Jean, watching their kids running across the park.

"Not that I'm aware of," Chad said. "I don't think that the people protesting this development were associated with the group that torched the Vail ski area. These were locals trying to block growth."

"What about Stan Cline?" Jean asked. "What is he like?"

"Stan seems to be a good businessman," said Chad, "although I've heard he isn't as charismatic as Brian Gowen. He has to work a lot harder at the politics involved to get things done."

"Like what?" Jean asked, as a white frisbee hit the table in front of her and skidded off the end. Matt came running, swooping down and throwing the disc in one fluid motion. Distracted, Jean followed her son with her eyes and noted the locations of the other three kids before resuming her conversation.

"When Stan presented his final plan on the development at preliminary hearings last fall, he had a hard time controlling his anger at the project's naysayers. Instead of discrediting their claims with facts alone, he inserted a lot of sarcasm and ridicule aimed their way. Of course, that wasn't very professional, but his attorney intervened and smoothed things over."

"So does Stan have a temper?"

"What, Jean? Could he have killed his partner?" Chad asked. "I suppose it's possible. I didn't see anything violent in Stan's behavior at that meeting. It was just a verbal outburst. I made a mental note to be careful about any business I did with him, and to always back up my position with notes and documents."

Chad turned toward Jean and placed his hand under her chin, turning her head toward his.

"Hey, sweetheart," began Chad, tenderly touching Jean's face, then switched to a more serious tone. "You're getting awfully interested in details about people involved in Brian Gowen's life," he said. "Someone killed him, probably someone he knew. It could be very dangerous for you to go around asking questions. I don't want you or the kids to get hurt." Chad sat up straight, which emphasized his height. "I think it's time to back away."

Jean threaded her arms around her husband's body and leaned her head against his chest. "I know," Jean sighed. "But I can't seem to stop wondering what happened. I guess I had better try to find something else to keep my mind busy."

§

After lunch, Jean and the kids stopped at the bank to make the campground deposit. A teller offered suckers to Kelsie and Ty before noticing the older kids standing nearby. She brought out two more for them, and they all thanked her.

On the way out of the lobby, a petite brunette dressed in a sleeveless yellow cotton-knit dress walked toward Jean. Slowing her stride, Jean took in the woman's neat appearance and thought she recognized her. The woman wore a Native American necklace made of various colored carved turquoise birds alternating with silver beads. Tiny blue turquoise birds dangled from the bottoms of liquid silver earrings. A narrow silver conch belt encircled her tiny waist, and her feet were clad with simple brown leather sandals.

"Are you Jean Branning?" asked the woman as she approached.

"Yes, I am," said Jean.

"I'm Cathy Gowen," the woman said. "I saw you at Columbine campground earlier this week but didn't meet you." Cathy paused, fighting the tears in her eyes. "I understand that you found my husband—my husband's body."

"I did," said Jean. "I'm terribly sorry about your loss." Jean wasn't quite sure what to say. What was the appropriate expression of sympathy, she wondered, when someone's loved one has been murdered?

"Thank you." Cathy said. "I wonder if you would be willing to tell me about—what you saw. Could you have coffee with me?"

Jean thought for a moment or two. "If you can meet me somewhere in about twenty minutes, I'll take my kids to the swimming pool. Is there a place that would be good for you?"

"Meet me at Jivin' Java. It's a block from the pool." Cathy extended her hand and touched Jean's arm. "I appreciate this."

"Don't give it another thought," Jean answered. "I'll see you there in a little bit."

Jean was already formulating questions for Cathy Gowen.

§

A short time later, Jean walked into the little coffee shop and found Cathy waiting. They each ordered espresso and biscotti, then settled back to become more familiar with each other.

"I told my daughter, Josie, where I'd be," Jean said. "I think the kids will be happy to stay in the pool for more than an hour, but Josie will bring them over here if they get tired of swimming before I get back."

"Oh, that should be plenty of time," said Cathy. "I want to know what you observed when you found Brian, and I'm hoping you can tell me about it. The sheriff has talked to me, but he hasn't told me much more than he believes that Brian was murdered." Tears again welled up in Cathy's eyes. It took a few moments for her to choke back threatening sobs. "I can't believe this could have happened."

"Are you sure you're up to this?" asked Jean.

"I need to know what happened," said Cathy. "Brian wasn't just my husband. He was my best friend. I have been going back and forth in my mind all winter and spring. I didn't believe that he could have been considering suicide, as the vicious gossips in this town have insinuated, but I was sure he was too experienced to be caught unprepared in a blizzard. We had an argument just before he left to hunt, but that was about him going alone. I was mystified by why he would consider doing that when he preached to Con and Jim to *never* hunt or fish alone. The buddy system was as important to him in the outdoors as it was to him in swimming. When he didn't come home, I started wondering if I had missed some clue or symptom of depression. I went over and over how he seemed before he left for hunting," Cathy said, her hands palms-up. "I couldn't think of any remarks he made or indications that he might be suicidal."

"I can't imagine how difficult this has been for you," said Jean.

"Brian was quieter than usual before he left," said Cathy, "but I knew that he was worried about something with the business. I even wondered for a while, though I didn't think it possible, whether he could have faked his disappearance and gone off somewhere to begin a new life. But his truck and all his belongings were found at the campsite, and I knew he couldn't stage something like that. He had very strong ethical values. Now I've learned that he was murdered. There wasn't anything I could do before this. If he had been lost or committed suicide, he was dead and I couldn't change that. But he was murdered, and his murderer is out there going about his life as though nothing happened." Cathy was angry, her voice growing louder as she spoke.

Jean's thoughts churned with all the possible motives and possibilities Cathy had presented, but nothing seemed to rise to the surface.

Grim determination transformed Cathy's expression, clearing her deep blue eyes of the mists of grief and tears. "I want whoever did it found and punished," Cathy said, slapping the table with both hands, which caused several customers to look their way.

Jean told Cathy the same information she had given to Sheriff Ramirez that morning. She didn't see how hearing the details of the discovery could be of much help, but she felt obligated to relate them to the victim's wife. As she did, she hoped to soften the macabre picture for Cathy. But Cathy's next question crushed that hope.

"The sheriff told me that Brian was shot," said Cathy. "Do you know where the bullet hit him?"

Sighing, Jean answered, "It looked to me like it hit him high in the back of his head. Of course, the coroner will determine what actually happened."

Cathy stifled a gasp, then took a deep breath. "They found Brian's wallet and keys still in his pockets," said Cathy. "All of his money was there, his hunting and driver's licenses, credit cards, everything—it was all there. He wasn't robbed. Not to mention, his rifle was buried by the tree, and it's valuable." Cathy gazed out the window at passing traffic, her hands clenched on the table, her knuckles white. "His glasses were broken. The sheriff showed me what was left of them, just to be certain they were Brian's."

Cathy shook her head and said, her voice straining with anguish, "How could anyone do this to Brian? This is insane!"

Jean squeezed her eyes shut, remembering the broken frames spattered with darkened grime. That one remaining lens had been just clean enough to catch and reflect the light that drew her close enough to find Brian's body.

Changing the subject, Jean focused her attention on asking Cathy some questions. "You said that Brian was worried about business. Do you have any idea why?" Jean nibbled at her biscotti and sipped the espresso for the first time.

Cathy looked at the ceiling. "He didn't tell me anything specific," she responded. "He had been working on the new condo development, and the planning costs were higher than he had expected because of some controversy over environmental impact. I know he had been going over the accounts of all of the businesses he and Stan owned, trying to determine if there was some pool of money that they could draw from until the project was ready to present to the bank for financing. He must have found what he needed because he had scheduled a meeting with the corporation's attorney the Tuesday after he planned to return from hunting."

"The boys—Jim and Con—told me that you are having financial problems because your business holdings aren't doing well," said Jean. "I know I'm sticking my nose where it doesn't belong, but will you tell me about it?" Jean continued to watch Cathy's reactions.

"I guess so. It will be a relief to talk with someone I think I can trust," Cathy responded, raising her eyebrows and tilting her head.

"Cathy, you can trust me to be discrete," said Jean.

"Thanks," said Cathy, "I appreciate that." She dipped her biscotti in espresso, vacantly stared at it, and set it on her napkin.

"Brian had a large life insurance policy," said Cathy, "but the benefits can't be paid without a death certificate. Since Brian's body has just been found, I hope they will send me a check as soon as they receive the certificate." Cathy grimaced. "Although, since he was murdered, they may insist on waiting till they know who did it. They'll probably make me their chief suspect, just so they can hang onto the money a little longer and earn interest." The sarcasm lacing her speech was matter-of-fact rather than bitter.

"Do you still have an interest in Brian's business?" asked Jean.

"Oh, yes. I want to retain Brian's partnership with Stan," Cathy answered. "I plan to stay here, and I'll need to have an income. I don't know whether I want to be an active partner, but I can't imagine selling out. I do receive income from the business, but profits have been way down in recent months. I may have to sell my house if something doesn't change soon."

"I thought you lived in Grand Junction," Jean said, confused.

"My house is in Grand Junction, yes," Cathy responded, "but I've rented it out and taken a small apartment here until Stan and I can sort things out and the business gets back on solid ground."

"It must have been difficult to move in addition to all the rest that's happened," said Jean. "Do you have any idea why your checks from the business are smaller than before?"

"It could be the development," Cathy said, pondering her answer. "Stan implied that that was part of the problem."

Jean studied Cathy for a moment, then plunged in. "How well do you know Stan Cline?"

Cathy sipped her espresso and sat back. "Brian and Stan met in college," Cathy told Jean. "Stan is a few years older than Brian, but they both played on the football team. I didn't meet Brian until he graduated with his degree in business, so he knew Stan longer than he did me." She smiled as she reminisced. "In fact, I met Stan before Brian. We had a few dates—you know, we went out to dinner, to a movie, dancing—but it was never serious between us. Then one evening, Brian showed up at my door when I was expecting Stan. Stan had been sent out of town for work, and he hadn't been able to reach me. He asked Brian to tell me what had happened. Brian and I talked for a while, then he asked if I wanted to go out for pizza."

"What did Stan think of that?" Jean asked, wondering if seeds of jealousy might have been planted.

"Brian talked with Stan before he asked me out again," Cathy said. "He told Stan that he was interested in me, but that if Stan's feelings for me were serious, he would take a hike. Stan and I were friends, but we weren't in love. He told Brian that he wouldn't stand in his way. The rest is history. Brian and I fell in love and were married within a year. Stan was best man at our wedding."

Tears filled Cathy's eyes, and she said, "It seems like a fairy tale now. We were so happy, except that we couldn't have children. I had endometriosis and fibroid tumors, and I couldn't get pregnant. Brian took a huge interest in Jim and Con, though, and he was much more than just an uncle to them." She smiled, remembering.

"And Stan never showed any resentment toward the two of you?" Jean asked.

"No, he was a good friend to Brian and always respectful toward me," Cathy said. "He's had a few serious girlfriends over the years, but he never married. Stan and Brian became business partners a couple of years after Brian and I were married. They worked together, played golf, hunted, fished—but it was always their friendship, and I was a separate part of Brian's life." Cathy added, "I've seen Stan more since Brian disappeared than I had in the past fifteen years. In fact, he has become my closest friend."

"Do you trust him?" asked Jean.

"With the partnership? Of course," said Cathy. "I don't understand why the profits are down, but Brian trusted him, and so do I."

The coffee shop door opened, and small bells hanging above the window jingled. Jean looked to see who had entered, thinking it might be the kids. Instead, a tall thin man with silver-streaked black hair focused intense blue eyes on Cathy and approached the table. Cathy turned to see who had come in.

"Oh, Stan!" said Cathy. "I wondered if you would get my message. I'd like you to meet Jean Branning." Stan Cline extended his hand to Jean, and she rose from her chair to shake in greeting.

"Aren't you the one who found Brian's body?" Stan asked.

"Yes," said Jean. "The news seems to have traveled fast."

"Jean is the campground host out at the new Columbine Campground," said Cathy. "I ran into her at the bank and asked her to have coffee with me. I wanted to ask her about—finding Brian."

Stan brought another chair to the table and joined the two women. A waitress approached, but he shook his head and she retreated.

"I'm sure that you must have been quite disturbed by what you saw," suggested Stan.

"It was difficult," Jean responded, then switched the focus to Stan and Cathy. "I imagine that the uncertainty of what happened to Brian must have taken quite a toll on both of you. I'm glad that at least the waiting to know what happened is over for you." Jean saw a look of concern come over Stan as he gazed at Cathy, who appeared to be mesmerized by her espresso. Collecting himself, he turned to face Jean.

"Yes, the waiting was terrible," said Stan. "Now we can start looking in earnest for answers to a lot of questions." His countenance darkened with anger and determination.

Jean excused herself to go to the counter for a glass of water. As she waited,

she listened to Cathy and Stan talking together in low voices.

"What answers, Stan?" asked Cathy, as she toyed with her cup. "Questions about who murdered Brian?"

"That, and some other issues I've been reluctant to address," Stan replied.

Cathy looked up at him. "Like what? Are you talking about the business?"

Stan sighed. "Yes, Cathy, the business," he said. "I told you that profits have been down, but that isn't quite right. The truth is that the records show money missing. I've been very hesitant to talk about it because everything seemed to point toward Brian."

"Brian? He would never jeopardize the business by taking money," Cathy said indignantly. "He was too honest and he loved what the two of you had built. You should know better than that. You were his friend."

"I do know better, Cathy," said Stan. "That's the problem. Even though it looked as though Brian was bleeding the accounts, I knew him too well to give the idea credence. I just didn't have any proof." Pausing, he added, "Not until his body was found."

"What do you mean?" Cathy was agitated, shredding her paper napkin with her fingers.

Jean returned to the table and sat, hoping that Cathy and Stan would forget she was there.

"If Brian had killed himself, then I could have believed that he took the money. He might have been ashamed or not known how to fix it. But he didn't. Someone else killed him. That means that Brian may have been aware of the problem, and perhaps he was killed because of it." Stan stopped, shaking his head. "Whoever was stealing stopped when Brian disappeared. I didn't want to say anything about the money because I didn't want to hurt or frighten you with suspicions that I couldn't believe myself. I knew how much you loved Brian."

"But who would want to kill Brian? Who would embezzle?" Cathy dissolved in tears, and Stan moved over to put his arms around her and comfort her.

Jean was silent, lost in thought. Who would want to kill Brian Gowen? And why had Stan said these things about the business in front of her?

§

Exiting Jivin' Java, Jean was upset by the exchange she witnessed. Her face pale and shoulders sagging, Jean walked to the swimming pool, arriving just as her progeny pushed their way out the swinging glass doors. Laughing and snapping towels, they didn't notice her at first. Backing out of Matt's striking distance, Ty nearly fell into Jean's arms.

"Oh, sorry!" Ty chirped, then saw that he had bumped into his own mother.

Jean tousled his wet hair, lingering to form spikes that stuck straight up. Looking around at all of them, she asked, "Anyone for an ice cream cone?"

Gleeful yelps confirmed their approval. The three younger kids ran for the van, but Josie stayed back to walk with her mother.

Ice cream revived Jean's crew, and they were successful navigating Safeway's aisles. They bought and stowed a week's worth of groceries, and drove back to the campground. On the way, Kelsie started singing *Rudolf the Red-Nosed Reindeer* to the disdain of her older siblings.

"It isn't Christmas!" Ty exclaimed.

"Then sing something else with me. I know! The other day...out in the woods...I saw a bear...a way out there," Kelsie began, and Josie repeated each phrase. As Kelsie continued the song, the boys gave in and sang, pretending to not notice that they were having fun.

At the wheel of the van, Jean reflected on her meeting with Cathy and Stan.

"What's wrong, Mom? You look so tired," Josie said, keeping her voice low so only Jean could hear.

"I am, Josie. I've been talking to Brian Gowen's wife and his partner," said Jean. "It seems as though not only was Brian murdered, but his and Stan Cline's company is missing a great deal of money."

"You're kidding. Is that why he was killed?" Josie asked.

"I don't know. Stan and Cathy are just now telling the sheriff about their business problems," said Jean. "Stan was trying to hide it because he thought Brian might have committed suicide."

"Could Stan have done it?" asked Josie.

"Done what? kill? steal? I don't know." Jean shook her head and repeated, a little softer, "I just don't know."

14

Jean and Chad took the family to the Steamboat Lake dance on Saturday night. Josie rode with Jim and Con, but since the young men were going straight to town afterward, she planned to ride back to camp with her family.

Jean marveled at the old-fashioned bandstand and dance floor. "I haven't seen anything like this since I was a little girl," she said, feeling nostalgic. A very large platform built of wood planking had been constructed adjacent to Steamboat Lake, and cars surrounded it. Pillars supported a pitched roof, and porch-style railings enclosed the perimeter. Strings of soft white lights hung from the edges of the roof and crossed under its center like spokes in a wheel.

At one corner of the platform, a four-person band stood on a raised stage with a spotlight focused on them. The lead singer was a woman, but the rest were guys. One doubled as singer and guitarist, another played bass, and the last was on the drum set. Off to the side, another young man controlled the soundboard, a confusing array of switches. On the main floor, people of all ages danced to a country western song. A table loaded with coolers full of water, iced tea, and punch sat in the corner opposite the band.

Jean felt as if she had stepped back in time.

Matt, Ty, and Kelsie made a beeline for the punch table, while Jean and Chad lingered at the edge of the floor and watched the dancers.

"If we go out there and try to dance, do you think everyone will start laughing?" asked Chad.

"Oh, come on!" exclaimed Jean, laughing. "We won't even be noticed as long as we don't knock anyone down. There are so many people on that floor that only a few could see us at any given time." Grabbing Chad's hand, she pulled him into the gyrating throng. He was reluctant to follow, but then concentrated on looking around for and imitating a dancer who seemed to know what he was doing.

"Not bad!" Jean laughed after his clumsy spin brought her back close to him.

"Just wait till I get the hang of this. I'll dance you off your feet!" Chad grinned down.

"You can dance me off my feet. Just don't dance on them," teased Jean.

"What?" Chad replied as he looked toward the dance platform's entrance.

Jean followed Chad's gaze and watched as two couples joined the crowd. She recognized the women. The blonde was Marni Cole, and the small brunette was her sister, Kristi Weller. She assumed that the men were their husbands.

Marni's escort was just less than six feet tall and rangy, with dark brown wavy hair. A reddish-brown mustache shaded wide, thin, unsmiling lips. Sunken gray eyes peered from a rugged face prematurely aged by the elements. He wore a white western-styled shirt, tight faded Levis, and pointy snakeskin boots with high heels angled sharply toward the arch. A turquoise and silver bolo tie, huge silver belt buckle, and massive turquoise and silver watchband glinted as he reached to pull Marni to his side.

The man with dark blonde hair, black eyebrows, lots of freckles, and close-set brown eyes smiled and leaned in to whisper and chuckle near Kristi's ear as he guided her to an open area on the dance floor. He was less than average height, and the extra weight he carried around his waist made him look even shorter. The man wore a short-sleeved blue-and-tan plaid shirt and khaki pants, appearing cool, crisp and sure of himself. He spun Kristi onto the floor, and it was clear that he and Kristi were good dancers.

"Those women are Jim's and Con's mothers," Jean said to Chad.

"They are? I wonder if the men are their stepfathers," said Chad. He glanced toward the men again then back at Jean. "The shorter one is Tom Weller. He is one of the people who opposed Stan and Brian's development proposal. In fact, he was quite nasty about it."

"Let's stop and get something to drink," said Jean. "I'm thirsty, and it will be easier for us to talk." They made their way over to the refreshment table. Jean scooped a few ice cubes into a plastic cup and pushed the button on the side of a large drink cooler to fill it with iced tea.

"Mmm...this is so good," she said, as Chad filled his own cup. Backing toward the railing, Jean looked down and saw that no one stood below her. As Chad joined her, she asked, "How was he nasty?"

"Weller was one of the main spokespeople for the local environmentalists," said Chad. "At first, he made a reasonable presentation of facts about the habitats that would be affected by the development. People were listening. Then he went off on a tangent about how Stan Cline and his company were traitors to the local community, had no sense of historical pride, and were interested only in making money at the expense of everyone around them."

"Is it true?" Jean asked, raising an eyebrow a she spoke.

"No, of course not. From what I've gathered from the people I work with and county planning officials, Stan and Brian have always been conscientious about what they were doing and how it would affect the community. They had become part of the Steamboat community and cared about it."

"It sounds like he made a fool out of himself," Jean suggested.

"Yes, he did," said Chad. "Almost everyone in the room was embarrassed for him. In the end, his accusations were what kept the whole approval process from dragging out any longer. It was becoming too personal."

Jean spied Josie and Con heading their way through the crowd. Jim wasn't with them, but she saw him moving toward his mother and stepfather. Jean also saw Marni point at Con and start after him with her husband in tow.

"Hi, Mom! Hi, Dad!" Josie called out, her cheeks flushed with exertion as she waved and smiled. "Why aren't you out there dancing?"

"We were. Didn't you see us?" Chad asked. Josie shook her head, and Con shrugged his lanky shoulders. "Well, we didn't see you, either, so maybe we were all just lost in the crowd."

"Yeah, that's probably it. We've been dancing for quite a while. I'm thirsty!" Josie stood up on her toes and peered into her father's cup, which was almost empty.

"The punch is right over there," said Chad, gesturing with his arm.

"Hey!" Con touched Josie's arm and pointed at Marni and her dance partner on the floor. "That's Mom and my stepdad." Con made his way to them as Josie moved toward the refreshment table. Con stopped to speak to them for a few moments, then led them back to where Jean and Chad stood.

"This is my mom, Marni Cole, and my stepdad, Lonnie." Con flung his hand toward them as he spoke. "Mom, Lonnie, these are Josie's parents, Mr. and Mrs. Branning."

"Call me Chad," he said as he extended his hand to Lonnie.

"Marni and I have already met at the campground," Jean said, shaking Lonnie's hand. "It's good to meet you, too, Lonnie."

"Hi, Jean!" said Marni. Lonnie just grunted in a man-of-few-words manner.

Chad turned to Lonnie and asked him about the upcoming rodeo. Lonnie started talking and predicted who would be in contention for the top prizes.

The women stood back chatting to each other.

"What do you think of the local night life?" asked Marni to Jean. "This is one of the few inexpensive things left to do around here. Besides fishing or camping, that is." She lifted one corner of her mouth in a halfhearted smile.

"So far, I'm having a ball," said Jean. "I haven't been to a dance like this in ages, and I'm glad that the kids have a chance to experience it. I thought local dances like this had gone the way of the Studebaker."

"Oh, no! The community has been having these Saturday night dances here since the days of the cave man. I don't think they'll ever stop." Marni laughed.

"Well, if attendance is always this good and it stays clean—you know, no drugs, alcohol, or those kinds of things—then I hope they do go on forever," said Jean. "I'm surprised there is such a range of ages here! You seldom see multiple generations enjoying an activity together in one place anymore."

Jean scanned the dance floor as she spoke, noticing a gray-haired couple dancing near two girls in their early teens. A few small children were laughing, holding hands in a circle, and moving in time with the music. One of the little girls spun around and collapsed in a fit of giggles. A pre-adolescent girl reached down to help her up. Near the band, couples ranging in age from teens to sixties, maybe seventies, showed off with complicated dance steps.

Josie came back with her punch, and Con excused himself to get his own. Josie followed him back to the table.

"We're sorry about your brother, Marni," began Jean.

"To be honest," Marni replied, "it's a relief that he was found. Now we at least have some idea about what happened to him. I was pretty sure he was dead, but I thought it was an accident, or…" Her voice trailed off.

"Or suicide?" Jean suggested.

"Yes." Marni paused, her smile fading and wrinkles deepening. "Jean, you found him. Do you think the sheriff can be sure that Brian was murdered, that it wasn't suicide?"

"I'm sorry, Marni," said Jean. "I could tell when I found him that he couldn't have killed himself. From what I know about forensics—which isn't much, but I do read about it because I'm curious—he was shot in the back of the head."

Marni turned white and began to sway. Lonnie caught her around her waist and held her up.

"The sheriff didn't tell us that," Marni said, beginning to regain color. "He didn't give us any details other than Brian was shot."

"I shouldn't have told you. I'm sorry," Jean said, touching Marni's arm gently.

"No, I want to know. Don't apologize," said Marni. "How did you know that he was shot in the head?" said Marni.

"Well, when someone is shot, the entrance wound makes a small hole, but the exit causes much more damage. It's traumatic. The bullet that hit your brother left that pattern," Jean said, feeling she was out on a limb saying way too much from her novice forensic perspective.

"Do you have any idea who Brian's enemies might have been?" asked Jean.

"That's all I've been thinking about," said Marni. "I want to know who shot him. I don't like the idea of that person getting away with murdering my brother." Marni's stern, angry expression took on a hint of anxiety. "I'm worried, too, that whoever did it might kill again."

Glancing at the men, who were still talking about roping and bull riding, Jean formulated more questions for Marni.

"Marni, do you remember the last time you saw Brian alive?" Jean asked.

"Yes, it was the day before he left to hunt," answered Marni. "He came to my office and asked to go over some of the records."

"What was he looking for?"

"Brian had been going through all of the account records from the past three years. He said he was looking for more investment capital for the condominium project, so he decided to see if he could take short-term loans from some of the other businesses. He wanted to avoid getting a bank loan to finance the development phase."

"Did he find what he needed?" asked Jean, trying to keep Marni talking.

"He was a lot quieter and more serious over that last month," Marni said. "He didn't tell me whether he was able to scrape together the funds he needed or not."

"What did he do that last day?" asked Jean.

"Brian had me pull the corporation's hard files for the last year," replied Marni. "All of the monthly totals for each business appear there. But he didn't tell me what he was looking for. He made some notes, but I couldn't see what he wrote."

"I wonder, has anyone else looked at the records?" asked Jean.

"Not that I know of, at least not until after Brian disappeared. Then Stan came in and took a look, but he didn't spend as much time at it as Brian had," said Marni. "Stan seemed worried and didn't say much. It wasn't too long until Kristi and I lost our jobs."

"And what did he say when that happened?" Jean asked.

"Stan said that there were some financial pressures on the business, and he would have to reduce the staff," Marni recalled. "We weren't the only ones to be let go, but somehow it felt like we were getting booted out of our family."

Marni explained. "Kristi and I worked for the corporation for a long time. Our boys weren't even in school yet when we moved from Denver to Grand Junction. In a way, Brian rescued us. I had divorced my first husband, and a few months later Kristi took Jim and left hers because he was abusive. Brian asked both of us to move to the Western Slope and work for him."

"Is that how Brian was able to spend time with Con and Jim while they were growing up?" asked Jean. "They told me how he had been there for them. They respected and loved your brother."

Tears welled up in Marni's liquid brown eyes, and she turned her head to shake off the sadness. As she did, Jean saw Kristi and her husband approaching.

"Hey, sis!" called out Kristi, her husband following. "Why aren't you out dancing?"

"We're just taking a break," said Marni.

"Hi, Jean!" said Kristi. "This is my husband, Tom Weller."

Chad and Lonnie surfaced from their conversation, and Kristi introduced Chad to Tom.

"Didn't I see you at a county planning meeting last fall?" Tom asked Chad.

"Yeah, at the condo development meeting. I believe you spoke for the local environmentalists during the hearing on Stan Cline's condo development," Chad replied.

Jean turned to look at Chad, miffed because he had just told her about this encounter. He could have said something sooner, she thought.

"I thought we would be able to stop that approval," Tom said, "but I guess we're going to have another big development on the slopes." He snorted.

"Why did you want to stop it?" Jean quizzed. "Doesn't a project like that help the community's tax base and bring in more sales revenue?"

Tom shifted his weight to both feet, straightened his posture, thrust out his chest, and inhaled. "Some people believe that any development is good just because of those points—the positive impact on the tax base and increased local sales. It doesn't matter to them that along with this influx of cash comes increased demands on the infrastructure." His animation increased and his face grew red. "More people living in an area requires more schools, more recreational facilities, more road building and repair, and more of just about everything that people think they need for a comfortable life. Unfortunately, in the process of obtaining all of these creature comforts, the native wildlife—the local fauna and flora—get trampled and shoved away. I wanted to stop the development because it was one more step into their territory."

Tom's reasoning confused Jean. Why protest this particular project, she wondered?

Jean asked, "But won't people find another way to expand the community if there is a genuine need for more vacation housing? It seems to me that a condominium development takes up a lot less space than single family cabins or vacation homes."

"This area is well on its way to becoming a vacation mecca," Tom sputtered. "The land-use plan is too vague, in my opinion, and will promote the kind of exponential growth seen in Vail and Aspen. All for progress and profit."

"Let me see if I understand this. Was your objection to the development because of environmental concerns or because of growth in general?" Chad tipped his head to the side as he waited for Tom to answer.

"Let's just say that this particular project did not appear to be justifiable." Tom's expression was inscrutable as he stared unblinking at Chad.

Jean observed the interplay of body language between her husband and Tom. It was obvious that Tom had said all he would on the subject and that his answers had not been complete. She could also see that Chad had picked up on Tom's evasion and would have liked to press the conversation further. But Kristi laid one hand on her husband's arm and looked up at him, eyes pleading for a change in topic.

"Honey, don't you think we've rested long enough? Let's go back out on the floor and dance." Kristi slid her hand down

Tom's arm to grasp his hand, and then began to back away from the small group. Tom resisted at first, then looked back at Jean and Chad, tipping his head and lifting the corners of his lips in a half-smile.

"Duty calls. It was good to have met you." Tom turned to his wife, and they disappeared into the throng.

"What was that all about?" asked Marni. "I would have thought he would be glad to see more construction here. After all, he's a realtor."

"A realtor?" Jean echoed. "You could have fooled me."

Lonnie put his arm around Marni's shoulders and squeezed. "We've spent enough time bending these folks' ears, Marni. Let's dance."

Jean raised her right hand in farewell, and Chad nodded his head at the pair. Jean stared after them, punch cup in her other hand.

"Was that an abrupt departure, or am I imagining things?"

"It looked to me as though Tom had some strong feelings in that conversation," Chad mused.

Jean shook her head in bewilderment. "But why? As far as I could tell, nothing was said. It was all a bunch of drivel."

"Maybe we pushed a button." Chad unwound his long body and stretched. "Well, let's follow the crowd and dance some more. It's getting late, and we should start back to the campground pretty soon."

"Umm...sleep sounds good all of a sudden. Let's watch for the kids and nab them as soon as we see them." Jean allowed herself to be led onto the floor and pulled into the warm comfortable arms of her handsome husband.

§

Descending the platform's steps to the dark parking area, Jean and Chad had to walk slowly to give their eyes time to adjust. The Branning family was one of the first groups to leave, and the younger kids ran between the parked cars in a race to see who could get to the van first. Josie was saying goodbye to Jim and Con at the base of the stairs.

Jean leaned against Chad's shoulder, looking up at the stars. The moon was absent, causing the stars and planets to seem much closer and brighter than usual. Treetops were silhouetted against the inky night sky, creating a dark frame around the lake. They could hear the soft lapping of the water at the lake's edge, and the call of a loon carried across its obsidian surface crowned with tiny diamonds.

"It is so peaceful here," Jean sighed. "I wish we could just stay out here all night." She breathed deeply, taking in pine-scented mountain air.

"We can at least go and stand by the lake for a few minutes," Chad murmured. "We wouldn't want to pass up any romantic opportunities, would we?"

Jean laughed quietly. "I've never known you to miss your chance, that's for sure."

Taking Jean into his arms, Chad's kiss was passionate. Holding her close, they listened to the night sounds.

Jean opened her eyes to the darkness and relaxed against Chad's safe chest. Drinking in the gentle waves undulating under the twinkling stars, Jean watched the hypnotic rocking of a log caught in the water's motion. Slowly she realized that the object was wrapped in cloth. Air trapped inside shiny fabric buoyed the object.

"Chad." Jean stiffened as she spoke, staring at what appeared to be the second body she had discovered in just a few days.

"Mmm," he sighed, as he buried his face in her hair and attempted to gather her more closely. "Your hair smells nice."

"Chad." Jean put her hands on her husband's chest and pushed him away. Chad looked down at her quizzically.

"Look, Chad; turn around." Jean clung to his arm, rotating him to the same direction she was facing, and pointed to the water's edge with her free hand. "I think it's a body."

Chad let his wife's hand go and moved toward the object. He walked into the shallow water, Jean just behind him on dry ground, and crouched down to investigate. He reached down with both hands and rolled the bundle over.

The unseeing eyes of the dead man glittered, mimicking the lake.

15

C had stayed near the body while Jean returned to the van. The kids were supposed to be there, waiting to return to camp, and Jean was frantic to see them, to know they were okay and make them as safe as possible. Then she had to find a sheriff's deputy.

The side windows were open, and Jean relaxed a little as she heard the kids bickering, happy to hear them acting so normal.

"Matt, stop hogging the seat!" Ty complained from the back bench.

"Quit kicking my seat, Matt!" Kelsie whined, pushing herself deeper into the middle bench.

Matt leaned forward, snagging Kelsie's hair as he grabbed the top of her seat to dig his knees harder into the seat back.

"Ow! Stop pulling my hair, you meanie!" she cried. "Josie, make him stop!"

Josie sat at the other end of the middle bench from Kelsie, oblivious to the ruckus, eyes closed, her Walkman's headphones covering her ears.

"Crybabies!" Matt sneered, refusing to budge.

Jean opened the sliding passenger-side door, and the over-head light flashed on, blinding and silencing the occupants. She leaned in over Kelsie.

"Look, we're going to be here awhile, and I don't want any of you leaving this van without permission." Jean's angry, worried eyes moved from face to face, beginning with Matt. "And you *will* stop fighting with each other," she ordered.

"Josie, can you reach over and get my cell out of my purse? It's under the front seat," Jean said.

Josie didn't move.

Impatient, Jean slid Josie's headphones back from her ears. Josie turned to see who had moved them and saw it was her mother. Jean saw her daughter bite back whatever she was about to say.

"Josie! Get my phone! Please!" Jean snapped.

Josie shrugged and crawled forward over the console to rummage in Jean's purse on the floor for the cellphone. She handed it over her shoulder to Jean.

"Thank you," said Jean, taking it and Josie's hand in both of hers.

Josie, her attention captured, glanced over her shoulder at her mom. "Mom?" she said, looking apprehensive.

Jean straightened, scanning the parking lot but seeing no one nearby, and slid the door closed. Lifting her cell, she pushed the on button and saw that like at the campground, there was no service by the lake. Earlier, she had hesitated about leaving her cellphone and purse under the front seat during the dance, concerned that it might be stolen. But what difference would it have made to have it with her or have it at all? She shook her head.

She walked to the back of the van and opened the double doors, retrieving several pink, blue, and white striped cotton Mexican blankets. A cover of Bobby Gentry's *Ode to Billy Joe* floated through the dark from the bandstand, and a chill ran down her back. She was uneasy about leaving the kids alone, but she had to find help and return to the side of the lake where Chad waited. Jean closed the doors as quietly as she could and walked to the driver's side door where Josie sat.

Maybe the murderer is still here, Jean thought. But in the van, the kids are closer to the crowd still dancing. They had some protection inside the locked vehicle. At least they can't see the body, Jean thought, shuddering. And soon, the dance would end and the crowd would head for their cars.

Passing the blankets through the open passenger-side window to Josie, Jean said, "Okay, kids. Get comfortable, be quiet. Lay down and try to go to sleep. And keep the doors locked."

The van's springs squeaked as the children unfolded the blankets and wrapped them around themselves.

"Josie," Jean said.

Josie handed the last blanket but hers to Matt and turned to look at her mom.

"Josie, you heard what I said, right?"

Josie nodded.

"This is important, Josie. You're in charge. Keep the kids in here."

Josie answered, "Sure. But what's going on?"

Jean spoke, hoping the sound of the band, now playing Garth Brooks' *The Thunder Rolls*, would mask her words enough that the younger kids wouldn't hear. "Your dad and I found a body at the edge of the lake. There's no cell service, so I need to go to the bandstand and find a deputy. They'll need to call for backup. It may be fifteen or twenty minutes before they get here. Then the sheriff's deputies will want to talk to us."

"Why are you leaving us alone? I don't understand," said Josie, looking frightened. "Are we going to be safe in here?"

"You're as safe here as you would be among the crowd," Jean said, hoping that was so. "No one else knows about this yet, and it would be better if you and the kids didn't go back and tell others. Move over into the driver's seat. If anyone approaches except Dad or me, lean on the horn."

Josie clutched her blanket and maneuvered through the open space between the captain's chairs to sit in the driver's seat. Jean backed away from the van and softly closed the door.

"Dad and I will be back as soon as we can," said Jean. "Keep your eyes open and listen for any trouble."

"Why? Do you think there will be trouble?" Josie's eyes widening. "Was the man murdered?"

Jean nodded her head and grimaced. "It looks like it," she said, and hesitated, torn about leaving. Then shaking herself, Jean spoke. "I have to go. Stay put."

Jean watched as Josie removed the earphones dangling from her neck. Looking back at her brothers and sister, she saw three pairs of wide-open eyes.

"Alright, troops. Booger," Josie said to Ty, "move up here on the floor in front of Toots. Toots and Matt, lay down on your seats. Heads down and not a word from any of you."

The van rocked as Ty climbed over Kelsie's seat and plopped on the floor, pulling his blanket on top of himself, covering his head. Matt sank to the side on his bench, but not without glaring at Josie in defiance. Kelsie, wrapped in her blanket and curled into a tight ball, burrowed as far back into her seat as she could. She pulled her blanket tight over the back of her head and clenched it with both fists under her chin.

"I'm scared," said Kelsie, sniffling.

So am I, thought Jean, still standing outside the van looking in mesmerized, feeling as though she was watching a home video.

"Kelsie," Jean said, "Josie said 'not a word.' I wouldn't leave you alone if I thought it wasn't safe. This is the best place for you right now. Go to sleep."

Jean tried to push away from the van, but her hands felt as though a strong magnet held them fixed to the metal.

"Roll up the windows, Josie," said Jean. "I'll come back as soon as I can."

Jean turned away and moved toward the bandstand, glancing back every few steps. With light from the dance area penetrating the windshield, she could see Josie reach up to adjust the rear-view mirror, then slouch in the seat. She seemed to shake her head as she turned to glance at the side mirrors.

Jean didn't like leaving them. It felt wrong, and they were scared. So was she. But she had to hurry now to find help.

144 | DONNA J. EVANS

The nose of the van pointed toward the bandstand, and light spread out enough that Jean could see the parking area in between. Taking care not to trip over rocks or pinecones, she hustled toward the light, feeling as though she moved in slow motion. Her body ached with tension as she kept looking back, pulled toward the van and propelled forward toward the tight bunch of people. She tried to pick out the deputy's uniform in the crowd but didn't see it.

It could only have been a few seconds later when, off to Jean's left, lurking in the darkness, she sensed movement before she saw it. Someone was slipping away from the lake edge and moving toward the parking area. All she could see in the darkness was a moon-like object, a white face reflecting light from the bandstand, floating above a black form. A dark hood extended forward over the head like a monk's cowl, and the face was partially eclipsed as it moved. Despite its bizarre appearance, the direction it was going suggested that it had searched the lighted area near the bandstand before veering toward an SUV on the lake side of the lot.

Jean stopped, hidden behind the trunk of a spruce, and watched as the figure approached a dark vehicle. She knew it was a person, despite the figure's unearthly appearance. When it opened the vehicle's door, the dome light remained unlit; the interior lights must have been turned off earlier. Pausing for a moment, the figure seemed to stiffen. Light from the bandstand glinted off the figure's eyes, and Jean thought they fixed on the van before the form slipped inside the SUV. Had this person seen her kids?

Jean heard a low rumble as an ignition turned. The crunch of gravel and quiet rhythm of the engine wasn't loud enough to drown her pounding heartbeat or the rhythm of *Thunderball* emanating from the bandstand.

She looked toward the bandstand, saw Deputy Bailey walking around its corner, and ran to him.

§

A couple minutes later, Jean ran back to the van, pinballing off car fenders and ignoring tripping hazards. She heard a muffled scream as she slapped the driver's window with her hands, and saw Josie curled up in a fetal position under the steering wheel, the sheen of her red hair visible in the darkness and her arms curled around her head.

"Josie!" Jean said. "Josie, open up! It's me! Mom! Are you okay?"

"Oh, Mom!" Josie gasped as she boosted herself up into the seat. "I'm so scared! I saw something so creepy!" Tears smeared her freckled cheeks.

"It's okay, honey. You're okay," said Jean.

Josie was so frightened she was panting for breath. Jean opened the door and pulled her daughter into her arms.

"What happened? What did you see, Josie?" asked Jean.

"Oh, Mom! It was awful!" Josie burrowed into Jean's shoulder and cried.

Jean stroked Josie's lustrous hair, calming her daughter as she had when Josie was an infant.

"What was awful, honey? Tell me," Jean said, her voice quiet but firm.

"I heard a car moving," said Josie, "so I tried to get as low as I could in the seat. But I was holding my breath, and I jerked my feet when I gulped fresh air. One foot came down on the brake pedal, and the brake lights flashed. I could see red light in the mirror."

Josie shivered, and Jean squeezed her shoulders.

"What happened then?" Jean asked.

"I straightened my legs and jumped up in the seat," Josie said. "I guess my foot was still on the brake pedal because the light stayed on." Josie whimpered.

"Josie..." Jean waited.

"I saw him...I looked in the bubble on the side mirror and saw his face there. It was all distorted, like in a fun house mirror. You know, like the one at the amusement park Funhouse in Denver? And his eyes glowed red," said Josie.

Jean realized that the brake lights had caught the attention of the hooded figure as he drove away. The red reflection in the rounded bubble mirror had contorted the face Josie saw.

But what had the departing driver seen? Jean had no doubt that the driver had seen into the van; there would be no mistaking this old van or Josie's remarkable long red hair.

16

"Josie, he's gone. You're safe now." Jean pulled Josie tighter. "I'm so sorry I left you and the other kids here alone! I didn't think anything would happen."

"Oh, Mom! Nothing would have happened if I hadn't panicked. I feel so stupid!" Josie sobbed.

"But you're okay," Jean said, patting her back. "It's okay."

"Can you believe that Matt and Ty and Kelsie fell asleep almost as soon as they laid down?" asked Josie, with a half-sob, half-laugh. She pushed away from her mother and looked in the back at her siblings. "I'm so glad they weren't awake when this—this thing—went by us."

"So am I," said Jean. "But now we need to tell the police what you saw. Maybe some other official will have seen the SUV on the road on their way to the lake. Can you stay here just a few minutes more? I'll go tell the deputy."

"Hurry, Mom," pleaded Josie.

"I'll be right back," Jean said, closing the door, and signaling to Josie to lock it.

Jean headed to the lake, where she had left Chad with the body. The rotating lights on the sheriff department's SUV comforted her.

The first police vehicle drew the attention of a few of the people who were still dancing to the loud music of the band. But when a string of emergency vehicles approached, including an ambulance, people began to stream off the platform. Fortunately, one of the two deputies in the first car was assigned to calm the people and keep them from moving en masse to the lake's edge. One of the newly arrived cars stopped at the entrance and set a barricade to prevent the dancers from leaving until the police were able to talk to them.

It was going to be a long night.

Jean returned to the van and waited with the children while holding Josie's hand. Chad was still at the lake answering questions about their discovery of the body. From the vantage point of the big van's front seats, she and Josie watched as people milled around by the bandstand, floodlights illuminating the area. From a distance, they could also see that another floodlight had been set up by the lake, near where several uniformed figures stood.

If that was the murderer who left in the dark SUV, Jean thought, then he must have seen Josie, at least the back of her head. Jean wondered if Josie could be in danger. He would not have had time to catch her reflection in the van's mirror—as Josie had his—since his car was moving. Could he identify Josie?

Of course, there is this big fossil of a van, thought Jean. And vans like this one are rare around Steamboat. There were large numbers of them running up and down the highways on the Front Range a decade or more ago, but now other models were well on the way to replacing them there, as well as here, by big, expensive four-wheel-drive vehicles. Ford Expeditions, Chevy Suburbans, Dodge Dakotas, even Range Rovers had become popular. At any rate, this old Dodge van stuck out like an iceberg in a desert. It would not be too difficult for someone to figure out who owned it.

Jean took a deep breath, exhaling slowly. Maybe the driver didn't see anything. The brake lights might have blinded him, at least to any characteristics of the person inside.

"Josie, I think that's Deputy Bailey coming toward us," whispered Jean. "Let's get out so we don't wake the kids up talking."

Jean and Josie opened and closed their doors without sound, and walked to the front of the van to meet the deputy. Josie was wrapped in her blanket and looked very young and vulnerable to Jean. Jean felt very, very old.

"Hello, Mrs. Branning, Miss Branning," said Deputy Bailey. "I've talked to your husband and heard how the two of you found the body. I understand that your daughter, Miss..."

Josie interrupted. "We met by Whiskey Creek the day Brian Gowen's body was found, Deputy Bailey. Call me Josie." She sounded young and tired but in control. Jean admired her daughter's spunk.

"Yes, I remember you. You were helping with the search." Bailey searched the shadows of Josie's face. "Your father told me that you saw someone suspicious a little while ago. I'd like to ask you about it. Are you up to it?"

"I guess so," said Josie. "I just want to get it over with. It was creepy."

"Okay. Then let's do it." Bailey pulled a pencil and small notebook from his pocket. He glanced back at the throng of people still gathered at the dance platform. They had retreated up the steps, and many people were sitting either on the chairs lining the rails or on the tables that had held the refreshments.

"Tell me what you remember seeing, Josie. Take your time," said Bailey. He leaned against the van, striking a more relaxed pose.

Jean was impressed with Deputy Bailey's concern for Josie and how he was attempting to put her daughter at ease.

Josie explained how she had stayed in the van with the younger children after Jean and Chad had found the body. She told how the SUV moving without headlights on through the parking area had caught her attention and frightened her, causing her to try to hide lower in the seat. When she related how she had crouched down near the pedals and stepped on the brake, flashing red light into the face of the unknown driver, Bailey stopped her.

"Did you see anything about him you might be able to identify?" asked Bailey. "The haircut, skin color, shape of his eyes?"

Josie shivered. "The mirror made his eyes huge. I might be able to recognize them if I saw them again." She paused to think. "All I know for sure was that it was a man, and he had light skin. It wouldn't have looked so red in the lights if it had been darker." Josie closed her eyes. "And he didn't wear glasses. His eyebrows looked big and dark in the bubble mirror." She opened her eyes again. "The rest of his face was just too weird in that mirror. And I couldn't see his hair. He had a hoodie or something pulled over his head."

"Did you turn around? Was he able to see your face?" Bailey asked.

"No. I was too petrified," said Josie. "I don't think he could have seen my face," Josie answered.

"What about the vehicle? Do you know what color it was?" Bailey asked.

"No. It could have been any dark color," Josie replied. "I just couldn't tell."

Bailey closed his notebook and placed it and the pencil back inside his pocket. He said, "I doubt if there is much danger of this man searching you out, Josie, but for the time being, you shouldn't go anywhere alone. Watch for suspicious behavior, and don't hesitate to call us for help if you need it." He turned to Jean. "Mrs. Branning, I advise you to stick close to your daughter."

"Yes, of course I will." Jean moved closer to Josie, reaching for her hand. She asked, "Deputy, do you know who the dead man was?"

"We can't be certain. The coroner will have to do a positive ID on him. However, he was carrying private investigator's credentials."

"A PI? Here? I thought they worked in big cities, not in the boonies," exclaimed Josie.

"You'll find them just about everywhere," said Bailey, with a tired smile. "Insurance companies employ them to investigate claims, spouses suspicious of their mates hire them...there are a lot of reasons why people hire private eyes, even in the boonies."

Bailey turned toward the lighted platform. "It looks as though our people have finished interviewing the crowd. Ma'am, we'll need for the two of you and Mr. Branning to sign statements. I know that tomorrow's Sunday, but can you come to the sheriff's office, say, around 2:30 in the afternoon, and we'll get it taken care of?"

"We'll be there," Jean said. Deputy Bailey turned to go, but Jean reached out and touched his elbow. "Was this murder related to Brian Gowen's?" she asked.

"I don't know, ma'am," said Bailey. "Even if I did, I couldn't tell you." He tipped his hat and turned away, striding toward the shoreline.

Jean watched Bailey retreat as Josie clambered back into the van. Could the same person have killed both men?

17

Jean remained in the van with her kids for the rest of the evening. When the sheriff's deputies allowed the Brannings to leave Steamboat Lake, Chad moved the younger kids back to their usual seats without waking them. Kelsie's head lay on Josie's lap, both in the middle seat, and Matt and Ty sprawled legs-to-legs on the back seat, with one of Matt's legs drooped over the edge. They drove in silence, although Jean glanced often at Josie, noting how pale she appeared. Back at camp, Jean watched Josie hurry into the camper to get her face wash and night clothes. But when Josie hesitated opening the door to come out and scanned the dark campsite before heading to the shower house, Jean knew her daughter was scared. Jean and Chad ushered the kids to the restrooms and put them to bed in the clothes they were wearing. By then, Josie was back, and she and the parents almost fell into their beds with exhaustion.

When Jean woke up the next morning, she had a throbbing headache. Chad was still asleep beside her, but she heard the kids' voices coming from the outer room, so she got up, grabbed a robe, and joined them.

"Geez, Mom!" exclaimed Ty, when Jean entered the kitchen. "Why didn't you wake us up for all the excitement last night?" He sat on one of the benches tying his sneakers.

"It seems to me that you must have been pretty tired to have fallen asleep so fast," responded Jean.

"Yeah, but you could have told us what was happening. Then we could have watched for the murderer," said Ty, chastising his mother for not including them in the action.

"Did Josie tell you about it?" Jean asked as she realized Josie wasn't in the trailer.

"Yeah, and she saw the murderer! She said his face was really spooky." Ty grabbed his baseball cap and stood to go outside.

"Do you know where she is?" Jean asked, feeling a twinge of uneasiness.

"She's in the shower," said Ty. "She went out just before you got up."

"Well, I don't want you to go very far from the trailer," Jean told Ty. "I'm going to take a shower, too, so stick around."

"Ah, Mom! Can't I go fishing?" Ty asked, dejected and a little belligerent.

"Not this morning," she said with unusual sharpness. Jean knew she was more irritable than the kids were accustomed to. She hadn't slept well the night before because her mind conjured scenarios, one after the other, in which Josie was in danger from the murderer. Between fatigue and worry, she felt frazzled. She made a mental note to control herself in front of the kids.

Jean gathered a towel, a bag of personal items, and a clean outfit. When she opened the door and descended the steps, the crisp air and blue sky of the early mountain morning did nothing to clear the clouds from Jean's mind. She was more concerned about the safety of her daughter and her family now than she had been the previous night. It was possible that the man Josie had seen wasn't the murderer. But whatever his purpose, his actions appeared suspicious. Jean brooded as she approached the shower house and paused to take in a deep breath before opening the door and confronting her daughter.

"Josie, it's me," said Jean, steam fogging the room. There was no reply, just the splatter of water as it struck the hard surfaces of the wall and floor. Listening, Jean could also hear the soft rhythm of soap and water being whisked over skin.

"Josie, can you hear me?" Jean asked, raising her voice.

"Yes." Josie's answer was sharp and clear.

Jean sat on the bench and removed her nail polish as she waited for her daughter to finish. She could have popped into the second shower, but she wanted to have a few moments to talk to Josie where the younger kids wouldn't be listening. Jean searched for the right words, trying them out in her head before discarding them.

The water ceased to beat its furious spray, and Jean could hear Josie squeezing water out of her long red hair. After a few whispering pats of the towel and some minor bumps on the walls, Josie pushed back the shower curtain and stepped out of the cubicle, one towel wrapped around her body, the other around her hair. The look on her face was both rebellious and defeated at once.

"Josie..." Jean began.

"Oh, Mom! I know!" protested Josie. "Here I am, almost a senior in high school, and I'm on house arrest! I didn't even do anything wrong!"

"You're not on house arrest, sweetheart. Of course you didn't do anything wrong!" exclaimed Jean. "It's just that we have to be careful, at least for a while, until the sheriff can figure out what happened last night."

Josie leaned down and let the towel fall from her head. Then she whipped her red hair back over her head and shook it. Glaring at Jean, she said, "Sure, and if they *don't* figure it out, I'm stuck at home forever."

Jean shook her head and sighed. "Not forever, honey. Give it some time so we can be sure no one is following you," she said. "Besides, the sheriff's department will make it known that there are no suspects yet, and the driver of that SUV will wonder if you saw him well enough to identify him."

"Great. So, we're going to be on the lookout for some creep who might or might not figure out who I am. In the meantime, what am I supposed to do?" Josie demanded.

"Be reasonable," Jean responded. "You can still go anywhere the rest of us go. You can work at the campground as long as there is someone with you or you're within sight. You might be able to do something with Jim and Con on the weekends. But we have to know where you are *all the time*," said Jean. "That includes when you leave the trailer to do something like take a shower," she admonished.

Jean and Josie stared at each other in a contest of will. It wasn't long, though, before the fire in Josie's eyes was smothered by tears, welling up unbidden.

"I just wish this wasn't happening," the girl lamented. "This summer is awful. I wish you hadn't brought us here."

Feeling the weight of Josie's reprimand, Jean was remorseful for having taken the campground host job and dragging her kids with her. Still, self-reproach wouldn't do any good now.

"But we are here, and for the time being, we can't change that," Jean responded, chewing her lower lip.

"Josie, will you promise me that you will always check in with me and have someone else with you when you go outside?" Jean asked.

Josie flopped down on the bench beside Jean. Leaning back against the wall, she squeezed her eyes shut and rocked her head.

"I'm so scared." The high-pitched tone of Josie's voice reminded Jean of the little girl her daughter had been not so long ago. Jean wrapped her arms around Josie and held her daughter, her cold wet hair, raising goose pimples, sandwiched between them.

"I know," Jean said. "Me, too." They sat clutching each other, then Jean let go and looked at her daughter. "But we can't let it get us down. We're both going to have to keep our eyes open. Our ears, too. Maybe we'll be able to find some clues that will put an end to this situation."

"You mean spy on people?" asked Josie.

"In a way. But just being more aware of the conversations of other people around us, and finding out more about the Gowens..." Jean's voice trailed off.

"Jim and Con have talked quite a bit about their family," said Josie. "Some of what they said is pretty sad."

Chewing her lip again, Jean pondered her next suggestion, not wanting to intrude on her daughter's growing friendship with the boys.

"I don't want to pry or gossip about them," said Jean, "but if you can think of anything they've said that might be helpful, I hope we can talk about it."

"So how do I draw a line between gossip and information?" Josie asked.

"I know I've always said 'Don't gossip.' But in this case, we're not spreading malicious rumors or being careless about other people's privacy. This may be a matter of..."

"Life or death?" Josie finished. "Whose? Mine?" She shivered.

"We're just taking precautions for your safety." Standing and stretching, Jean placed shampoo, soap, and a razor in the shower stall, then moved her towel to a dry spot on the bench nearby. "It's time we get busy. We have a lot of work to do today. The campground needs a good clean-up before the next batch of campers shows up, and I have more paperwork to do than I want to think about." Turning, she looked down at Josie. "Want to help?"

"Why not?" Josie shrugged. "I guess I don't have much choice."

§

Jean delegated the cleaning tasks and worked on bookkeeping. After matching the weekend's registration forms to payments received, she stood up and stretched her whole body. Her headache was gone but she was tired. Was it the dancing the night before? Stress? Or just not enough sleep?

Stress, Jean thought. I thought this was going to be a nice, fun, relaxing job living in the mountains. With a strong twinge of guilt, she fretted over having brought her family into such an awful situation. But how could she have known? What was happening now was set into motion long ago and had nothing to do with her when it occurred. There was no point in blaming herself.

Sighing, Jean watched out the window as Matt drove the small tractor with Ty perched on the back edge of the utility trailer. Josie and Kelsie wore work gloves and picked up litter using long sticks with spikes at the end, dropping it into garbage bags. Chad exited the men's bathroom carrying a mop and bucket.

Her eyes scanning the grounds, Jean watched campers folding, packing, and loading their gear, preparing to drive either home or to the next campground on their itinerary. In a way, she envied them. Her family had been at Columbine for one week, and things couldn't possibly get any worse. At least she hoped not.

Jean resolved to spend more time at the campground doing fun things with the kids. Then she remembered they had to be in Steamboat that afternoon to sign statements.

Okay, Jean thought, I have to get this work done. She began to add the names of weekend campers to the registry she was keeping for Forest Service mailings. Only a week, and look at how many people had stayed here. She scanned the list, taking more time at the beginning when so many of Brian Gowen's relatives had been here. She shook her head. None of the names told her anything.

Jean's musing was disturbed by the crunch of tires on gravel. Looking up, she saw Bob Duncan getting out of his Forest Service pickup. Jean reached up and opened the sliding window above the counter. Chad walked with long strides toward the office.

"Hi, Bob. I haven't seen you for a few days," said Jean.

"Well, it sounds to me like you've been busy. I heard that you found Gowen's body. And you and your husband also found that guy on the lakeshore, didn't you?" Bob glanced to his side as Chad approached.

"Bob, this is my husband, Chad." The men shook hands.

"Happy to meet you, Chad," said Bob. "I'm glad you're here after all that has happened the past week."

"I hope I'm up to the task of keeping her out of trouble. She seems to be giving me a run for my money," Chad said with a little sarcasm and flashed Jean a quick smile, one eyebrow raised.

"Come on, Chad, I didn't plan any of this," Jean said, folding her arms over her chest, irritated at her husband's tone.

Chad just smiled and winked at Jean. Jean stood unresponsive, feeling patronized, her ire toward her husband intensifying.

Turning to Bob, Chad said, "Seriously, I'm concerned about Jean and the kids. Tomorrow, I have to go into town for work, and I don't like leaving them so far away from help."

"We have the office phone," said Jean, "and there are other campers here." She dropped her crossed arms and twisted at the waist, sweeping one arm around to encompass the campsite. "As long as we stay close to each other, we'll be fine," Jean added.

"You may be right, Jean," said Bob, "but I'm going to come by several times a day to check on you and your family. The sheriff's department is sending a deputy up at least once a day as well."

"That makes me feel a little better about the situation, but just how close will help be if they need it?" Chad asked.

"I can't say," Bob replied. "There's a lot of territory to cover, but I'm guessing that either a sheriff's deputy or someone from the Forest Service can be here in less than thirty minutes, at least for the next few days. By then we should have a better idea of who and what we're looking for." Bob shifted his weight and surveyed the campground. "In the meantime, be cautious and call if you have any reason to believe you may need help. We'd rather make a run that didn't result in any action than arrive too late."

"All right, you two," said Jean. "I know the drill. But what if things are happening too fast to call?" Jean folded her arms across her chest again and tilted her head.

"Then leave a note or some clue as to what is happening," said Bob. "There's too much ground to cover if we don't have some idea where you might be."

"It seems to me that Josie is the one who should be listening to this," Jean said. "She's pretty upset about the whole deal. And even though she's frightened, she has that sense of invincibility that most teens are endowed with." Exasperated, Jean spread her hands and shook her head. "Half of her believes that she can take care of any problem, and the other half is terrified."

"Well, no matter how she feels about it, we all need to make sure that she doesn't go off anywhere alone. She just can't afford to take that risk," said Chad, setting his jaw and squaring his broad shoulders.

Bob lifted his wide-brimmed hat and smoothed his hair before replacing it. Taking his key ring from his trouser pocket, he started moving toward his pickup but stopped and turned toward the Brannings.

"I hope we're being overly cautious and nothing happens," Bob said. "But it doesn't hurt in a situation like this for all of us to remain alert."

"Oh, *we will,*" Jean said with force. "That's what mothers are best at. In fact, human mothers are a lot like bears—you had better not get between them and their young."

Bob chuckled. "Just keep those claws sharpened." Nodding a quick farewell to Chad, he slid into the driver's seat and reached for his seatbelt. In a moment, he had the engine running, and the truck retreated down the road.

"He's right, you know," Jean said. "And so are you, Chad. This may be a wasted exercise, but we just can't take the risk of being unprepared."

They watched in silence as a chipmunk scurried over a fallen tree, then spiraled up the trunk of a tall pine farther away. The heavy-laden boughs swallowed the tiny creature and hid him from sight.

"I wish I had a hiding place like that—or maybe a nice cave. I'd just tuck the kids in it and hibernate for a few weeks." Jean leaned against Chad, seeming to draw strength from his size and masculinity. But she was ambivalent about relying on him now for direction. The past year, his absence had redefined her role as wife and mother, and she was reluctant to yield that newfound autonomy and independence.

"Maybe we should consider the possibility of you taking the kids home," Chad suggested in a quiet voice.

"Home! Home?" Jean pulled away, putting her hands on her hips. "This is home, at least for this summer. We just got here a week ago, and I don't intend to let anyone or anything ruin our summer together!" She turned to walk away.

"Not even a murderer?" asked Chad.

Jean winced and kept walking.

18

By the time the Brannings finished their chores, ate lunch, and cleaned up their own campsite, the temperature had risen a lot. Bees buzzed as they gathered nectar from wildflowers basking in the sunshine. Camp robbers perched in the trees and hopped around on the ground, scouting for stray morsels left on tables and around fire rings. In the shade, flies made nuisances of themselves. The small biting flies were the worst. They left angry, itchy welts around ankles and on hands.

Jean and Chad rounded up the kids, which was easy since all were under strict orders to stay within sight of the trailer. Chad opened the van's side door for the kids, standing aside as he waited for them to get inside.

Jean locked the trailer and hurried to the van, her purse and a camera case slung over her shoulder. Chad opened the front passenger door and waited for Jean to climb in. Jean realized that men didn't perform this courtesy as much as in the past, and she was capable of doing it herself, but she was grateful for her husband's thoughtful gesture.

"I thought we might take some pictures of the kids this afternoon by the lake," Jean said. "We need to be thinking about getting a good photo for our Christmas card." Her manner was light and cheerful.

"Christmas already? It's only June," Chad said, one eyebrow raised.

"It's never too early to start," said Jean. "We usually scramble to get something developed in time to send out. Maybe this year we'll be more organized."

"Why by the lake?" Chad asked. "We just found a dead man there last night. Isn't there a better place?"

"I love the lake," Jean said. "I have a lot of favorite childhood memories from there, and from the dance last night. I don't want the horror of murder to overwhelm what is beautiful, not for me or the kids."

"Umm," muttered Chad, closing the door behind her. By the time he got around to the driver's side, Jean had selected a cassette tape for the ride into town, a collection of Chopin piano compositions. But as Chad started the engine, and the sound from the speakers sprang to life, Jean looked over her shoulder and caught the frown on Josie's face as she reached for her Walkman and earphones. Glancing around at the rest of her progeny, she saw that Matt wore a look of bored resignation, Ty was already engrossed in a book of mazes, and Kelsie was plumping up a pillow so she could take a nap.

The trip into town was quiet, other than the music. When they passed Steamboat Lake, Jean noticed a sheriff's department Jeep and a Colorado State Patrol car parked by the bandstand. Jean's attention riveted on the officers, and she only stopped watching when it became impossible to rotate her neck any further.

"I married an owl," Chad said, one corner of his mouth lifting.

"What?" Jean responded, distracted by her thoughts. She wondered whether the sheriff's deputies had discovered any clues to the second murder on the shore or in the water. Could this murder be related to Brian Gowen's? The most obvious connection was location. But what motive was there for either murder? Why murder a private investigator? If the same person killed both men, why change murder weapons? With an almost imperceptible shake of her head, Jean set one question after another aside to revisit later.

When they reached Steamboat Springs, Chad drove straight to the county sheriff's office. He parked the van and announced, "We're here. Let's go in, kids."

"Ah, Dad, do we have to?" whined Ty. "Can't we just stay out here and wait for you?"

"Nope, not this time. Everyone has to come inside," said Chad.

Jean turned around and gently shook Kelsie's leg. "Come on, honey. It's time to get out of the van." Kelsie burrowed her face into her pillow. "Uh-uh, sweets," said Jean. "That won't work. You have to come, too."

Josie took her headphones off and gave Kelsie's rump a quick shove. "You're awake," she said. "Stop being such a baby."

That made Kelsie sit up. With a sudden spurt of anger, she said, "I am *not* a baby. Why do you have to be so mean, Josie?"

"Whatever," replied Josie, as she grabbed the door latch and pushed the door open, then slid her feet to the ground.

Jean shook her head in disappointment. She had known that the camaraderie her offspring had exhibited for much of the past week was too good to last, but there were such things as miracles, weren't there? They're children, she reminded herself, normal, healthy, well-adjusted siblings. A flash of memory from not so long ago screened a series of pictures in vivid color across the canvas of her mind. Tiny cherubic faces, four of them, sleeping innocently for precious moments. The scenes changed, and the angelic countenances became angry, demanding organisms, which nothing could placate. Food, clean diapers, a soothing voice, gentle rocking. Nothing worked. She had learned that it was simply their time to be fussy.

Sighing, Jean locked the van and joined her family at the entrance to the building. Chad held the door as the kids entered, then guided Jean through the doorway with a gentle touch of his arm on her elbow.

"Hello," Chad said to the receptionist. "I'm Chad Branning; this is my wife, Jean, and our daughter, Josie. We've come to sign statements concerning the body found at the lake last night."

"Of course, Mr. Branning," the receptionist said. "Sheriff Ramirez is expecting you; he'll be with you in a moment." Shifting her gaze to Jean, the receptionist added, "Weren't you here earlier this week? About the Gowen murder?"

Jean nodded. "Unfortunately, yes. This seems to be becoming a regular thing."

"Oh, I hope not," the woman said. "I mean, we haven't had any murders in this county for the longest time. Two in one week! My goodness, there couldn't possibly be another one, could there?" asked the woman, eyes wide with alarm.

"Let's hope not," Chad said.

The receptionist buzzed the intercom and left the room, closing the door to the hallway behind her.

"She's a bit of a fruitcake, isn't she?" Chad whispered to Jean.

"I have to admit that was a strange conversation. She seemed very professional the other day," Jean said.

"I suppose the discovery of two dead bodies is the biggest news this town has had in a long time. She's in an ideal position to pick up tidbits of information and send it out through the gossip mill," said Chad, keeping his voice quiet.

"Maybe, but I bet she wouldn't keep her job long if she did." Jean's attention on the woman and her access to sheriff's business, she asked her husband, "I wonder just how long she has been working here?"

Chad looked at his wife, cocking one eyebrow, and said, "What do you have in mind? Wringing information from her sealed lips?"

"Actually," said Jean, "I was thinking of unsealing them with some good coffee, then maybe…"

"Softening her up like dipped biscotti?" Chad chuckled.

"Something like that," Jean admitted.

"In all seriousness, Jean, you need to stay out of this," said Chad. "You could endanger yourself, not to mention the kids."

"Everyone is saying that we are already in danger," argued Jean. "I just want to make sure that it's over soon—very soon."

"Let the professionals do it," Chad said, his words clear and clipped.

The door opened, and Sheriff Ramirez beckoned the Brannings inside. Jean turned to remind the younger kids to behave and not leave the room. She sensed they were offended by her public admonition. Did she see the glimmer of halos slipping over their foreheads? Shaking her head to clear the image, she told herself she'd been thinking about cherubs too much. It was time for a reality check.

§

A reality check was precisely the next order of business. A third chair had been added to the sparse collection of furniture in the sheriff's office, and Chad, Jean, and Josie were asked to read their individual statements, which had been typed since the night before. A body with a slit throat, a silent figure slipping through the night, a dark vehicle. lights off, moving with stealth through the parking lot...was this reality or a nightmare? Paper rustled as Chad placed his summary on the sheriff's desk and signed it. A vein pulsed on his temple, and he clenched his jaw, muscles flexing. Jean closed her eyes a moment longer than necessary, wondering if she dared ask whether the body had been identified, before she placed her signature on the page she had been given.

Josie sat frozen in her chair, her face almost as white as the paper she held except for the freckles sprinkled across her nose and cheekbones.

"Josie, are you alright?" asked Jean with concern.

Josie stared at her mother with wide eyes. "This is surreal."

Relaxing a little, Jean patted Josie's leg. "I know. I feel that way too." She gestured at the page her daughter clutched. "Does the statement seem accurate to you?"

Josie nodded. "Except for one thing. I don't think I told any-one about this last night. I just remembered as I read this." She closed her eyes.

"What, honey?" Jean asked.

"I'm not sure how to explain it," Josie said. "I think I saw something in the car...the SUV, I mean. It was hanging from the mirror in the center of the windshield. The brake lights made something glitter. It was kind of weird, like...like one of those mirrored disco balls at the roller-skating rink. Only it was small." Opening her eyes, Josie looked at the sheriff, nor-mal color returning to her face. "It twinkled with red light, from the brake lights, I think."

Sheriff Ramirez sat back in his chair and watched Josie, as if he was trying to read her mind, his hands splayed and fingers touching. The quiet room seemed to have an energy of its own.

"What do you think it was, Josie?" the sheriff asked.

"A crystal," said Josie. "I'm pretty sure it was a crystal. A lot of people have them hanging from their mirrors."

"Could it have been some other ornament?" asked the sher-iff.

"No, I'm sure it was a crystal," Josie answered. "And it was round, or maybe oval."

"Are you sure enough to add this to your statement?" Ramirez leaned forward with his forearms against the edge of his desk, a pen bridging his forefingers.

"Yes, I'm sure," Josie said, her voice firm.

Ramirez swiveled his chair and grabbed the mouse on his computer. After a few clicks, he scanned a document, posi-tioned the cursor in the manuscript and began to type. A few more clicks of the mouse, and then silence, except for the whir of the printer. When the printer finished, Sheriff Ramirez leaned down and retrieved the document. He looked it over and handed it to Josie. She read it, then leaned forward and accepted a pen from him. After she finished signing, she sat back in her chair, took a deep breath, and addressed the sheriff.

"Do you have any idea who it was that I saw last night?" Josie asked.

"Right now, no. But your recollection of the crystal will help us narrow down the pool of small, dark, SUVs that proliferate in this county. Few have baubles dangling from their mirrors."

"Am I really in danger?" Josie asked, fingers laced together in her lap, knuckles white.

"I don't know, Josie," replied the sheriff. "It's best to assume you are for now. Give us some time to track this guy down."

Josie's shoulders sagged in capitulation, all the rebellion seeping out of her. It was easier to accept the situation as stated by a stranger than by her parents.

Sensing that the interview would end soon, Jean asked, "Sheriff, have you identified the body?"

"Yes, we have." Ramirez opened a file near the edge of his desk. "This information hasn't been released to the press yet, so don't share it with anyone. We're still trying to inform some of his family, who happen to be traveling. But the man's name was Walter Norby. He was a private investigator working on his own out of a Denver office."

"Wal-ter Nor-by," repeated Jean, dragging out the syllables. "That's an unusual name, but it sounds familiar for some reason." She tried to recall the various places she may have heard the name. Could it have been in a newspaper or on the television? No, it was more recent.

"Oh, I remember!" Jean exclaimed. "Someone by that name was registered at the campground."

The sheriff paused, pen over paper, ready to write down any details he might want to add to his notes.

"Do you remember when and how long he was there?" the sheriff asked.

"Well, I know it was early in the week," Jean responded, "but I'd have to check the records to be sure of which days."

"Did you see him when he registered, around the campground, driving in or out?" prompted Ramirez.

"No...but I think he was close to the front of the campground...in #2," Jean said. "I need to check my log to be sure. I should have a car description and license plate number, too."

"As soon as you get back, please do that, then give me a call," said Ramirez. "It will help us reconstruct his movements for the past week."

"Sure, though we're going out for dinner before we head back. It may be late evening before we get home." Jean glanced at Chad, who nodded.

"Fine. Just do it as soon as possible." The sheriff rose from his chair and went to the door, opening it to the hallway. Looking at Josie, he said, "And you, young lady...stay close to camp and with someone you trust until we tell you otherwise. Let's keep you safe."

Josie nodded.

§

The Brannings ushered the children outside onto the sidewalk. The kids waited as Chad unlocked the door for them. Just as Josie began clambering in, Jean saw the sheriff exit the office and walk toward a woman holding a camera. It was Ginger Waverly. The family had been oblivious to her presence until that moment, but Jean heard what the sheriff said to her.

"Ms. Waverly, if you or your news station publishes or broadcasts pictures of this family in any form, I will charge you with reckless endangerment," Sheriff Ramirez warned. "Now do the responsible thing and leave them alone. They have enough to worry about without your harassment."

"Harassment? That is exactly what you're doing, Sheriff—harassing *me*. I have a story to cover, and I intend to do it," said Ginger. "For instance, have you identified the victim of last night's murder?"

"Hurry it up, kids," said Chad.

Jean slid into her seat as Chad closed the door behind the last of their four kids, then shut her door. Closing her eyes and leaning back against her headrest, Jean pondered what to do next and began sorting what she knew. It was the unknown that chilled her to the bone.

19

After a quiet meal at a small Italian restaurant, the Brannings drove north out of Steamboat Springs. The evening was beautiful, with sunshine sparkling off the tops of pale green quaking aspens and the evergreens' long shadows sliding across the road. Jean noticed many deer along the river and stream banks, drinking their fill after a long day of grazing. The pastoral scene stretched for miles.

The family arrived at camp before dark, and the kids asked if they could go down by the stream.

Chad said, "Let's all go for a walk."

"I have to check on that information the sheriff asked about and call him," Jean replied.

"Then the rest of us will go," said Chad. "Will you be in the office until we get back?"

"Yes, I have work to do," Jean said. "Quite a few new campers arrived this afternoon. Either warmer weather is bringing people outside, or we're getting publicity," she said with sarcasm.

"Well, whatever is bringing them, let them keep rolling on in," said Chad. "The more people, the better I'll feel." Chad turned to follow the kids down the hill. Pausing, he said over his shoulder, "We'll be back before dark."

Jean watched the kids bound down the hill, Josie off to one side by herself, with sunlight shimmering on her lustrous red hair. Maybe we should cut it and dye it, Jean thought. Then the murderer couldn't recognize her.

Unless the killer already knew who Josie was.

§

Sure enough, Walter Norby had been at the camp from Sunday until Wednesday. Jean had remembered correctly that he occupied #2, near the entrance of the campground, before the loops branched off. His arrival and departure coincided almost exactly with those of Brian Gowen's family.

What does this mean, Jean asked herself? He could have come for a vacation, just to fish. That's pretty unlikely, though, she thought. Her bet was on some association with the Gowens. Maybe he was working for one of them.

Or maybe he was investigating the Gowens. Could he have been working for the life insurance company? That might make sense, Jean thought. The insurance company, according to Brian Gowen's widow, was already balking at paying out on the policy, and they would probably be willing to spend a little money to find a legitimate reason to deny the claim. But why would someone kill an insurance investigator? Jean shook her head, disgusted at the thought of greed motivating murder.

Jean lifted the telephone receiver and dialed the sheriff's office. An answering machine picked up her call, and she left the information about Norby on a recording for Ramirez. She placed the receiver back in its cradle, then grabbed the stack of the day's registrations out of the drop box. As she tapped the edges of the envelopes on the counter to straighten them, a loose flap stuck out over the top. Choosing that envelope to start on, she pulled it out of the pile. She saw that the form on the outside of the envelope had not been filled out. Maybe it's a blank one thrown in with another, she thought. But as she stuck her fingers inside to search for a check or money, she yelped with pain.

Drawing her hand out of the envelope and back toward her body, blood dripped on the desk and splattered her shirt. She grabbed tissues from a box and pressed them around her finger, soon having to reposition them to catch more of the flow. She squeezed the finger and raised it above her shoulders to slow the bleeding.

Something at the bottom of the envelope had sliced her middle finger. Making a compress from a clean tissue to staunch the bleeding, she emptied the contents of the envelope. A small piece of paper and a double-edged razor blade fell onto the work surface. Jean stared at the razor for a long moment before shifting her focus to the paper. Bold letters, written in red ink, read "Go Home."

Jean fought panic churning inside her, threatening to boil over. She frantically surveyed the area outside her office for signs of someone watching. Finding no one, she again dialed the sheriff. As she did, she heard an approaching vehicle. She hesitated, adrenalin rushing in anticipation of the need to flee. But as the familiar Forest Service pickup became visible, she collapsed into her chair. Breathe, Jean told herself, realizing she had been holding her breath. Not too fast, you'll hyperventilate, she thought. In-two-three-four, out-two-three-four; in-two-three-four, out-two-three-four…slow it down; keep it even. The Lamaze childbirth exercise calmed her, and as Bob Duncan approached, she was able to breathe out a cleansing breath.

"Evening, Jean." Bob smiled down through the window. But his face sobered as he looked at her. "Have you hurt yourself?" he asked.

"I suppose you could say I hurt myself," she said. She looked down at the bloodied tissue, then up again at Bob. "Actually, though, someone else did it," Jean said, hands shaking.

"Was someone just here, Jean?" Bob asked, glancing down the road and toward each loop.

"No, there wasn't anyone else here. But come inside and look at this." Jean gestured, still squeezing her injured finger, at the items on her desk.

Bob circled the building and entered through the door. He stood beside Jean, taking in the envelope, razor blade, and note. His eyes widened.

"I'll be…it's a threat," said Bob. He straightened and looked down at Jean.

Jean turned to examine the tissue on her right hand, almost soaked with her own blood.

"Here, let me take a look at that," Bob said.

Bob dropped to one knee beside Jean's chair and unwrapped the tissue from her hand. "It looks as though the bleeding has almost stopped. Good thing you bled, though—it helps clean out the wound," said Bob. "I don't think it needs stitches, but you need to keep it bandaged." Glancing around the interior of the office, he spotted the Red Cross First Aid kit mounted on a bracket on the wall. He retrieved it and began to treat Jean's wound.

"Tell me what happened," Bob said, as he cleaned Jean's hand with hydrogen peroxide, then applied antibiotic ointment and wrapped the injured finger in a sterile bandage. Jean had just finished her story when she heard the sounds of her family returning from their hike.

"Oh, no! I don't want the kids to come in here and see all the blood," Jean said, anxiety showing in her expression.

"I'll head them off," Bob said, rising to his feet.

Bob went outside and approached Chad. "Howdy, Chad," he said. Jean heard no tension in his voice.

The kids passed Bob on their way into the trailer to make popcorn and play a game of rummy. Then Jean heard Bob explain to Chad what had happened, and both men returned to the office.

"Jean?" Chad said as he crouched low enough to take his wife's bandaged hand into his before gathering her into his arms.

Fighting tears, Jean nodded her head into her husband's shoulder. After a few moments, he leaned back and took in her appearance. Jean saw his gaze shift to the desk. The muscles around his jaws twitched, and his face reddened with anger.

"Someone planted this here to scare you," he said, his voice gruff.

Again, Jean nodded her head.

Bob shifted his feet and cleared his throat, reminding Jean and Chad that he was in the room.

"We need to get a deputy here to collect these things," said Bob. "I'll go use the radio in the truck. Don't touch anything." He left them alone.

Still crouching, Chad leaned back against the counter. "Jean, this is serious," he said. "You need to take the kids and go back home."

"That's exactly what this...this person wants us to do. He wants us to be terrified and leave," Jean said. Her initial shock and fear dissipated as her anger rose, and she began questioning the motive for the attack.

"He...she...whoever it was, must think you know something," said Chad. "Or that Josie does. This could have happened to her just as easily if she had been helping you tonight."

"I suppose that's true, but what *do* we really know?" Jean asked, raising her palms in emphasis, the bandaged finger upsetting symmetry. "We've found two bodies. Josie saw a distorted reflection in a mirror. But we don't know the identity of the murderer, or if there was more than one killer, or who was driving the SUV."

"Whoever did this thinks you're a threat," Chad said.

Jean sensed that Chad's position was becoming intractable. Experience told her that he was about to insist that she leave, and she had no intention of doing so.

"Take the kids and go home," said Chad, raising his voice. "I don't want any of you hurt!"

"But Chad, I took this job so our family could be together," said Jean, her voice steady. "I won't be chased off after only a week. There has to be another way."

"Well, I could quit my job, and we could all go back," Chad said sarcastically, "but that would create a financial problem for us. Besides, this job is, in fact, temporary, and I have already started sending out resumes. I don't think I'll be here past the end of August."

"That's all the more reason for us...or at least me... to stick it out," said Jean. "Who knows where you may have to go next, Chad? You might not find a job close enough for weekend commuting."

Jean heard boots crunching on gravel, and Bob cleared his throat as he approached the window.

Bob said, "Andy Bailey will be here in just a few minutes. He was already on his way up to check on things."

"Good," said Jean.

Jean rose from her chair and went outside, hoping fresh air would help her control her rising anger. Chad followed, and Jean turned to face him.

"I need to clean up a little," Jean said. She walked alone to the attached bathroom.

Jean stared into the mirror above the sink. Her cheeks and neck were red, her eyes flashing. If she left with the kids, would she really be any safer? Maybe, because the murderer—at least Walter Norby's killer—might be somewhere in the vicinity. It may have even been the person Josie saw. More important, Josie might be safer if they left. But it would take only a few hours to drive over the mountains. If someone wanted to find her, it wouldn't be difficult. And if she and Josie were to go back home, they wouldn't have the Route County Sheriff's Department to provide support and protection. Jean and the kids would be on their own.

But if Matt, Ty, and Kelsie were to go to Jean's mother's house for a week or two, they would be well cared for. As far as Jean knew, there was no reason for anyone to pursue her younger children. And her mother would watch them. By sending them away, they would be out of harm's way. She would also have more time to pursue questions of her own. The old proverb saying there is safety in numbers could be applied to her and Josie: Two are safer than one. They would just have to stay close to each another.

The sound of tires on gravel brought Jean out of her reverie. Rushing, she washed her hands as best she could without getting the bandage wet, then grabbed a sweatshirt she had left on a hook and covered her bloody shirt. Resolved to do battle with Chad, if necessary, she went back to the office to face the men.

Deputy Bailey had arrived in his Jeep, and he was wearing clean surgical gloves to collect artifacts of the threat from Jean's desk and place them in a self-sealing plastic bag.

"Hello, Deputy," Jean said, entering the room.

"I'd say good evening, Mrs. Branning, but it doesn't seem that good." He seemed to appraise Jean's condition. Jean knew that she must look worn, but she felt she was functioning. "Let's sit down and talk about this," he said.

"It's getting pretty dark. Why don't I go build a fire, and we can talk there?" suggested Chad.

"Good idea. Let me put this bag in the Jeep, and I'll be right over." Bailey went to his vehicle, placed the bag on the passenger's seat, and reached for his radio. He called the dispatcher to confirm his location and relay that the situation was under control.

Chad organized pine needles, kindling, and split logs in the fire circle, lit a match, and flames soon shot up, generating comforting heat. The kids were still playing cards and hadn't noticed the deputy. The adults situated themselves in camp chairs facing away from the trailer so their conversation would not be overheard.

"Tell me how you received this envelope, Jean." Bailey had his notebook out and pencil in hand, ready to write down what she said.

Jean explained how she had found the envelope among other registrations when the family returned to camp, and she had chosen to begin with it because of its open flap. She pointed out that there was no camper information on the outside, which had annoyed her, and she had assumed that someone had put money in without filling out the form.

"When was the last time you went through the registrations?" asked Bailey.

"I caught up with all the paperwork before we went to town today," Jean said. "There weren't any envelopes in the drop box when we left here shortly after lunch."

"So, this must have been dropped here between, say, 1 p. m. and the time you returned?" said Bailey, scribbling in his notebook.

"Yes. We got back about 7:30 this evening, I think," said Jean. "We had dinner in town. It wasn't dusk yet, and we figured there was time for Chad and the kids to go for a walk before it got too dark."

"That's right," said Chad, poking at the fire to keep it burning. Resin popped in the heat, sending sparks outside the ring, and Bob stood up to stomp them out. "The kids and I were gone for close to an hour. And Bob was already here when we came back."

"It was just before dusk when I got here. I wasn't using my headlights," said Bob.

"Okay. So, the window of opportunity was about 6 1/2 hours." Bailey tapped his notebook with his pencil. "I will need to talk to the campers staying here tonight. Do you have a list of registrants and sites?" he asked Jean.

"No, but I can put one together just by taking them from the outside of the envelopes," said Jean. She started to stand up, but Chad stopped her.

"Let me go do that for you," offered Chad. He stood and began walking toward the office before Jean could protest.

Chad looked back as the deputy called out, "Watch for anything else that looks suspicious. I don't think you'll find anything, but be careful, just in case."

With a single nod, Chad continued into the darkness. The others could see him through the window after he flipped the light switch on in the office.

"Did you see anyone suspicious around here this morning?" asked Bailey.

"No, it was a quiet morning," replied Jean. "We did the chores and paperwork but didn't see anything unusual."

"Did everyone who left today check out before you went to town?" inquired Bob.

"I'd have to check the campsites to know for sure. They are supposed to leave by noon, but there could have been some stragglers."

Jean heard Matt say, "Rummy!" inside the trailer. Creaking trailer springs indicated the kids were on the move, so she got up and went to the door to tell them to get ready for bed. Kelsie skipped down the steps toward the bathroom with Josie following. Jean could hear Matt and Ty having a pillow fight. Kids, Jean thought...they're so resilient.

Chad returned, paper in hand, and gave it to the deputy.

"It's getting late. I want to talk to these people tonight before they go to bed. Some of them may be gone early tomorrow, and it would be difficult to find them." Bailey stood and turned toward the upper loop.

"Want some company, Andy?" asked Bob.

"Sure. You'll need to know if anything turns up," said Andy, "so we might as well do this together."

"Will you come back and talk to us before you leave?" asked Jean, noticing that Chad was eyeing her with suspicion.

"We'll check back in with you," said Andy. "In the meantime, maybe you can try to determine if there were any late check-outs."

"Okay, and I'll have some hot cocoa for you when you get back," said Jean. "It's too late for coffee."

Jean picked up the metal coffeepot sitting on the picnic table and went to fill it with water. She could see the bright beam of a flashlight guiding the two men through the trees.

Chad stood with his arms crossed, watching Jean. She bent, placing the coffeepot on a flat rock just inside the fire ring. Then she turned to go to the office.

"I'm coming with you," said Chad.

Jean glanced over her shoulder and shrugged. She knew what he was going to say. And she was ready.

§

Within an hour, Bob Duncan and Andy Bailey had returned. The kids were in bed, and Chad and Jean had come to an understanding concerning how they would protect their family, but not before Chad had demanded that Jean go and she had balked, angry at his attempt to domineer over her. She surprised herself by not giving in, which had always been the case in past arguments.

Jean had already called her mother and planned to meet her in Granby late the next morning to send the younger kids home with her. With reluctance, Chad had agreed to allow Josie to stay, under the condition that she was not to be left alone. He had borrowed a satellite phone from his office, and Jean and Josie were to keep it with them at all times. And if there were any further threats, both Jean and Josie would go home to Loveland.

Bailey and Duncan had visited every campsite and managed to speak to someone at each of them. Most of the campers had not noticed anything unusual, but one woman reported that she had seen a man near the office as she went to deposit her registration. He was medium height, had dark hair, and left the area in a tan Isuzu Trooper without ever entering the actual campground. Bailey was hopeful that the lead might produce a suspect.

Exhausted, Jean and Chad went to bed hoping that the murderer would be arrested soon and they could get on with the family summer they both wanted so much.

But to Jean, Chad seemed subdued. Maybe he was tired. Or maybe, she speculated, he realized that she was changing, gaining confidence and self-reliance, and couldn't be as easily convinced to agree with him as she had in the past. Jean wondered how these changes would affect their relationship and marriage.

Jean's dreams that night were not about her and Chad but of her hands gathering and braiding Josie's lovely hair, only to have its strands slip away and disappear.

20

The next morning, at the picnic table, Jean told the kids to pack for their stay with her mother. No one was happy about going since they had only been in the mountains for a week, and they were just becoming accustomed to it. Ty grumped about not being able to fish, and Matt complained that Grandma never let them do anything. Kelsie was a little less reluctant to go because she loved playing with her grandmother's cocker spaniel, Goldie.

The boys were also angry because Josie didn't have to go with them.

"Why does Josie get to stay? She's the one who saw the murderer," Matt argued. "Why are we getting punished?"

"Matt, you're not being punished. I don't want you to be cooped up in the trailer," Jean said, trying to sound calm and patient, though inside, she was anything but. "The sheriff is working very hard on this, and hopefully, it won't be long until we can live a normal life again."

"Geez, Mom! What do you mean? Nothing's normal anymore!" Matt exploded. "Dad doesn't live at home, we're here for the summer, and somebody is killing people!"

This was the first time Matt had vented his frustration, and Jean realized that it ran deeper than the current situation. He hadn't expressed feelings about his dad working away from home until now, though it didn't surprise her that he resented Chad's absence. But, she thought, I can't cave on this and let the kids stay here. Who knows what might happen?

"We have to be patient while the authorities solve these murders," Jean said. "Your Dad and I will be less worried about you if we know you're with Grandma. Now get your things into the van and let's get going.

Jean hated having to split up the family, but this seemed to be the best solution. She and Josie could handle the campground alone for a week or two, and they could go into town a little more often since the younger kids wouldn't be clamoring to go fishing and on hikes. They might get to know some of the local people and, perhaps, figure out what was going on. With regret, Jean realized that Brian Gowen's funeral was today, and she would miss a good opportunity to observe his family and community.

Admit it. Jean told herself. You're hooked on figuring out who murdered these two men. It's just too tempting to be this close to a real-life mystery and not get involved.

You've read too many whodunits, woman, Jean thought, shaking her head.

§

Two-and-a-half hours later, Jean was at the highway junction outside Granby looking for the restaurant where her mother was meeting them. After lunch, the kids would go home with her. By the time they arrived, the boys had resigned themselves to this change in plans and were brooding.

Jean didn't see her mother's champagne-colored Crown Victoria parked at the restaurant, but she took the kids inside. They were seated in a booth and ordered cold drinks—strawberry lemonade for the three younger ones and unsweetened iced tea for Jean and Josie. Jean told the waitress that they would wait until her mother arrived to order lunch.

The boys excused themselves to go to the rest room, leaving Josie, Kelsie, and Jean sipping their drinks. Jean was preoccupied as she toyed with strategies for learning more about the Gowen family. She also needed to find out what Walter Norby had been investigating.

Jean, thinking about the murders, gazed out the window. The sight of her mother's gleaming car broke the spell, and Jean watched as her mom maneuvered the boat-like car into a parking space, wondering what had possessed the older woman to buy such a big vehicle. Then she noticed a tan Isuzu parked off to the left. The man and woman sitting inside appeared to be arguing. Intrigued that the woman looked familiar and the vehicle was the same model as the one seen at the campground the day before, Jean watched the pair. They were a long way from Columbine, Jean thought. It was unlikely that they were connected.

Had it not been for the woman, Jean would have lost interest. But the passenger door opened and a sleek, angry woman slammed it shut. It was Ginger Waverly.

Jean watched as Ginger marched into the restaurant and spoke to the hostess, who pointed to a sign marked 'Restrooms,' and Ginger disappeared down the hallway. Then Matt and Ty reappeared.

Jean's mother entered the restaurant, stopping to speak to the hostess. She scanned the room and pointed toward the Branning's table. With a smile, the hostess escorted her to join them.

"What a lovely day!" said Jean's mother. "I haven't driven over Trail Ridge Road in a long time, and I thoroughly enjoyed it.

"Hi, Grandma!" A chorus of voices sounded the greeting. Jean rose and hugged her mother. Disengaging, the two women slid onto the benches, Grandma leaning in to wrap her arms around Kelsie and give her a squeeze.

"You didn't mind the drive?" asked Jean.

"Oh, not at all. Despite the fact that I live so close to the mountains and enjoy spending time in them, I rarely take the opportunity to do so."

Jean smiled at the formality of her mother's speech. Natalie Maynard had been brought up in an affluent family and taught requisite social mannerisms. But she loved nothing better than tromping through the muck along streams and lakes to spend hours casting a fly over rippling water, and that image seemed incongruous with her deportment. Natalie was a lady, but an interesting lady, and Jean appreciated her vitality.

"Mom," Ty blurted, in a quiet voice, "Matt and I were getting a drink of water and joking around, and a woman yelled at us to go away so she could use the telephone."

"Maybe you were being too loud," Jean said. Looking toward the front of the restaurant, Jean saw Ginger being guided to a table. Jean leaned over to Ty and whispered, "Is that the woman?"

"Yeah; she was really mean. She even got her spit on me when she talked!" Ty made a face. "We weren't doing anything wrong," he insisted.

"That's Ginger Waverly," Jean told her mother. "She's the field reporter who's covering the murders." Just then, Ginger saw Jean staring at her, and appeared to be shocked and, maybe, afraid. Her face became an inscrutable mask, though, as she was seated at her table.

Jean wondered what Ginger was doing in Granby. She would have expected her to be in Steamboat gathering more material for her story. But she wasn't. Who was that man in the Trooper? Maybe I should go over and ask her. Then again, Jean thought, maybe I shouldn't be so curious.

Natalie was chatting with the children. They were telling her all about fishing, the wildlife, the campground...everything except the murders. The waitress came and took their orders, and when the food arrived, silence descended over the table as everyone ate.

After patting her mouth with a napkin and folding it in a smooth rectangle by her plate, Natalie talked about the possibility of visiting the zoo. The kids loved going there, especially since new exhibits had been added. Matt teased Kelsie about the runaway crickets that had dropped into her hair the last time they had visited Tropical Discovery. She squinted her eyes and wrinkled up her face, forcing her shoulders to shiver.

The family scooted off the bench seats and Jean went to pay the bill at the cash register. After a quick trip to the restrooms, they gathered just outside the restaurant and walked to Natalie's car.

"Well, Jean, it's time for us to go," said Natalie. "We have a long drive ahead of us, and I want to stop in Estes Park to buy some of the salt water taffy the children love so much."

"That sounds great, Grandma!" said Ty. Then he sobered. "But Mom, are you sure that you and Josie will be okay?"

Jean put her arms around Ty and hugged him. "We'll be fine. Josie and I will watch out for each other," Jean said.

"I want all of you to go and have a lot of fun," said Jean. "Make sure you clean up after yourselves and mind Grandma. It won't be long before you're back at camp." She leaned down to kiss and hug Kelsie. Jean put one arm around Matt's shoulders for a quick squeeze.

The kids dug in the back of the van to retrieve their belongings, and Natalie opened the trunk of her car so they could stow their things.

"Don't worry about the children," Jean's mother reassured. "I'll keep them busy, and they will be accounted for at all times. Do call us. The children will want to know what is happening, as will I."

"I'll call every evening, Mom," said Jean. "Thanks so much for taking them without much notice. I wish I could send Josie, too."

"Be careful, Jean," said Grandma. "There's no telling how much danger you and Josie may be exposed to. Remember to lock your doors at all times."

"We will, Mom," Jean said with a laugh, thinking about how little protection flimsy camper doors and locks provided. Leaning over and speaking through the open car window, she said to her children, "'Bye, kids! I love you!"

Natalie started the engine, closed the power windows, and drove away, with the kids turning around to wave at their mother and Josie. Jean and Josie stood side by side waving until the kids were out of sight. Then, without a word, they glanced at each other and walked to their van. As Jean started the ignition, she saw Ginger leave the restaurant and walk to a red sports car. She let herself into the car and drove out of the parking lot. There was no sign of the Isuzu.

Josie fastened her seatbelt, picked up her Walkman and slid earphones on. She leaned back in the front passenger seat and pushed the start button, prepared for the long drive back to Columbine Campground.

Jean turned the ignition key, shifted into reverse, and backed out of the parking space. She pulled forward to the exit, stopped, and eased the van through a deep gutter into the street.

A couple hours of driving would allow Jean to sift through events surrounding the murders and frame questions. If I can just find some answers, she thought.

21

J ean was surprised that Chad had acquiesced to her plan to keep Josie with them at Columbine. They argued, and Jean wasn't accustomed to pressing so hard. They had enjoyed a congenial, even happy, marriage, but looking back on it, Jean realized that she had left most of the decisions and family policy-making in Chad's hands. And she had passively agreed with the direction in which he led them.

But over the past nine months, before coming to be Columbine Campground's host, she had, by necessity, become more self-reliant and made most decisions affecting herself and the kids alone. Chad was not home every day to participate. Their marriage's dynamics were changing, and Jean felt challenged and apprehensive. They had not been able to communicate as extensively while living apart as she would have liked. Because of that, there were events and thoughts that each had internalized, not because they were secretive, but because of lack of proximity. Since they were only together on weekends, their paths were diverging. Jean knew that she had become more likely to question, more decisive, and less malleable. She liked this change in herself. But she also felt that Chad was backing away, becoming a passive observer of who she was becoming.

Jean wondered if their relationship would revert to their earlier pattern when—or perhaps, if—they were able to reunite full-time. She hoped they could find a comfortable middle ground. Jean felt good about her success in adapting and expanding her role, and would be reluctant to relinquish her new-found authority.

Despite this, Jean recognized that the kids needed to see their father as a strong figure in their lives, and she wanted to support Chad because she loved him.

Now she was faced with another intrusion in her life, this time in the form of a malicious stranger who wanted them gone. She was determined to stand firm against this new threat.

§

Josie slept most of the way back to Steamboat Springs. She roused when Jean pulled into a gas station. "Where are we?" she asked.

"We're in Steamboat. Do you want to get something to drink before we go back to camp?" Jean asked.

"Sure, that sounds great."

Jean got out of the van and removed the gas cap. After inserting the nozzle into the tank and starting the flow of gasoline, she relaxed against the van, waiting for the tank to fill. She noticed that a small black SUV was slowing well before the intersection on the other side of the traffic light, and her attention piqued. The sun glaring off the windshield made it impossible to see the driver.

Don't be paranoid, Jean told herself. There must be dozens of dark SUVs in town. The driver was probably taking his time, not in a hurry like most people.

As the SUV turned away on the cross street, Josie exclaimed, "Mom! Did you see that? There was a crystal hanging from the mirror!"

Jean hung up the nozzle and hurried inside to pay for the gas, then rushed back to the van and drove onto the street, squealing tires as she followed the SUV's path. But she was too late, and they soon lost track of the SUV.

"Do you think that was the one you saw the other night?" Jean asked.

"I think so, but I'm not sure." Josie fidgeted and craned her neck, looking in driveways and down cross streets.

Returning to the main highway through town, Jean found an ice cream parlor and parked the van. She and Josie went inside and sat at a table near the window. After they ordered two small chocolate shakes, Jean sat back. She rotated her neck and tried to relax her back. Seeing what might be the phantom SUV had given her a strong adrenaline rush, and she watched traffic, wondering whether it might have returned to track them down.

"I'm worried, Josie. I think I may have given away our ability to recognize the vehicle," said Jean. "Even if he didn't know before that you had seen it, he does now. I shouldn't have followed him."

"Oh, Mom! You didn't have time to think about it," said Josie. "Besides, maybe he didn't see us. We didn't see him after he turned the corner."

"Maybe not," said Jean, "but I think he was watching us before we saw him."

"Well, someone already knew who we were. Otherwise, you wouldn't be wearing that bandage," Josie said, gesturing toward her mother's hand.

The waitress brought the shakes. Jean unwrapped her straw and stuck it into the thick mixture. The door opened behind Josie, and Con walked in, wearing gray slacks and a pale blue-and-white-striped oxford shirt.

"Yo, Josie, Mrs. Branning!" Smiling, Con raised his hand in greeting. "What are you doing here? I thought you'd be at the campground."

"We just got back from Granby," Josie said, looking at Jean, who nodded, then smiled at Con. "Would you like to join us?"

"Thanks." Con grabbed a chair and placed it at the end of the table away from the window. "I just went by the garage to check my work schedule. Jim and I were supposed to start today, but we had the funeral…" Con's voice trailed off as he turned toward the window.

"Josie and I wanted to be there, but something came up and we couldn't," said Jean. "How did it go?"

"It wasn't as bad as I'd expected. I think everyone in the family is in shock because Uncle Brian was murdered. But it was, well, kind of a relief to get the funeral over with. It's been a long time not knowing, but now I can accept that he's dead." Con continued to look at the napkin holder he had been fiddling with.

"How is your Aunt Cathy?" Josie asked.

"She's okay, I guess," said Con. "She's sad, though." A waitress came to the table and Con ordered a chocolate shake and fries.

"Say, Mrs. Branning," Con said. "What happened at the dance Saturday night? Your van was still there when the police came, but none of your family was in the bandstand."

"We were there," answered Jean. "Chad and I found the body when we were about to go home. We had to stay until the police finished interviewing us."

"Yeah, we did too. At least Jim and my parents and I did. Jim's parents were already gone." Con's order arrived. He picked up a fry, bit into it, and set it down. Removing the lid on his shake, he used a spoon to taste it. Then he drew designs in the top with a fry while it melted.

"I haven't heard anything yet about the guy you found. Have they identified him?" Con asked.

Josie nodded but said nothing.

"Go ahead, Josie," said Jean. "You can tell him."

"He was a private investigator," said Josie.

Con's eyes widened. "Wow! Do you know what he was doing there at the lake?"

"I don't think anyone does," Josie said. "He was from Denver. His name was Walter Norby, but the sheriff hadn't released his name last night. I don't know whether they've notified his relatives yet."

"Man," said Con. "I get how this guy's family must feel right now." He lifted a spoonful of his shake to his mouth and swallowed. "It's funny, but I don't feel the sort of shock about Uncle Brian being murdered that I did last fall when he didn't come back from hunting. I guess I knew he was dead, and I dealt with the grief back then; but now I'm angry about his murder."

Jean felt sad for Con. No one ever expects someone they know—let alone someone they love—to be murdered. Waiting to know what happened makes it worse, she thought.

"Yeah, I'd like to find whoever shot Uncle Brian and…" continued Con.

"Leave it to the sheriff, Con," said Jean. "He's working on it, and he'll find the murderer if he can be found." Jean recalled having been told the same thing. Fat chance, she thought.

"It's been about eight months since he died," said Con. "The trail must be cold."

"Give it some time Con. They're trying," said Jean.

"Yeah, but do they care?" Con asked, sullen.

§

Jean was apprehensive as she drove back into the campground. She thought about the threat, the razor blade, and note she had received the day before, and she was a little more uncertain about her decision to keep Josie with her. But Jean believed that she was in the best position to assure Josie's safety. And she was determined to keep this job and stay near her husband. She would keep Josie close by and be vigilant.

It was too early for Chad to be back from work, but a new batch of campers had already begun to arrive. Jean decided that she and Josie should make a quick trash run around the site. They started the tractor and drove around the loops to empty all of the garbage cans, including those in the bathhouses and rest rooms, and hauled the trash to the dumpster. Then they returned to the office.

"Do you want me to start supper?" Josie asked.

Jean almost said yes, but stopped herself. "Not unless you want a meal right now. Let's grab a snack and get the paperwork done. We can fix something simple when your father gets back." She didn't think for a second that she had fooled Josie. Jean would do whatever she could to keep her daughter within arm's reach.

"No, we just had those shakes a little while ago." Josie shrugged. "Mom, what do you want me to do right now?"

"Well, you can do the registrations," said Jean, "or you can grab a book and read while I do them."

"I'll get my book. And a lawn chair," said Josie. "I'll be right back."

Jean watched Josie walk to the trailer. She was sure that emotions would flare if this enforced closeness had to go on too long. Josie was accustomed to more freedom, and Jean needed time alone on a daily basis, too.

After they were settled in the office, Jean began to open registration envelopes. She used a letter opener this time and either dumped the contents onto the desk or looked inside the envelope before sticking fingers in to retrieve forms and payments. She recorded information from the envelopes, then scanned the names for any she might recognize. Finding none, she went to work organizing files and doing some general tidying. As she did, she thought about the second dead man.

Why would Norby come to Columbine at the same time as the Gowen family? Jean found a clean sheet of paper and recorded her speculations in a list as she pondered the answers.

Who was Walter Norby, PI? What was he investigating? Maybe it was Brian Gowen's murder or someone in the Gowen family—Cathy, his parents, sisters, or nephews. Or he could have been looking into the Gowen & Cline business. The connection between Brian and Norby was that Norby was murdered soon after Brian's body was found. They were murdered in the same county. But maybe there was no connection, and Norby was here on vacation.

Who had Norby been working for? Brian's life insurance company? Jean knew that they had been suspicious of suicide, at least until Brian's body was found. Had Norby been hired before Brian was killed, or maybe by Brian himself? Maybe by Brian's parents, Joyce and Henry Gowen, or his wife, Cathy? Then there was his business partner, Stan Cline. He would have the means to hire a PI. Or Norby could have been hired by the murderer, who was spooked about the family gathering at Columbine Campground.

Why was Norby murdered? Jean wondered. She thought that he may have known something important, or was close to finding it, but what? If Stan's story about embezzlement was true, maybe Norby had confronted the thief. Or had he figured out who murdered Brian? Was he blackmailing the murderer? Jean didn't think that Norby's was a random killing, but she wrote it down, too.

Jean traced over and over her final question, making the lettering dark and bold: Who killed Walter Norby?

"What are you doing, Mom?" Josie leaned over Jean's shoulder and read the list her mother was constructing.

Jean startled. She had been focusing so intently that she had tuned out her surroundings. Not an auspicious beginning for the close watch she needed to keep for Josie's sake, Jean thought.

"Oh!" Jean replied. "I'm trying to organize my thoughts about Walter Norby. It looks like a multiple-choice exam," she added, holding it at arm's length.

"I've been wondering, Mom," Josie said. "I was thinking about those first few days we were here. I never saw the guy who was camped in #2, but that had to be Norby. Why would he have chosen that spot if he didn't want to be seen?"

"I don't know," said Jean. "If he was working on a job while he was here, maybe he wanted to see, not be seen."

"Do you suppose he talked to anyone while he was here?" Josie asked.

"Maybe, if he was working for someone," said Jean. "But I doubt he would've contacted anyone right here in the campground. And he wouldn't have used a cellphone if he had something important to say, because he couldn't be sure it was secure. Besides, there's no service here."

Jean tapped her pencil on the desk. "I wonder if he used the payphone…and whether I can get the telephone company to send a record of outgoing calls."

"But how would you know if he was the one to make any of them?" asked Josie.

"If I can get a list of numbers called," answered Jean. "I can dial them and try to identify who they belong to."

"Boy, I hope there aren't very many," said Josie, "because that could take a long time."

"I don't think there would be," Jean said, "because when people go camping, they usually avoid telephones unless they have a strong reason for making a call."

Josie looked at the list and said, "Do you think the sheriff knows who Norby was working for? Can we ask?"

"Sure, we can always ask," said Jean. "The worst they can do is tell us it's confidential…and remind us to keep our noses out of it." Her mouth twisted up at one corner. Then Jean sobered. "But we can't stay out of it. We're in it up to our necks."

"No, we can't," Josie said. "We have to keep asking questions." Josie put her hand on her mother's shoulder.

Leaning over and pointing at Jean's list, Josie said, "This note's weird, Mom. How could Norby have been working for Brian since he's been dead for months? He wouldn't have been getting paid, would he?"

"Probably not," answered Jean, "unless he continued to pursue the investigation after Brian disappeared. Maybe Brian paid him in advance. If Norby was working for Brian or Stan, what was he looking for?" Jean tapped her fingernails on the wooden surface.

"Brian could have been trying to find out who stole from the company," said Jean, "which may be the reason he was killed. Stan may have been doing the same, investigating Brian to find out if he was the embezzler."

"If that's the case," said Josie, "isn't Stan in danger?"

"Only if the person stealing the money killed Brian and Norby and thinks that Stan might know why," Jean said. "But does Stan know?"

"And then there are Stan and Cathy…" Jean said.

"What about them?" Josie said, surprised.

Jean realized she had let her suspicions slip into the conversation, and she would have to confide in her daughter. After all, Josie was as tangled up in this as she was. Maybe more so.

"Remember when I had coffee with Cathy?" asked Jean. "She told me that she and Stan dated before she met Brian. While we were there, Stan came in, and Cathy became pretty emotional about Brian's murder. I can't be sure about Cathy's feelings, but Stan sure acts like a man in love. And Cathy was leaning pretty hard on him for support."

"Stan and Cathy...in love..." Josie's voice drifted off. Snapping back, she said, "But Con and Jim told me that Cathy and Brian were in love. They admired their relationship."

"It's been eight months since Brian has been gone," Jean said, pondering. "It wouldn't be unusual for them to spend time together, considering Stan's and Brian's friendship and business partnership. A lot could happen in that time, especially since there's been so much uncertainty about Brian's disappearance."

Frowning, Jean asked another question. "What if Stan and Cathy were attracted to each other before Brian's murder?"

Josie put a hand over her mouth, shocked, and said, "Mom, that's awful! If Brian knew, wouldn't he have been really angry?"

"Maybe that was the real problem he was confronting before going hunting," said Jean. "After all, he didn't go with Stan like he normally would have."

"Are you thinking that Stan might have killed Brian?" Josie asked.

"Or maybe even Cathy," Jean said. "After all, what do we really know about her that we haven't heard from Cathy?"

Josie's eyebrows pulled together in deep thought. "Well, we know what Jim and Con told me, and they've known Cathy their entire lives. They both like her. She's always been very nice to them, and they believe that she and their uncle were very much in love. They worry about her because she's having money trouble," said Josie. "But wouldn't she have thought of that if she was the murderer? That money was going to be a problem?"

"Not if she didn't know about the embezzling. And that means that Cathy couldn't have been the embezzler. She wouldn't have put her assets in jeopardy by killing Brian unless she knew she had a stash of money somewhere." Jean paused to think. "She could have murdered him because she loved Stan.

Jean tried to recall conversations in which the missing money was discussed. "I wonder if there was really any missing money," Jean said. "Cathy told me at the coffee shop that she was aware of Brian's worry about something concerning the business, but she didn't seem to know why. Stan was the one who said there was a discrepancy in the books, and he didn't mention it to anyone until Brian's body was found, not even to Cathy. At the dance, Marni, Con's mother, told me that Brian had been going through financial records right up to the day before he went hunting. She was doing the accounting; she could see the figures." Jean tapped her pencil on the desk, increasing the tempo. "But no one except Stan has had access to the financial records since Brian's death." She turned the pencil around and doodled in the margins of her list, drawing money signs, guns, and knives. "Could Stan have embezzled, Brian discovered it, and then Stan killed him to keep from being exposed?" Jean pondered her question.

"If he did, why was Norby murdered?" Josie asked.

"Maybe Norby blackmailed Stan," Jean said, tapping her pencil faster. "Stan might have killed him to keep him quiet. We need to find out who Norby was working for." She started tapping her pencil again.

Josie, following Jean's lead, pivoted from the question of Brian's murderer to Norby's. "But why at the lake, especially with the dance going on?" Josie asked. "Wouldn't he have been afraid of being seen?"

"Having so many people around would have been good cover if the murderer planned well enough ahead of time," said Jean. "The pool of potential suspects with opportunity, just by being at the dance, is huge. What we need to figure out is the motive."

"Mom, do you think Stan could have killed Brian for the money...and for Cathy?" Josie shook her head and scuffed the floor with the toe of her shoe.

"Other people have done it," said Jean. "I don't know, but I think we have to consider him as a major suspect."

"You're beginning to sound like a detective yourself—motive, opportunity, suspects." Josie grinned.

"Thanks. I suppose I am," Jean said.

Jean hoped that her and Josie's sleuthing would not result in an ending like that of the detective found dead on the shore.

22

C had returned to camp early that evening. As he got out of the car, Jean saw deep worry lines on his face smooth when he spotted her and Josie leaving the office. Discarding his jacket and briefcase on the picnic table, Chad turned to his wife.

"Hi, honey," Jean greeted Chad, putting her arms around him. She tilted her head back to kiss him.

"You're lucky the boys aren't here, or they'd be grossed out," Josie teased. "'Ooh, ick!'" she groaned, mimicking her brothers.

Chad laughed. "They'll realize what they're missing soon enough. Besides, they've seen us do this for years, and a hug and a kiss are nothing new to them—or to you. You just get your kicks out of razzing us." He moved away from Jean to gather Josie into a tight bear hug.

Josie hugged back for an instant, then pounded lightly on his chest with her fists in mock protest. Chad released her with a laugh.

"I'm getting a little old for this, Dad," said Josie. "Isn't it about time I reserve my hugs for a boyfriend?"

"And who might the lucky fellow be?" Chad inquired, stroking his chin.

"I'll let you know when I figure it out myself," Josie bantered, grinning.

Chad turned to Jean. "How did the drive go today?" he asked.

"Good," said Jean. "We met Mom in Granby as planned, and the kids went home with her." Jean squatted by the fire ring to light crumpled paper and kindling. "They'll have a great time at her house. I think they were rebelling because we had just arrived here for the summer and had plans to fish and explore." Glancing up at Chad, she added, "They were happy to be with you, too. They've missed you a lot since you've worked over here on the Western Slope." Jean turned to the fire, leaning forward to blow on glowing embers until a tiny flame sprang up, then added some dry twigs to fuel the fire and waited for them to ignite.

Sighing, Chad lowered himself into a chair. "I know. I've missed all of you, too. I wish they could have stayed, but Natalie will keep her eyes on them."

Josie handed a can of beer to her father, and Chad flipped the top open with a forefinger.

Finished placing a few split logs in a pyramid over the growing conflagration, Jean stepped back and watched flames lick at the base. "I know," she said. "We agree on that."

Chad downed half the beer, muffled a long belch, and said, "I ran into the sheriff at lunch today. In fact, we ate together at Burger King. They've found some partial prints—other than yours, Jean—on the razor blade. He said they're trying to match them through DMV and the State Crime Lab. If they aren't able to, they'll contact the FBI lab."

"It sounds like they're serious about finding whoever left that surprise for me." Jean's calm voice belied the intensity of her inner tumult. She felt as though a sinister apparition was fading in and out of their lives at will. The specter knew who they were, but they could not identify their nemesis. Not yet at least, she reminded herself.

"Sheriff Ramirez is committed to finding the person who did it," said Chad, sprawling in his chair. "He told me that he was surprised to find prints on the blade, since both murders had very little physical evidence left behind. He thinks the murderer may be a different person than the one who left the envelope here."

"The murderer…then he thinks that one person committed both murders?" Josie asked, inspecting her fingernails.

"He can't be sure, of course," Chad replied, "but he thinks it's doubtful that two murderers would be circulating in the community among the same group of people."

"Why would anyone besides the murderer try to scare us off?" Jean said, stirring the fire.

"I don't know. Maybe someone wants attention," said Chad. "Or maybe it was a malicious prank."

"What if someone did it to try to protect the murderer?" Josie asked.

"If that was true, the person would have to know who the murderer is," Chad hypothesized. "That could put him or her in danger." He stood and walked to the portable cooler, took out another beer, and popped the top. Leaning his head back, he took a swig, burped with his mouth closed, and returned to his chair.

"But suppose the person did it for that reason," said Jean. "Who might pull a stunt like that? In a way, it's an effort to protect us as well. It would have been easier for the murderer to just...eliminate us." Silence held for a long moment.

"I know what you're thinking, Mom," Josie said. "Jim and Con wouldn't do a thing like that," she defended. "They just aren't the kind of guys who could hurt anyone."

"But there are others who might. Cathy might try to protect Stan," said Jean. She saw Chad's eyebrows lift and made a mental note to fill him in. "Any of Brian's family could have done it if they thought another family member was the murderer."

"Why scare us away, though?" Josie asked.

"That's a good question. Maybe we know something that we don't realize we know," said Chad. He looked from his wife to his daughter, then back again. "What do you two think we're missing? You're closer to these people than I am."

"Search me," Jean said, raising her hands palms-up. "If I knew what it was, we could get this whole mess over with."

Jean leaned in to stir the fire again. Having rolled the logs to expose checkered gray coals glowing red-hot, she jabbed the point of her stick into the dirt outside the ring, smothering the burning tip.

§

The next morning, Jean was again disoriented by her surroundings. Instead of waking to the glow of the sun sweeping upward into a crystal-clear blue sky, she looked out into a dull grayness that saturated the air. During the night, clouds had stacked up against the mountains, dropping a light but steady drizzle. Moisture collected in trees and on buildings rather than pattering down in a steady rhythm. From experience, Jean expected the blanket to tighten and thicken, producing a steady rain.

Chad was still asleep beside Jean. She rose, trying not to disturb him, pulled on a white terrycloth robe, and slipped her feet into fleece-lined moccasins. She filled the coffeepot at the sink, grateful for the water hookup and water heater. When she was a child, most of her mornings camping had begun with the squeak of the hand pump as one of her parents filled a pan to heat water, but now she had an electric pump. Of course, they had started pots of coffee as well, filling the air with the bitter scent of fresh brew to savor when they were dressed for the day. Feeling nostalgic, her lips curved into a smile as she thought of those carefree days.

Jean's forehead furrowed as she reminded herself that the kids were not going to come back and have a pleasant experience here this summer unless the murderer was caught. Gloom descended on her as she lamented events that had sucked her and her family into the fog. Determination won over defeatism, and Jean turned to planning her day while she mixed biscuit dough.

First, she needed to be sure that she and Josie stayed as close as bindweed on a chain-link fence. Jean wasn't about to risk her daughter's safety by letting her out of her sight. They would have to do the cleaning and the office work together as a team. Jean promised herself that they would stay in constant visual and voice contact. When the work was done, they would find something else to do. She wasn't comfortable with the idea of hiking or fishing. They would stick close to camp until they knew who had threatened them. Jean hoped that Josie would go along with this plan without too much pushback.

Whisking eggs and chopping vegetables for an omelet, Jean's thoughts turned to the note and razor blade. It didn't seem to fit with the murders. For one thing, if Norby's murderer drove the dark-colored SUV Josie had seen at the lake, then it made little sense that a tan Isuzu had been seen at the campground just before she found the envelope. Unless, of course, there were two people involved in the murders. Or two murderers working on their own. Or the murderer had two vehicles. It seemed to her that finding the driver of the tan Isuzu might allow her family to loosen up on security a little. Of course, there was that incident in town when the driver of the dark SUV seemed to be watching Josie.

Jean shook her head to clear confusion, then tried again to focus. She decided to call the sheriff and tell him about the tan Isuzu she had seen yesterday in Granby, and Ginger Waverly's discomfort at their chance encounter in the restaurant. Maybe there was a connection between the man driving the Trooper and the one seen at the campground. Besides, that SUV in town had a crystal hanging from the mirror. It might not mean anything, but the sheriff should know about it.

Tossing sauteed green peppers, mushrooms, tomatoes, and onions onto one half of the omelet, she flipped the other half over and sprinkled grated cheddar cheese on top. She pulled the oven door open and slid the pan of biscuits out, set it to cool on a wire rack, and snatched a crumb to nibble on. Reaching into the cupboard, she found honey, then opened the refrigerator for salsa and orange juice.

"Hey, sleepyheads! Breakfast is ready!" Jean called.

"I'm up," called Chad. He went into the bathroom and closed the door.

"Can't I sleep some more?" Josie moaned, her sleepy voice muffled by her pillow.

"Not if you want your omelet while it's fresh and warm," Jean said. She set the table for three people and poured orange juice and coffee. She moved steaming plates of veggie omelets to the table, followed by the biscuits. Jean heard the squeak of Josie's bed as she swung her feet over the side. A few moments later, Josie slid onto the bench between the table and window.

"Mom, how long do you think it will be before the kids can come back?" asked Josie.

"What? Are you already missing them?" Jean asked with mock surprise.

"Oh, all right—I admit it," Josie said, frowning. "It's lonely without them. There's no one to tease or play cards with or chase down the hill."

"I hope it won't be long," said Jean. "I miss them, too. It's pretty quiet with just the three of us, isn't it?"

§

Even though there weren't many people in the campground, chores seemed to drag on and on. Jean and Josie cleaned and scrubbed all of the bathhouses and gathered the garbage, then walked around both loops shortly after checkout time. Stay-over campers occupied about a third of the spaces, but the weather was so dreary that Jean doubted they would have many new arrivals. It was Tuesday, which was a slow day for check-ins anyway.

The mother-daughter duo returned to the trailer and prepared clam chowder and crackers for lunch. After washing dishes from breakfast and lunch, they walked together to the office. Sitting at the desk, and Jean picked up a stack of folded papers.

"You know," said Jean, "I've been so distracted by what's happened this past week that I haven't even begun to study these Forest Service maps. It's a good thing no one has asked me for advice on where to go or directions on how to get somewhere. I couldn't have helped much." Jean unfolded one of the large white squares and looked for a spot big enough to spread it. Not finding one, she laid the map on the counter by the window, with the top part propped against the glass.

"Look at all of these forest roads." Jean pointed to lines marked with numbers. They followed the contours of the hills and valleys for the most part, which appeared as ripples and waves. But there were places where the roads took off on their own, zigzagging up and down the sides of mountains in shorter, perhaps quicker, routes.

"I can remember some of these roads," said Jean. "Hmmm...I think that 402 was the road that went straight up the hillside in one place. I remember it because it has the same number as the highway we take when we turn off I-25 to go home through the south side of Loveland.

"One time, I was with your dad on Forest Road 402. It wasn't too long after we were married. We came up here to spend the Fourth of July with my family. We borrowed Grandpa's Jeep and went off by ourselves," Jean said, smiling and gazed out the window, remembering that time years before.

"The Jeep kept vapor locking, making us stall as we went up the hill," said Jean. "And there were deep ruts where runoff had eroded the tracks, so deep that if we had slid into them, we might have either broken an axle or been high-centered. Even though the ground looked dry, less than an inch below the surface it was greasy and mucky. When we got out of the Jeep, the topsoil slid out from under our feet. We had a terrible time getting out of there." Jean grinned. "I learned from that road that if you go down a hill, you had better be sure your vehicle can climb it again or you could be stuck there for a long time.

"That was a very long day," Jean said, laughing. "I also learned that your father is a daredevil when he gets into backcountry. It seems to challenge him to find ways to get over roads not fit for use anymore. I think it must be the engineer in him."

"That's cool," said Josie, grinning. "I didn't know that about Dad. He always seems so, well, cautious."

"He was a lot younger then," said Jean "Being a father has reined in his thrill-seeking. But, you know, when we have the money, he still goes skiing and takes us with him. And he rides his Harley sometimes. He had to give up flying, though, and he seldom rock climbs anymore." Jean bowed her head, sad because attending to family needs and his job loss had pushed him to give up some of the things he loved most and had enjoyed long before they met.

"Do you remember any other places?" Josie asked.

Jean pointed to a section of the map, "There's an old, broken-down cabin somewhere over in this area west of the main road," Jean said. "The road winds around some hills, then descends into a meadow filled with wildflowers. That meadow camouflages a slimy green bog full of decaying vegetation. The trick is to step on the gas and get through fast without getting stuck, then wind around the edge to get to the cabin."

"Is there a road through the meadow?" asked Josie.

"It's a trail, really," said Jean. "You can see the tracks going into and out of the wet area pretty well, but unless tires have beaten the vegetation down recently, it looks as though the edge of the meadow is the end of the road." Jean tapped her right forefinger close to where the meadow was located on the paper. "With all of the Forest Service Road closures in recent years, I wonder if it's still open to public vehicles."

"Who owns the cabin?" Josie asked.

"I don't think anyone does now," said Jean. "It's on National Forest land. I heard that a trapper built the cabin in the late 1800s." Jean gazed at the map but instead saw images from her memory. "There was a stock trail going over the mountain behind the cabin. Basque sheepherders using it followed bright orange streamers tied on tree trunks. Names and dates as far back as the late-19th century were carved into the aspens, and the bark was scabbed and scarred by them."

Turning to Josie, Jean added, "In a couple of weeks, big flocks of sheep will be moved through the valleys. One night, my brother and I couldn't sleep because of all the noise they made. We made up names for their 'music,' like *Sonata in Baa-*

flat and *Rhapsody in Ewe.* Coyotes yipped nearby, waiting to pick off some of the weaker or straying sheep."

Jean realized she hadn't told Josie these stories, although her daughter had grown up listening to her grandparents' camping and fishing tales. There was a lot Josie didn't know about her mother's life. Maybe she'd want to learn, thought Jean.

"Do you suppose we could do some exploring? I know we don't have a Jeep, but we could use the van and go hiking," Josie began. Then she grimaced. "Oh, I forgot. We can't because of that jerk."

"You're right—we can't do it now," Jean sighed. "But we'll soon have our chance to explore," she said.

Sounding a lot more confident than she felt, Jean hugged her daughter and said, "This'll be over soon. I know it will."

23

B ob Duncan pulled up to the office about midafternoon. He finished talking on his radio, then got out of the truck. Glancing in the office's front window on his way around the office to the door, he saw Jean examining a book on Western Slope wildflowers and Josie flipping through another on trees. After a quick knock, he let himself in.

"Hello, Jean, Josie." Bob had left his hat in the pickup cab, but he pushed the hood of his rain jacket off his head. "The weather is pretty miserable today, isn't it?" he asked.

Jean realized that rain was beating down on the metal roof in a steady rhythm, just as she had predicted when she woke up that morning. "Oh, I like occasional days like this," she said, smiling. "It makes me want to slow down and do more reading and thinking." She paused to compose another positive statement. "Besides, it will be good for the trees and flowers."

"That it will. And it will put off the danger of forest fire a little longer," said Bob.

Jean turned her chair around to face Bob. Josie stayed seated in her chair away from the door, next to a wall.

"How can I help you, Bob?" Jean asked.

Bob grabbed a folding chair from beside the wall near Josie and set it down with the back to the door. "I'm expecting Andy Bailey to meet us here in a few minutes," he said. "He has something he wants to talk to the two of you about, and he asked me to come, too. He should show up any minute."

"We've avoided talking about the whole mess all day," Jean said, sighing. "But that hasn't stopped us from thinking about it."

"I know," said Bob. "This has to be difficult for you and your family. You've only been here a little over a week, and a lot has happened to you. I don't suppose you have this kind of experience *every* place you go?" Bob's question trailed off, then he laughed. "Do you cut notches in your fire-stirring stick for each body you find?"

"I have never been anywhere near a murder...murderer...body...oh!" stammered Jean, indignant at this assertion and feeling unfairly accused. Taking in a deep breath, she realized Bob was trying to be funny, and released another big sigh. "Nothing like this has ever happened to me before," she responded, flustered.

"Take it easy," Bob said, smiling. "Most people don't ever have to deal with a situation like this. I was just teasing."

Jean made herself relax. "Thanks for trying to lighten my mood. I'm just tense and worried. I'm sorry."

"Hey, Mom! It's been a while since I heard you apologize like that. Maybe Bob should come around more often," ribbed Josie.

A sharp rap on the door caught them all by surprise. Josie jumped. Between their conversation and the sound of the rain on the roof, none of the three had heard a vehicle approach.

Bob moved his chair aside and stood to open the door. Andy Bailey waited outside, avoiding the torrents falling from the eaves. He ducked through the doorway and pushed back the hood of his slicker.

"This rain is foul," stated Andy.

"It could be worse," said Bob. "We could have lightning."

"Okay, so at least we don't have to deal with fires out of this storm. I guess the nice weather had me spoiled," said Andy.

Noticing that Andy was looking around the room for something, she pointed to a small stool and said, "Help yourself."

"Thanks," said Andy. He grabbed the stool from under the counter, pulled it out next to Jean, and squatted low to rest on it with his shoulders against the counter's edge.

"So, I hear you have some questions for us," opened Jean. "We have some for you, too."

"Let me start, then," said Andy. "We found a match for the fingerprints on the razor blade. They belong to a man from Granby named Lee Zimmerman. Have either of you heard of or met him?"

Jean and Josie shook their head. "No," said Jean, speaking for both of them.

"We have an APB—an All-Points Bulletin—out on Zimmerman," said Andy, "but no reports have come in yet."

"You know who left the envelope?" Josie asked.

"We have a fair hunch that he was the one," said Andy. "He owns a tan Isuzu Trooper, which fits the description of the vehicle seen here just before you found the razor."

"Granby...then I saw him with Ginger Waverly," Jean said.

"In all likelihood, you did," Andy replied. "But we can't assume that she knew what had happened. At least not before he did it."

"Why not?" Josie asked.

"Because he's Ginger's half-brother," Andy said. "Their meeting in Granby may have had nothing to do with the threat to you or the murders."

"Or maybe it did," said Jean, scoffing.

"The news reporter's half-brother? What reason would he have to threaten us?" asked Josie.

"That's what we need to find out. As soon as he's located," said Andy, "we'll bring him in for questioning. But until then, Bob and I will stay with you just in case he comes this way."

"Does he know you're looking for him?" Jean asked. She wondered whether the APB would have scared him away.

"He might," said Andy. "He's a freelance writer and photographer, so he probably has a police-band radio. That would allow him to hear the transmissions giving his description."

"Then I suppose you had better stay," said Jean. "But let's go into the trailer where it's a little more comfortable and get some coffee. It's already been a long day."

Jean stood, reached for Josie's book, stacked it with hers, and set both at the end of the counter. She and Josie put on rain jackets and followed the two men, who were closer to the door, outside. The rain poured down on them and rolled off the surfaces of their water repellent outerwear. They trod on layers of decaying pine needles and plants which formed a porous, spongy mat of humus and kept their shoes relatively dry.

Once inside the camp trailer, they removed their wet jackets, hanging them on hooks next to the door. They squeezed in around the table while Jean made a fresh pot of coffee. Reaching into a cabinet, she pulled out a package of Oreo cookies and filled a small plate with them. She placed a bowl of sugar and a small carton of half-and-half on the table, then put four mugs and a small stack of teaspoons alongside them. She ripped several sheets from the paper towel roll on the counter for napkins. Then Jean sat down with the others as she waited for the coffee to perk.

"Do you think this guy murdered Gowen and Norby?" Jean asked. All three lifted their eyes and stared at Jean. "If he did, then as soon as he's arrested, we should be out of danger, right?"

Andy cleared his throat and hesitated. "We've been doing a lot of investigating, as I'm sure you know," said Andy. "We've matched those prints on the razor blade to Zimmerman, and as soon as we pick him up, we'll question him. He may or may not be linked to the murders."

Andy shifted, twisting his shoulders to look out the window. Satisfied that there was no one there, he turned around and continued. "Norby was murdered with a broad-bladed knife. In addition to having his throat slashed, he had been stabbed once in the right side. That wound allowed the coroner to gauge the size of the blade. He speculated that the murder weapon was a hunting knife because of the depth of penetration and width of entry. A kitchen knife may have made the wounds, but it isn't likely that someone would run around carrying an unsheathed knife. A hunting knife makes more sense." With a shrug, Andy added, "We haven't found the murder weapon yet. We're checking the lake."

Jean grabbed a potholder and poured steaming coffee in the waiting mugs, then distributed them to Josie and their guests.

"Near Norby's body," said Andy, "we found blood smeared on a patch of grass and a few marks where a sharp object had been thrust into the ground. The murderer may have given the knife a cursory cleaning and taken it with him."

"Have you found out who Norby was working for?" Josie asked.

All eyes turned toward the young woman sitting in the corner of the bench. Andy replied, "It appears that he was hired by Brian Gowen. The Denver Police Department found a record of checks written last summer and early fall by Gowen and deposited in Norby's account. They were standard fees for his service, nothing exorbitant. The deposits stopped a few days before Gowen's disappearance."

"Weren't there any files containing notes on what Norby's assignment was?" Jean asked, hoping to keep Andy talking. This was information she would have trouble obtaining on her own.

"No, they didn't find any files concerning Gowen," said Andy. "We didn't find anything significant in Norby's car, either, which was abandoned at the back of the parking area by the bandstand. He had a cellphone, but there wasn't any record of calls made around Steamboat."

Jean thought of the request she had made to the telephone company for a list of outgoing calls made from the payphone. Now it seemed even more important to check for calls Norby may have made. Her hunch about him using the campground's payphone might be right.

"What about Gowen's murder? Has the murder weapon been determined?" asked Bob, who had been quiet for a long time. He sipped his coffee and set the mug down on the table, warming his hands on the outside of it.

Shaking his head, Andy replied. "No, we have a problem there. He was killed by a rifle bullet that entered high in the back of the head and exited on the front left side. Unfortunately, we didn't find the bullet, which we need in order to determine the make of the rifle. Since the body was moved from the scene of the murder to its hiding place, we need to find the primary murder scene to look for a bullet or casing."

"Isn't there any solid evidence to go on?" Jean asked, emphasizing her frustration by slapping her hands on the table to the rhythm of her words.

"Well," said Andy, "there's that metal button found under the tree blocking the logging road where the body was found. We're checking to see which clothing manufacturers use them, and what type and brand of garment it came from. That will take some time, though."

"Brian's murderer could get away with it, couldn't he?" Josie exclaimed, raising her hands to cradle her head.

"It's possible," said Andy. "Unless Norby's murder is tied to his, we have a very cold trail." He stood and stretched. "It's time to check in with dispatch. Maybe there'll be some news for us."

He grabbed his jacket from a hook by the door and slipped it on before stepping out into the rain.

"Are you ready for more coffee?" Jean asked Bob.

"Thanks. It's been a long time since I had real brewed coffee, not that drip stuff," said Bob.

Jean smiled, saying, "It's one of the luxuries of camping in the mountains. There's a little more time to do things. Besides, food tastes better up here." She poured fresh coffee into all of the mugs, then sat down by Josie. Andy returned and went through the process of removing his coat.

"Nothing yet," said Andy. "The sheriff is talking to Ginger right now. Hopefully, she'll be able to help them locate her brother."

"How long has Ginger been working in Steamboat Springs?" Jean asked.

"She's been on-air about two years, more or less," said Andy. She's been a real in-your-face kind of news gatherer. I suppose that's how city reporters have to behave, but a lot of folks here have been offended by her manner." Andy sat down and drank from his steaming cup.

"Has her brother spent much time here? I know he lives in Granby, but..." Jean said.

"I don't think he's stayed in the Steamboat area for long periods of time, if that's what you're asking," said Andy. "I imagine he visits his sister, but there aren't any records of him being charged with crimes or being cited for traffic violations. Andy glanced over his shoulder, checking again for movement outside. He said, "It's just a gut feeling, but I don't think that Lee Zimmerman is our murderer. He may have planted the razor, but there are too many unanswered questions about Norby and Gowen, and to the best of my knowledge, Zimmerman had no association with them."

"Then why would he try to scare us off?" Josie asked.

"We'll have to wait and ask him," Andy said.

§

The afternoon passed slowly as Jean, Josie, the forest ranger, and the sheriff's deputy waited for news that Lee Zimmerman had been apprehended. The camper's windows fogged, and the air was becoming humid and fetid. Jean cracked opened a couple windows, and cross ventilation began taming the unpleasantness. Fatigue had finally silenced the group, but the cooler fresh air helped revive them a bit. Jean imagined that thoughts in the others' minds were running rampant like in hers.

Andy left the trailer periodically to check the radio. Jean worked on a crossword puzzle, then began preparing supper. Josie played solitaire on her end of the table, shuffling and sliding cards with a soft rhythm. As the day wore on, rain continued and the light faded.

There was still no word about Zimmerman's whereabouts when Chad arrived home from work.

"What's going on?" Chad asked, looking around the table as he removed his dripping coat.

Jean let Andy explain his and Bob's presence. She listened as she continued with supper preparations. Potatoes baked in the oven, and she had begun to fry some pork chops in a cast iron skillet. A fresh salad was waiting in the refrigerator, and all that was left to do was warm up some canned green beans. If the evening drags on, Jean thought, I'll make fudge for a snack rather than having dessert.

"I appreciate the fact that Andy and Bob are here to look out for you," said Chad. "But Jean," Chad chastised, "I wish you'd called me to tell me what was happening."

Jean could see that her husband was exasperated. His jaw was clenched and face red with anger. Frown lines demonstrated deep concern.

"I didn't think to call you," said Jean, realizing that in his absence, she often delayed calling him when crises arose—she took care of them on her own.

"I'm sorry, Chad," Jean said. "It's just been a matter of waiting, and there was no reason to believe that this guy is anywhere nearby. Even if he was..." Jean shook her head and spread her hands.

"Chad, I've already told this to the others," Andy said, "I—we—don't think Zimmerman is the murderer. We'll have to check it out, of course, but there are too many complications in this case that he couldn't have had anything to do with."

Chad sighed. "I have to agree with that. From the little I know, I think it's unlikely that he killed Norby or Gowen."

"Besides, the man in the SUV was older," said Josie.

All eyes turned to the young woman.

"What?" said Jean.

"Are you sure?" asked Andy.

Josie, looking sheepish, said, "Yes, I'm sure. I can't explain how I know, but he just looked older in the rear-view mirror."

"Do you have any idea how old he might be?" asked the deputy.

"He was at least as old as my dad, maybe even older," said Josie. She glanced at Chad.

"Maybe mid- to late-forties, then," said Andy. "Do you remember anything else about him?"

"No. I guess his age was an impression," said Josie. "I can't think of anything else I haven't already said."

"Alright," said Andy, getting up from the table. "I'm going out to the radio, and I'll pass this information along." Andy pulled his damp jacket on again and went outside. The camper bounced a little as he descended its steps.

Jean set plates and tableware out, and placed a roll of paper towels for napkins near the window, next to salt and pepper shakers. She refilled coffee cups, shifted food from the stove to the table, and sat down next to Chad, who wrapped his arm over her shoulders. She leaned closer to him, grateful for his presence, sorry for leaving him out.

Supper was ready when Andy returned. Zimmerman hadn't been found yet, so the three Brannings, the deputy, and the ranger ate a quiet meal as darkness fell.

There was nothing they could do but play gin rummy and wait.

24

The aroma of fresh coffee woke Jean as the sun rose the next morning. Birds sang, and she didn't hear rain spattering on the roof, a welcome reprieve from the previous day's weather. She rolled over in the empty bed, wondering why she heard deep voices in conversation in the kitchen. Then she remembered. Taking turns on watch all night. Deputy Bailey, Ranger Duncan, and Chad had made sure that no one approached the trailer unnoticed.

Jean slid out of bed and put her clothes on. Maybe there would be time for a shower later, she told herself. She left the bedroom and slipped into the bathroom, hoping she wouldn't be seen but knowing the small trailer didn't offer much privacy.

Pulling a brush through her hair, she leaned toward the mirror and examined the dark circles under her eyes while pulling her hair back. Tension was getting to her.

As Jean entered the kitchen, the men greeted her. They seemed to be in a cheerful mood. Chad put his arms around her and squeezed her tight, with Andy and Bob smiling as she looked past her husband's shoulder.

Chad released Jean and swung to the side with one arm draped over her shoulders. He said, "Andy just learned that

Lee Zimmerman has been picked up. He was driving over Cameron Pass and blew a radiator hose. He didn't know anyone was looking for him, and he waited in his Trooper until a state patrolman came along. Zimmerman is now at the Jackson County jail. Sheriff Ramirez is sending a deputy to pick him up and bring him to Steamboat Springs for questioning."

"Does this mean that Josie and I are out of danger?" Jean asked.

Andy's smile faded. "We need to talk to this guy and find out if he planted the razor...and why. Even if he did do it, you are still going to have to be very careful until we find Norby's murderer. Like I said, I don't think Zimmerman is the perpetrator on that score."

Jean slipped out from under her husband's arm and turned to the refrigerator, removing milk, eggs, bacon, and frozen hash browns. Carrying her clothes and a small bag, Josie opened the door and stepped outside, headed for the shower to dress.

"Well, the least I can do is fix breakfast for you and Bob, considering you stuck around all night to keep us safe." Jean busied herself separating bacon strips in the heavy black skillet. Waiting for answers to what Lee Zimmerman knew was going to drive her up the wall, so she ventured a suggestion.

"If Josie and I were to visit the sheriff's office this afternoon, do you think that he would tell us what he's learned?" Jean asked.

"If it has to do with you, he might," Bob speculated.

"Why don't we plan to have dinner together in town, then?" Chad said to Jean. "You and Josie can do a little shopping, if you want, and then meet me at about six at that steak house on the edge of town."

"Sure," Jean answered, "that sounds wonderful. I think Josie will enjoy getting away for a few hours. I know I will."

"Just be aware of your surroundings," cautioned Bob Duncan, who had been silent during the conversation. "This isn't over yet."

"I know," Jean replied. "But we have things to do."

She didn't tell the men that some of those things included talking with Brian Gowen's family members.

§

In contrast to the previous day, when Jean felt trapped under the moisture-laden clouds, morning seemed to melt away under a clear azure sky. Sunshine did a lot to bolster Jean's optimism, and she observed that Josie was more energetic and positive today, too. They hustled through light chores, then swept and mopped the bathhouse floors free of mud and debris tracked in from the drenched forest floor. There wasn't much to do in the office.

As Jean worked, she tried to sort what she was thinking into some kind of order. She thought back to the list she had made after Norby's murder. One question had been answered: Norby worked for Brian Gowen. That meant that Norby probably knew what was happening in Brian's business, and perhaps he even knew who had embezzled. If the same person had committed the embezzlement and Brian's murder, then Norby may have been killed when he confronted that person. But why would Norby go to the murderer instead of the police? Maybe Norby wasn't an honest detective. Perhaps he had been trying to blackmail the murderer. Jean wished the list of calls would arrive from the phone company. Maybe she could figure out who Norby had talked to while he was at the campground.

Andy's gut feeling that Lee Zimmerman was not the murderer made sense to Jean. If he was, then he would have been more likely to kill Jean or Josie than to try to frighten them away. Jean shuddered. She remembered that a doctor had once told her that after a person crosses the line with violence and deliberately kills, or tries to kill, someone, the mental process leading to subsequent violence is streamlined. The neuron pathways forged to bypass inhibitions make killing easier. No, Zimmerman's actions, if he was guilty, simply confused things.

Jean wanted to talk to Cathy Gowen when she went into town, as well as Marni Cole and Kristi Weller. She needed to find out more about those last few days before Brian died. And it wouldn't hurt to talk to Stan Cline. She wondered if Norby had ever contacted him to see if Stan wanted him to continue the job he started for Brian.

Josie, who had been in the shower at the back of the office building, popped in the office door, sunshine glistening off her freshly washed hair.

"Hey, Mom! What're we doing for lunch? I'm ready to go," said Josie.

Tension dissipated in Jean's neck and shoulders as she laughed at her daughter's exuberance. "Let's grab a sandwich and get out of Dodge—I mean, get in the Dodge," Jean replied, grinning. She followed Josie out the door and locked it behind them.

"Oh, Mom! That's cheesy," groaned Josie. Then she grinned, too.

Jean and Josie made the drive into Steamboat Springs without much conversation. They found a local oldies station and listened to 60s music together. When music from the 50s and 60s had become popular again, Jean's and Josie's tastes had found common ground. Jean had to admit, though, that near simultaneous resurrection of bright neon colors, bell bottoms, and clogs, along with 60s era music, made her feel old.

Jean's first priority was to find Cathy Gowen. She had checked the office telephone book for an address, but Cathy was a recent transplant to Steamboat, so her number was not yet listed. Jean considered stopping at the cycle shop where Jim and Con worked but decided instead to go straight to Stan Cline's office. If he was available, perhaps she could ask him some other questions as well.

Jean slowed the van in front of a two-story office building sheathed with smoky glass. Perpendicular to the street, a sign identified the building as belonging to Gowen & Cline, Inc. The building was set back from the street, and Jean pulled into the asphalt parking area to its side, which provided easy access to the main doors.

Jean admired the visual effect created by modern architecture set against a natural background. A grove of aspens was intended to perform the dual purpose of filtering the hot summer sun striking the building as well as allowing solar energy to warm the façade in the winter when the leaves fell. Blue and white columbines grew at the bases of the aspens, adding texture and color to the bark-mulched ground. A windbreak of Colorado blue spruce would grow and shelter the building from cold westerly winds. And the smoky, transparent exterior walls of the building reflected its surroundings, creating a sense that the building was, in fact, an extension of forest.

Jean and Josie locked the van and walked to the main doors. Large potted plants thrived in sunlight filtered through the smoked glass walls. Everything was clean, uncluttered, and new. A receptionist sat at a large desk inside the cool building, her back to a black glass wall.

"May I help you?" the woman asked.

"Hello, my name is Jean Branning, and this is my daughter, Josie. We don't have an appointment, but we'd like to see Stan Cline if he's available. Is he in this afternoon?"

"Let me call his secretary and check. Just a moment, please." The receptionist touched a button on the switchboard and spoke into her headset. After a few moments, she turned to Jean. "Yes, Mr. Cline will see you. Take the elevator up to the second floor. You'll find his office opposite the elevator."

"Thank you." Jean and Josie turned toward the direction the receptionist had pointed and found the elevator. Jean pushed the up button, and the door opened. Once inside, it took a few seconds to ride to the second floor. Stepping out, they found that Stan's secretary's office was walled on three sides, having been left open on the side facing the elevator. The secretary, a woman in her late fifties, with salt-and-pepper hair swept up and arranged in a neat chignon, greeted them with a smile. A small sign on the desk identified her as Gina Tesone.

"Hello, Mrs. Branning, Miss Branning," said Gina. "Mr. Cline is out of the office right now, but I talked with him, and he said he'll be back in a few minutes. Would you like some coffee or tea while you wait?"

"Thank you," Jean responded, "Tea would be nice. Josie?" she turned to her daughter.

Josie shook her head, smiled, and said, "No, thank you."

"Would you prefer a cold soda? I have Coke, 7-Up, and Dr. Pepper."

"A Coke sounds great," Josie replied. "Thanks."

Jean and Josie walked to the end of the room and sat on dark green overstuffed furniture. It was a cozy space given the reading lamps, end and coffee tables, and magazines provided. Opposite the sitting area was a heavy oak door. Jean assumed it opened to Stan's office. Gina disappeared into a cubbyhole at the side of Stan's office which appeared to be a small kitchen.

When Gina returned, she carried an oak tray laden with a teapot, two white bone china cups and saucers, spoons, a sugar and creamer set, a tall crystal glass filled with Coke over ice, and a small plate of chocolate chip cookies. She placed the tray on the coffee table in front of Jean and Josie, then sat down to join them.

"I heard that you found Mr. Gowen's body, Mrs. Branning," said Gina. "We have missed him a great deal since he disappeared. It is unimaginable that anyone would kill him. He was a very good man." Gina poured tea for Jean and herself, and handed the glass of soda to Josie.

"Please call me Jean. And my daughter's name is Josie," Jean said. "Have you worked here for a long time?"

"I've been with Gowen and Cline for ten years. I worked in Grand Junction until last November, when this building was completed and opened as the head office."

"Have you enjoyed living in Steamboat Springs?" asked Jean.

"Yes, I have," replied Gina. "I like the atmosphere of this city much better. It has the ski area, of course, and since we aren't on an interstate highway, there aren't as many people driving through." Gina paused a moment. "Of course, those of us who worked in the Grand Junction office made the move together, so we haven't felt as though we were in an entirely new community." Again, Gina paused, this time appearing troubled. "Unfortunately, some of the people who worked for the company in Grand Junction were laid off early this year..." she said, her voice trailing off.

"I've met Marci Cole and Kristi Weller," Jean said. "Did they move here last fall?" Jean already knew the answer, but she thought that this question might help get Gina to open up.

"Yes, they did," said Gina. "It's a shame they went through all the work and expense of a move, then lost their jobs. But it couldn't be helped." Gina said, shaking her head.

"I've heard there are financial problems, both in the company and for Mrs. Gowen personally," Jean said.

"Yes, but that was true even before Mr. Gowen disappeared, or so he led me to believe," said Gina.

"Oh?" asked Jean, raising one eyebrow as she lifted her tea cup to her mouth, wondering if Gina hadn't trusted Brian as much as she'd suggested.

Josie sipped her Coke and nibbled on a cookie as she listened to the conversation.

"Well, Mr. Gowen had me print out all of the financial records for each of the businesses in the corporation. At first, he was trying to find a way to finance that condo development being built near the ski area. But he stopped talking about that and started focusing on people. He began to look at personnel records, appointment schedules, travel requests," Gina said.

"I was aware he was reviewing financial records, but I didn't know that he had gone beyond that. I wonder, did anyone else know what he was doing?" asked Jean.

"To my knowledge, no one except the two of us knew that he was examining personnel records. But I have told the police." Gina paused to think. "I also recall mentioning this to the life insurance investigator who came, oh, I think it was about a month ago. He seemed to know that there were some internal problems in the corporation. He asked for a copy of Mr. Gowen's appointments for the month prior to his disappearance."

Jean felt as though an electrical charge had shocked her, that she was fine-tuned to an emergency radio frequency. She wondered how she could get her hands on a copy of that appointment calendar. Should she ask the secretary, or maybe Stan Cline himself? Jean wondered.

Careful to not appear eager, Jean asked, "Was this the first time you were contacted by the insurance company?"

"No, I received a call after the New Year," Gina replied. "A claims person asked if I had any information about Mr. Gowen's whereabouts—was there any indication that he may have planned his disappearance, was he distraught—that sort of thing. That conversation was very different than the one conducted in person. The man who came—let's see, his name was..." Gina stood up and walked to her desk. She flipped through a small alphabetized business card file until she found the insurance contacts. "Yes, it was Walt North. Mr. North seemed to be most interested in whether Mr. Gowen had been investigating his employees prior to his disappearance."

Jean and Josie exchanged startled looks, eyes open wide. While Gina wasn't looking, Josie raised her shoulders and mouthed, "Norby?"

Jean's mind raced. Walt—Walter...North—Norby. Could Walter Norby have posed as an insurance investigator, as Josie suggested?

Returning to the conversation area, Gina frowned and continued, "I thought that was rather strange since Mr. North's ostensible purpose for being here was to assess a life insurance claim."

"Has the sheriff or one of his men talked with you since the murder of the man last Saturday night?" asked Jean.

Gina said, "Yes, I was asked if I knew anything about Mr. Gowen's reasons for having employed him as a private investigator."

Jean leaned forward and looked into the secretary's confused eyes. "I think it may be possible that you have met the man. Do you remember what Mr. North looked like?" Jean asked.

"Oh, yes!" said Gina.

"Would you be willing to look at some photos at the sheriff's office and see if you can identify him?" asked Jean.

"Yes, but I would feel silly going there and asking to see pictures of the man murdered last Saturday," Gina said, shifting in her seat, her face reddening.

"Let me talk to Deputy Bailey. I'll see if he can arrange it." Jean sat back in silence for a moment, then threw caution to the wind. "I realize I have no right to ask, but is there any possibility of my getting a copy of Mr. Gowen's appointments—the same list you printed for Mr. North?"

"I don't see why you could possibly want that information." Gina said, sitting back and glaring at Jean.

"Gina, I know this is an unusual request," said Jean, "but I may be able to help figure out what's been going on. I just want to help," she added.

Gina capitulated. "I suppose I don't see any harm in giving it to you." She sighed, shaking her head and adding, "I've already been far too open with you. I hope it's not a mistake."

Gina returned to her computer, moved the mouse and clicked it a few times, then Jean and Josie heard the sound of a printer spitting out its product. The secretary took a sheet of paper from the tray and passed it to Jean, saying, "I would appreciate it if you don't tell Mr. Cline that I gave this to you, however. I'm not quite sure why I am."

Jean glanced at the dates, assuring herself that she had the entries she wanted. "I'm not sure why I want to see this, either. It may not make any sense to me." Jean folded the paper and tucked it into her purse.

"There's one more thing," said Jean. "May I get the phone numbers from the insurance people you've spoken to, including from Walt North? I'd like to make sure that Cathy has the contact information she needs."

Gina looked at Jean, then said, "I'll have them for you this afternoon. And that's the last I can do for you."

"Thank you," said Jean. "I won't say anything to your boss; I'll leave that to you, when you're ready. But I'll talk to Deputy Bailey today about showing you some photos."

The muffled sound of a door closing at the end of the hallway reminded Jean that she was still waiting to see Stan Cline. Less than a minute later, he walked into the office.

"Mrs. Branning, Miss Branning, come on in. I apologize for the wait, but I had some business to take care of," said Stan. He gestured with an open hand for them to precede him into his office, then closed the door behind them. "How may I help you?"

Stan appeared fatigued and drawn. There were lines on his face that Jean didn't remember from her first meeting with him and Cathy at the coffee shop. Dark rings circled his glassy, red-streaked eyes. His body seemed shrunken, although he still looked tall. He must be very tired, thought Jean.

"I want to visit Cathy Gowen," said Jean. "But her telephone number is unlisted. I wonder if you might be able to tell me how to contact her?" said Jean.

Stan reached for a notepad and began scribbling. "Certainly. Cathy has been quite distraught. It may help for her to have a woman to talk to." He ripped the sticky note off of the pad and leaned across his desk to hand it to Jean. "Here's her address and number. She has been screening her calls, so you may have better luck if you just drop by."

Jean was somewhat surprised that Stan was being so helpful. Then again, he cared a lot about Cathy. She wondered if that was why he looked so haggard.

"I want to ask you another question, if I may," said Jean.

"What is it?" Stan replied, sinking back in his leather executive's chair.

"The man my husband and I found dead Saturday night was a private investigator named Walter Norby. Did you ever meet him?" asked Jean.

Frowning, Stan answered. "No, but I did receive a call from him last fall. He told me that he had been working for Brian and wanted to know if he should continue the investigation. I told him no. At the time, I was just beginning to get an inkling of the problems with the company's finances. I didn't know what it meant or who it would point to. I was afraid that Brian might have been involved, and I didn't want to risk his reputation." Stan tapped his pen against the opposite hand, not noticing the black ink spreading on his fingers.

Jean asked, "Didn't it seem contradictory for Brian to have hired an investigator if he was guilty of embezzlement?"

Wearily, Stan slumped in his chair. "At the time, I was afraid that if Brian was implicated in some wrongdoing, Cathy might be named as an accomplice. Of course, I know now that she couldn't have been the recipient of any skimmed money. She has had a very difficult time since Brian's disappearance—murder—as we now know."

"You love Cathy, don't you?" Jean said quietly.

"Yes. I've always loved her. I've always loved Brian, my friend and partner, too. I don't know what I was thinking when

I told Brian that I wasn't seriously interested in Cathy back in those early days. I think I was too goal-driven to realize that she was everything I could ever want in a woman." Stan smiled, sadness etched around his eyes. "I never found anyone else worth considering. It was difficult watching the two of them—my friend and the woman I loved—together. But they were a very happy couple, and I took solace in not having stood in their way."

"You've sacrificed a lot for them," said Jean. "Did Brian know about your feelings for Cathy?"

Stan frowned. "No," he said. "At least I don't think he did."

"Cathy is free again," said Jean. "What happens now?"

"I've spent a great deal of time with her since last fall," said Stan, "and yes, I want to spend the rest of my life with her." He straightened, seeming to regain some of his vitality, but just as fast, he lost his glimmer and shrugged. "Cathy's become very suspicious of everyone since Brian's body was discovered," he said. "If I can't prove that I wasn't involved, then I don't believe there's any hope for us."

Josie sat motionless listening to Stan's confession.

The intensity of Stan's anguish over what he perceived to be a hopeless situation made an impression on Jean. She trusted Stan. His pain was too naked to ignore or disparage.

"My family has been affected by Brian's and Walter Norby's murders," Jean said. "It was bad enough finding the bodies, but we are concerned about our safety unless the murderer is caught. Can you tell me anything that might help me know who I can trust?"

"I'm sorry you've become involved," Stan said. "Maybe if I'd been more open about this last fall, Norby would still be alive and this would all be over." He sighed, shifting his body. "I think, though I can't prove it, that Brian was murdered by someone associated with the business who had access to the computers. The best I can tell, money was being moved from all of the businesses within our corporation. After analyzing the last three years' records, I found that a pattern emerged early in the second year showing leveling income in some of the businesses. This happened despite an increase in production and sales volume. At first, only a few of the individual businesses were affected, but soon, the same thing happened to all of them." Tapping his pen on the desk blotter, he continued. "Using the first of the three years as a benchmark, I estimate that about two million dollars are unaccounted for."

Jean and Josie looked at each other, stunned. The amount was staggering. The idea that someone could have gotten away with it was mindboggling.

Stan continued. "Money appears to have been moved by electronic transfers to accounts payable. I found five different destinations. There may have been more."

"But why wouldn't the bookkeepers and accountants have noticed?" Jean asked incredulously. "It's hard to imagine that much money evaporating without someone seeing it was happening."

"Brian and I had been working on several big projects," replied Stan. "I wasn't paying close attention to actual numbers. He apparently wasn't, either. And it appears that the transactions were made after books had been balanced each month.

Someone went back in and doctored them after they had been reviewed, when no one was likely to scrutinize the numbers. As far as dates of transfers, they were always on the fifth of the month."

"No one noticed?" Jean asked. "I would have thought that mental math would have triggered some sort of question from someone," she observed. She was skeptical that no one had become suspicious.

"I thought the same thing," Stan said. "That's why I gave pink slips to everyone in accounting and bookkeeping and hired an outside service. Remember, though, the money stopped slipping away when Brian disappeared. When I found out he had asked for printouts of the financial records, I decided that I should try to find what he was looking for."

"Do you know if anyone found Brian's copy of the records?" Josie asked, speaking for the first time since entering Stan's office.

"No, nothing has been said about them," Stan replied. "I think if the records had been in his camper, the police would have found them and mentioned them to me. And Cathy would have told me."

"Then whoever took the money may have wanted to stop Brian from exposing him," Jean summarized. "What about Norby? Did he see the records?"

"I don't think so. When he talked to me, he didn't give any specific information," said Stan, nostrils flared. "In fact, he was very evasive when I asked what he had been doing for Brian." Stan rubbed his jaw. "I intuitively distrusted the guy."

Jean stared at the edge of the desk and spoke her thoughts aloud as they formed. "Norby worked for Brian," she said. "He knew who Brian was suspicious of, or perhaps Norby discovered the identity of the embezzler himself. At least, he knew he was looking for an embezzler."

Jean paused, raised her eyes to meet Stan's, and said, "When you didn't want to continue employing Norby, maybe he worked on his own."

"And tried to blackmail the embezzler," added Josie.

"And was murdered," Jean concluded.

"So, the murderer and the embezzler are the same person," Stan said.

"I think so," Jean affirmed. "But who?"

25

Jean and Josie arrived at Cathy's apartment, and Josie rang the doorbell. Jean hoped Cathy would at least come to the door and check the peephole to see who was there. After ringing a second time, they stood and waited. A muffled sound penetrated the closed door, then the click of the deadbolt and slow movement of the door knob signaled Cathy's appearance—a weary, unkempt Cathy. Wearing jeans and a wrinkled, plaid, flannel camp shirt, Cathy's hair was off balance, smashed on one side from lying on it, indicating that she had not made the effort to wash and blow it dry that morning. Without makeup, she looked much older than Jean had estimated. But stress and grief can give that impression, Jean surmised.

"Hi, Cathy," said Jean. "This is my daughter, Josie. May we come in?"

Cathy didn't reply but backed up and made room for the Branning women to pass through the doorway into her living room. The room was tidy, Jean observed, contrary to the appearance of its mistress. A table lamp lit the small cloistered space. On the same table, a mug sat on a coaster beneath the lamp, a shriveled teabag, edges dried and discolored, resting in a teaspoon on a saucer. Cathy's television was off, and no sound emanated from her high-end entertainment system.

Cathy waved her guests toward the couch, then sat in an easy chair perpendicular to the leather couch. As she did, she pulled her legs underneath her, grabbed a toss pillow, holding it tight against her ribs, and grasped her elbows.

"Cathy, my daughter and I got your address from Stan a little while ago. I'm sorry that we're intruding on you, but I hope you'll let us ask some more questions about Brian's disappearance."

Cathy stared blankly for a few moments, then breathed in deeply. The extra oxygen seemed to ease the stranglehold her mind was placing on her body. She relaxed her hands from their steely grip, and, pushing the pillow aside, dropped them to her lap. She straightened her legs, sliding her feet to the floor, and raised her head, her eyes appearing to refocus in the present.

Cathy sighed, paused to take another deep breath, and began again. "Yes, let's talk. I'm not coping well. I've begun to distrust everyone around me, but not you." Looking at Jean, she said, "I wonder why."

"Maybe it's because I wasn't here when Brian was killed," Jean suggested.

"I suppose," said Cathy.

"Are you sure you're up to this?" Jean asked.

"I have to be," said Cathy. "I've been going over and over who could have killed Brian but can't figure it out. I need to know. Maybe it will help to talk to you." Tears filled Cathy's eyes, threatening to spill over. "I'm even suspicious of Stan, and he has done everything he can to help me all these months. I'm afraid I've hurt him terribly."

Jean wondered whether she should reply, and said what she was thinking. "I don't think Stan will hold this against you. He seems to be a very kind, intelligent man." She paused, watching Cathy's reaction. "He cares very much about you."

Tears ran down Cathy's cheeks, and she lifted her hands to cover her face. Through the sobs, she said, "I know he loves me. And I love him. That's what makes this so horrendous. What if he killed Brian? Because of me!" Cathy's small body succumbed to convulsive heaves.

"I don't believe he did it," said Jean. "And you don't believe it either, Cathy." Jean stood and said, "Let me get you some fresh tea."

Jean picked up Cathy's mug and went through a doorway into a small kitchen. She rinsed and filled the mug with water, then put it into the microwave to heat while she looked for a tea bag. With the steaming mug in her hands, she returned to find Cathy more composed. Josie had sunk into the shadows in the corner of the big sofa. This was heavy conversation for a teenager, Jean thought. She hoped Josie was coping.

Cathy accepted the tea, concentrating on balancing the hot brew. "You're right, I don't believe Stan killed Brian. But someone I know must have done it."

"It seems like it. That's why I want to talk to you," Jean said. "I think the person who did it also killed Walter Norby. Did you know he worked for Brian last fall?"

Cathy seemed surprised. "No. He was a private investigator, wasn't he?"

"Yes," said Jean. "He was helping Brian track down the missing funds—and the embezzler. Did he ever try to contact you after Brian disappeared?"

"I don't think so. But I was so upset then," said Cathy.

"I'm sure you were," Jean said. "He did try to talk to Stan, but he—Norby—didn't give Stan any information. He was checking to see if Stan wanted him to continue the job he'd started for Brian. Stan declined. He never heard from him again," continued Jean, "but I think Norby may have talked to Gina Tesone just before he died. If I'm right, he pretended to be an insurance investigator working on the claim for your husband's life insurance policy. He asked Gina for a printout of Brian's appointment calendar dated just before Brian's disappearance."

"That's odd," Cathy said, frowning.

"I'm here," said Jean, changing topics to avoid a continuing discussion of Norby, "because I want to ask you about the time just before Brian left to go hunting. Do you remember anything out of the ordinary—other than him being worried—that might be a clue to who killed him? Did he have any strange calls, messages, meetings, even visitors?" Jean waited as Cathy closed her eyes.

"Brian spent a good bit of time in his study," Cathy said. "He must have been going through the records. I remember he received a call one night, and he was very angry afterwards."

"Do you remember when that happened?" Jean asked.

"It was just a couple of days before he left for hunting." Cathy said, leaning forward. "I remember, too, that Brian had an argument with his sister, Kristi, the night before he left. She called him for some reason—I don't know why—and he moved into the study to talk." She looked embarrassed. "I was walking by his door, and I eavesdropped when I heard him telling her—almost yelling it—that she was a fool. That's all I heard." Cathy added, "I haven't thought of that phone call since Brian disappeared. It didn't seem to matter."

"Maybe it doesn't," Jean said. "Can you remember anything else unusual?"

"No," said Cathy, shaking her head. "Brian packed to go hunting, and we talked about taking a vacation to Hawaii or Bermuda before the end of the year. He seemed to relax a little, to lighten up. We talked about the office move from Grand Junction to Steamboat Springs, and whether we should sell the house in Grand Junction." Sadness spread over her face. "Brian and I designed that house together, you know. I've wanted to keep it just because of the memories." Tears threatened to surface again.

"Cathy, who knew where Brian would be?" said Jean. "Do you know who might have been able to find him while he was hunting?"

Struggling to steady her voice, Cathy answered. "I think everyone in his family knew. They'd all gone to the Whiskey Creek camp at one time or another. And even if they didn't hunt there with Brian, they'd camped and fished."

"Can you think of anyone else?" asked Jean.

"No...except Stan." Cathy's face crumpled.

"Cathy, I don't think you need to worry about Stan," said Jean. "Everything he's done since Brian disappeared has been to protect you. I don't believe he was involved."

"I want to believe that." Cathy leaned her head back, her hair falling away from her lined face. "Oh, this is so strange!" said Cathy. "I hadn't thought of Stan as more than a friend since the night I met Brian. But in the past few months, he has become very important to me. But with Brian being found, I feel as though I'm grieving for him all over again. I feel so guilty. It seems disloyal to love someone else so soon." She ran her hands through her rumpled hair. "The funeral was just on Monday."

Jean changed the subject again. "Cathy, do you know if anyone in Brian's family drives a dark colored SUV, one of the smaller ones, like a Honda CR-V or Chevy Blazer, or some other brand?

"Umm...I think Marni's husband does," said Cathy, "and I know Kristi has one. Any of them could drive one because we all have access to the car dealership and can borrow one if needed or try out a vehicle for a few days. Why do you ask?"

"It would take a while to explain," said Jean, "and Josie and I have some errands. I'm sorry, Cathy, but we need to leave. Besides, I think we've been here long enough."

Jean rose and Josie followed. "Thanks for talking to us, Cathy. You've been a big help."

Jean hugged Cathy and the two Branning women left, the door closing as soft as a whisper.

§

"Geez, Mom," said Josie as they walked down the sidewalk to the van, "that was really hard to listen to. I felt so uncomfortable being there," said Josie, shuddering as though shaking off bad vibes. "Do you think Brian was killed by someone in his own family?" Josie's voice seeming strangled, her face pale.

"Maybe," said Jean. "I've read that in most murders, the victim knows the killer."

"What do we do now?" Josie asked.

"Let's talk to the sheriff and make sure we can rule Lee Zimmerman out," said Jean. "And we need Andy to show a picture of Norby to Stan's secretary to find out if he was the man who called himself Walt North." Jean started the van and pulled into the street.

"I wonder why Brian was angry with Kristi," Jean said. "But I don't think she could have killed him. She wouldn't have been strong enough to move his body, not by herself."

"What about the telephone numbers you asked Gina for?" Josie asked.

"Let's stop and see if she has the list ready. Stan's office is right over there," Jean said, pointing.

Jean parked parallel to the curb and stepped down onto the street. As she reached the office door, she stopped, turned around, and walked back to the van. "Come in with me, Josie. I don't want you to be alone out here on the street."

Josie slid out the door without protest, following her mother into the building. In a few minutes, they had collected the list, exited the building, and were driving away.

Josie latched her seatbelt and picked up the paper Jean had set between them on the console. She scanned the phone numbers and times. "There aren't any names on here. How are you going to know if Walter Norby made any of these calls?" asked Josie.

"We won't know for sure," replied Jean, "but if we can figure out who he might have called, we may be able to narrow down the list of suspects."

"Mom, you're beginning to sound like a detective," Josie laughed. "Are you sure you haven't been reading too many mysteries?"

Jean glanced sidelong at Josie, sensing her daughter's question concealed apprehension.

"I never thought I would try to solve a real crime myself. Maybe reading all those books will help," Jean said.

"Mom, it's dangerous to do this. How are you going to protect yourself—or me—if the murderer comes after us?" Josie asked.

Jean didn't have an answer. She parked in front of the sheriff's office, and said, "Why don't you put that list of numbers in my purse with the appointment calendar? We'll take a good look at it tonight when we get home."

Jean and Josie entered the sheriff's office and were greeted by a different receptionist than they had met before. Jean asked to see the sheriff, and she and Josie were authorized to make their way to the all-too-familiar office.

"Come in," said Sheriff Ramirez from his doorway. They went inside, and he shut the door behind them. "I'm glad you stopped by. I want to talk to you about what we learned from Lee Zimmerman."

"Was he the one who left the note and razor blade?" asked Jean.

"Yes, he admitted doing it," said Ramirez. "However, he could not have killed Walter Norby. He was in Denver Saturday covering a protest march at the Capitol Building. He had dinner with friends before driving back. He didn't arrive in the Steamboat area until 2 a.m., and by that time Norby was already dead. His alibi for Norby's killing is airtight."

"Why did Zimmerman do it? Why threaten me?" asked Jean.

"His sister, Ginger Waverly, has been trying to get a position as a news anchor at one of the big Denver stations," said the sheriff. "Zimmerman says that he was trying to stimulate media attention. He thought that if he could create drama surrounding Gowen's and Norby's murder cases, his sister would have more air time and be able to land a better job."

"That wasn't smart," commented Josie.

"No, it wasn't," said the sheriff. "Now a judge will decide what his immediate future holds. And his sister has been forced to resign from her position with the local station, so who knows what she will be doing next? Certainly not working for a major station."

"At least we don't have to worry about any more surprises in the registration box," Jean said.

"No, but I'm still concerned about finding the person Josie saw the night of Norby's murder." Ramirez looked at the mother and daughter. "I've had my deputies watching for a SUV with a crystal hanging from its rearview mirror, but so far, they've drawn a blank. There's been no sign of the vehicle, other than your possible sighting."

Jean hadn't told the sheriff when she called that she and Josie had tried to follow the SUV. She decided not to mention it now. Instead, she changed the subject to what she had learned about Walt North.

He leaned toward Jean. "Are you sleuthing, Mrs. Branning? You're in dangerous territory," he cautioned. The sheriff backed away, adding, "All the same, I'll have Andy take a few photos over to Gina Tesone and see if she can identify North, actually Norby, as the man who came to the office."

Ramirez turned to Jean's daughter. "And Josie, I suspect the SUV driver is still in the area. Don't go anywhere alone."

Josie nodded her head and said, "I understand, Sheriff."

"Have you found the murder weapons?" Jean asked.

"No," said Ramirez. "The gun found with Gowen was his own hunting rifle. And we haven't found anything at the lake, either."

Jean stood to leave, and the sheriff and Josie rose with her. "Thank you for working so hard on the razor blade incident," said Jean. "I'm relieved to know that there was never a serious threat from that direction."

"That's our job," said Sheriff Ramirez. "Not yours, Mrs. Branning. Let us handle it," he said.

As Jean stepped onto the sunlit sidewalk, she wondered where the SUV was. It seemed to her that the key to solving the case was locating the elusive vehicle and its driver. She wondered if the sheriff's staff had compared a list of Brian Gowen's relatives with motor vehicle records. Even if they had, she didn't think they would be able to search for the vehicle if it was locked up in some garage. They would require a reasonable suspicion of guilt. She doubted that the SUV would turn up anytime soon, and if it did, who could guess whether it would have had a fresh paint job?

Jean reminded herself that Josie was the only one who could possibly identify the driver. Did the SUV driver know that Josie had even seen him in the van's mirror? If he suspected as much, killing a third person might not seem like such a big deal.

Jean doubted she had any choice but to try to identify the murderer.

26

The rest of the afternoon slipped away as Jean and Josie browsed along the main street. After refreshing themselves with Italian sodas, they wandered along the covered sidewalk, admiring half-barrels and hanging baskets overflowing with petunias, impatiens, alyssum, lobelia, fuchsia, and other flowers. Jean bought some t-shirts for the younger kids, and Josie purchased a pair of Teva sandals that looked like they would hold up outdoors. They'd better last, Jean thought, considering their price.

Before Chad had left for work that morning, Jean and Josie arranged to meet him for dinner at a Chinese restaurant. Over hot-and-sour soup, cashew chicken, and Szechuan beef and broccoli, the three Brannings discussed their day. Chad had called Natalie to check on the kids, and he said that all seemed to be going well. The kids were enjoying time with their grandmother, but as expected, they felt confined by her extreme caution.

When the Brannings finished eating, Josie excused herself to the restroom. Jean watched as her daughter opened the door and went inside, glad that they had been seated within view so that she did not have to escort Josie as though she was a little girl.

"Well, it's official. My job here comes to an end on the last day of August," Chad told Jean, as he poured steaming oolong from the small metal teapot. "The good news is that I've been recommended for a temporary job similar to this one with the same firm in Saratoga. It begins in September. I have to travel to Wyoming soon for an interview, but I'm pretty confident that I'll be offered the job."

"Saratoga… the distance from home in Loveland won't be much different from last winter's commute to Steamboat," Jean said. "At least you'll be able to come home on weekends."

"That I will," said Chad, watching Jean. "My salary would be about the same, and we'd still have the same employee benefits. I'll keep looking for a permanent position near home. But if I'm still working in Saratoga next summer, you and the kids could spend it there whether or not there's a campground to host."

Jean tried to be cheerful about Chad's news. Still, she couldn't help but be disappointed about the continued separation. Leaning to pick her napkin up from the floor, she spread it on her lap, smoothing it with her hands, trying to remove its wrinkles as though she was wiping away the complications in their lives that she couldn't control.

Jean asked, "Have you looked for any possibilities in northern Colorado? It would be so nice to have you home again."

Chad sighed. "I've been talking to headhunters, and searching internet listings and the Job Service database. So far, there haven't been many openings in my field. I'll keep looking, but if I'm offered the job in Saratoga, I'll accept."

"I have to admit it's a relief not having to deal with unemployment again. At least, I hope not," Jean said, qualifying her statement. "But another year apart—I know you don't like this any more than I do. This is all the more reason to have the family together this summer. But this extended separation is changing the fabric of our family."

"I haven't changed," Chad said in a low, quiet voice.

"No, I don't think you have," Jean said slowly, looking at Chad. "But I am changing, and so are the kids. We have to make decisions without your influence, do things and go places without you. Concerts, plays, soccer games, stargazing, Little League—you're missing important events in the kids' lives. This is Josie's last year at home." Tears filled Jean's eyes.

"They miss you; they're sad," Jean said. "And I've stopped explaining your absence to other people because they're skeptical of the truth that we don't want to be apart." She took a slow drink of tea, searching for the words she needed to say.

Chad waited.

"When we were growing up," said Jean, "our fathers were able to work for the same employer most of their lives. Today, employers don't seem to have any loyalty to employees." She looked into her cup of tea and swirled it, as if trying to read the future in its depths. "I suppose what I'm trying to say is that corporate America is destroying the American family. Our family."

"I wouldn't go so far as to say that the family is being destroyed," Chad said, "but I do agree that it is being altered. A lot has shifted over the years. Just as being a stay-at-home mom puts you in the dinosaur class," Chad said, flashing a grin, "men are struggling with the conflict of blending career and home-life. I've heard women say 'you can have both family and career, but you can't have all of both'—or something like that. I suppose that men have always fought a battle to balance both, but since society no longer expects men to be the sole providers, those of us who want to keep it that way are forced to do so without support. That means compromise in terms of jobs, location, salary, maybe even lifestyle. I don't want you to have to get a job, but it may come to that."

Jean's anger rose. Had he forgotten that she was already working? That's how she was able to be here with him tonight. She'd just heard him say he wanted her to continue her traditional stay-at-home mother role, but Jean wasn't sure she would be able to go back or even wanted it anymore. There were things she wanted to do, to learn, to experience. But she still wanted to be with her husband; she loved him. Jean was confused.

Chad, seeming to sense his gaffe, reached across the table and took Jean's hand in his own. "I'm grateful for the sacrifices you're making."

Jean struggled to hold back her tears.

Josie came back from the restroom, slid into her seat, and said, "My gosh, you two! Leave you alone for a few minutes and you act like a couple of lovesick teenagers! What would your mothers say?"

Josie's needling broke the tension, and Jean and Chad, who had let go of Jean's hand, dissolved in laughter. This is one of the perks of having kids, Jean thought.

Jean walked alone to the van, and Josie got into Chad's car to ride back to camp. As Jean backed from her parking space, a Dodge LeBaron convertible rolled into the parking lot and stopped a row back. In her mirror, Jean saw Jim Sheets get out of the rear of the car and open the front door for his mother, Kristi Weller. A moment later, Tom Weller exited the driver's door and followed his wife and stepson.

Jean turned the ignition key and backed from her space, pressing her brakes before shifting from reverse to first gear, and rolled away. Chad and Josie followed close behind.

Glancing again at the mirror, Jean broke into a cold sweat as a solitary male stepped out from the row of parked cars after Chad and Josie passed by.

The man stood motionless, watching Chad's Metro drive away.

§

Jean was withdrawn after returning to the trailer the night before. She had been aware that Chad was observing her. He apparently recognized that she was tired and upset, and he gave her space—as much as possible in the small trailer. When they turned the lights out, Chad had gathered her into his arms and held her until they both fell asleep. His warmth and quiet concern for her had given her the comfort she needed without insisting that they talk about what was bothering her.

Jean woke up the next day thinking of the documents awaiting her, the list of camp payphone calls, and the copies of Brian Gowen's calendar and phone numbers that Gina had given her. The call record had arrived in the mail the day before while she and Josie were gone. She and Josie had a lot to do.

Over coffee, Jean told Chad most of her plans. The daily chores had to be done, and she would stay at camp all day. She did not mention the telephone records and appointment calendar she intended to scrutinize that afternoon. It wasn't that Jean wanted to keep secrets from Chad, but she knew that if she told him she was continuing to investigate, he would raise objections and try to talk her out of it. Jean didn't have the patience or energy to argue. She wanted to get on with her inquiry.

Chad told her he would be home at the usual time. He kissed her, held her tight, then left for work.

Josie roused as Chad shut the door. "What time is it?" she groaned.

"You missed the worm, girl. The sun's been up for, let's see," she said, looking at her watch, "at least an hour."

"Oh, Mom!" Josie muttered, sticking her finger a little way into her mouth as if to gag herself.

"Sorry," Jean said, "that one's pretty old."

"And lame," said Josie.

Jean went to make her bed as Josie climbed out of hers. "There's orange juice in the fridge," said Jean. "How about cold cereal this morning? Cap'n Crunch Peanut Butter?"

"Okay," said Josie.

"I thought I'd wait until the cleaning is done to take a shower. We're going to have a hot day." Jean listened, wondering if Josie would take the hint, and smiled when she answered.

"Yeah, I can take my shower later, too." Josie opened a drawer to get clean underwear and pulled the t-shirt and jeans she had worn yesterday over them.

There wasn't much to do in the trailer with only the three of them to pick up after. Jean had a second cup of coffee while Josie ate.

"Mom, do you mind if I call Con and Jim?" asked Josie. "I haven't talked to them for days."

Jean considered this. She was reluctant to let Josie have contact with any of the extended Gowen family, but she was certain that Jim and Con were not threats. They had been at school when Brian died. Jim was busy with football season, and Con had been editing the college paper. They wouldn't have had time to leave campus. In fact, Andy Bailey had mentioned these alibis when they were waiting for Lee Zimmerman to be apprehended.

"Sure, honey," said Jean. "You can use the office phone this once. But I don't want you to make plans yet to meet with them, at least alone," said Jean.

"I know," Josie shrugged. "I just want to talk to them."

"Then we'd better get to the office," said Jean. "They'll be leaving for work soon."

Bees were already moving among the wildflowers as the sun warmed the forest air. Without a whisper of a breeze, tall evergreens stood motionless. From nearby patches where sun hit the trees and soil, Jean heard intermittent crackling sounds as vegetation heated up. A doe passed through the shadows along the fringes of the campground on its way uphill after drinking at the stream.

"It's going to be a hot day," Jean said for the second time. "I hope it rains this afternoon. I'd hate to think that we're in for a dry summer."

"But there aren't any clouds!" Josie observed, looking at the blue sky visible above the trees.

"You haven't seen a thunderstorm roll through here yet," Jean said. "After a morning like this, cumulus clouds form over the mountains and sit, growing darker, taller, and more ominous."

The office was as they had left it yesterday at noon. Jean remembered the lists were in her purse in the trailer and went back for them, first checking to see that no one was lurking inside or nearby. Josie went to the office to call the boys.

When Jean returned to the office, she found Josie seated, looking shocked and upset.

"What is it, Josie? Are Con and Jim alright?" asked Jean.

"Yeah, Mom, they're okay," answered Josie. "No one answered at Con's house, but Jim's mom was home and called him to the phone," said Josie, rocking gently in her chair. "They're coming up this weekend to camp and fish." Josie wasn't smiling.

"I'd better set aside a tent site for them," said Jean. "We're pretty busy on weekends." Jean smiled at Josie, who wasn't smiling in return. "Aren't you happy they're coming?" asked Jean.

"I think so," said Josie, turning to face away from Jean.

"Come on, something's bothering you," said Jean. "Tell me."

"Well, Jim had to get off the phone because Con was picking him up for work," Josie said. "I asked Jim whether he had a car of his own he could drive. Jim told me he does, but one of his family's cars—his stepdad's—is in the shop for at least a week, waiting for parts, so his stepdad is using Jim's."

"Why is that a problem, Josie? I don't understand," said Jean.

"I asked what kind of car his stepdad has," Josie said. "Jim said it's an SUV. A black Ford Explorer." Josie's freckles stood out against her pale face like splatters of chocolate on milk.

Mother and daughter stared at each other, saying nothing.

"The call upset me," said Josie. "I'm scared."

"I know, Josie. Me, too," said Jean. "But, you know, we have a few more pieces of information to examine today before coming to any sort of conclusion. Let's get our work done and look at those lists and things afterward."

Josie looked around the room for a diversion. "So, where should we start this morning?"

§

With chores completed, Jean and Josie were dripping with sweat. After long, cool showers, they made sandwiches of tomato, avocado, and provolone on sourdough bread. Each grabbed a Coke and went outside to sit in the shade. Small puffy clouds flitted across the blue sky, but only the treetops sensed their movement.

"It's going to rain," said Jean.

"Good," Josie responded, fanning herself with a *Seventeen* magazine. "Maybe it will cool down."

"If it doesn't cloud up too soon, how about wading in the spring down the hill?" asked Jean. "Let's get the work done so we can play."

"Play?" Josie snorted. "I'm not a kid anymore."

"Hey," said Jean, "you're never too old to play in the water, or golf, or stroll through the mall..."

"I get your point," Josie said, groaning. "But can't I stay outside while you do the office stuff? It's so hot in there."

"Sorry, sweetheart. You'd be too far away," Jean said, shaking her head.

Josie followed her mother, her head hanging despondently, feet shuffling. She took a chaise lounge inside to stretch out on while she read. Jean turned on a fan. Within fifteen minutes of entering the office, Josie was sound asleep.

Poor kid, thought Jean. This waiting is exhausting her. She's being a good sport, though.

Jean did the paperwork, then reached into her pocket for the telephone record. Uncapping a yellow marker, she highlighted phone numbers with 970 prefixes, which included the Steamboat area. That meant she'd ignore the entire Denver-Metro area in her first search, but she could go back and check them later, if need be.

Eleven calls remained on the list, several of them to the same number. Jean picked up the phone and dialed the first one. After a couple rings, a woman answered: "Steamboat Medical Group, Ellen speaking. May I help you?"

"I'm sorry. I dialed the wrong number," Jean said, and broke the connection.

The next numbers were for a movie theater, a massage therapist, the swimming pool, a pharmacy, and a pizza parlor with delivery only. Jean wondered, do some of these campers really think they can get pizza delivery all the way out here?

Only three numbers remained unaccounted for. Jean drank chilled water from a Thermos and wiped perspiration from her forehead. She noticed that Josie glistened with sweat as she lay on the extended chair.

Jean punched buttons for another number. A woman answered and said, "Gowen and Cline, Incorporated. This is Gina. May I help you?"

Jean caught her breath. Could she have been wrong about Stan? Quickly, she formulated a question. "Hello, Gina. This is Jean Branning. I wonder if I could ask you something..."

Jean heard Gina take a deep breath. "I'm sorry. I've felt so guilty since I saw you yesterday and gave you that calendar. I had no right."

"Please don't blame yourself, Gina," said Jean. "I'm the one who overstepped."

"Well, I can't possibly answer any more questions, Mrs. Branning," Gina said.

"I understand. And I apologize." Jean hung up after a courteous farewell. She closed her eyes and shook her head. Am I really doing this? What if the murderer answers, and I give myself away? If I need to, I can hang up as soon as the phone is answered, without any conversation. Just two more calls.

She dialed again. An RV supply company answered, and she hung up.

Jean was down to her last local call. Please don't let it be some innocuous company phone, she thought.

Jean dialed. Four rings, then the answering machine picked up. A man's recorded voice said, "You've reached the Weller residence. Tom, Kristi, and Jim Sheets are not available right now, but if you leave your name and a short message, we'll return your call as soon as possible."

Jean jabbed the "End Call" button with her index finger, almost missing in her anxiety to sever herself from the machine. The shock of hearing the voice of someone she knew rattled her. But wasn't this what she'd hoped for? Waves of nausea sickened Jean, and darkness threatened to overwhelm her. She leaned forward, lowering her head between her knees.

"Mom? Are you okay?" Josie asked.

Jean heard alarm in her daughter's voice, which sounded as though it came from a long distance away.

"Mom?" Josie's pitch rose and increased in volume.

Jean lifted a hand, signaling Josie to wait a moment. Slowly, Jean raised her clammy head. Relieved that the tunnel vision was receding, she sat back and rested.

"Mom, what happened?" Josie asked again.

"I'm fine. I just felt faint for a moment," Jean answered. "It must be the heat."

Jean didn't want to tell Josie that she suspected Jim's stepdad. There could be some mistake...I should check the date and time of that call. Kristi could have made it while she was camping here, Jean thought. Or Josie could have called Jim. But it was more likely that she would have called Con. Wait to tell Josie. Think, Jean told herself.

"Drink some water. Maybe that will help. Do you want me to get some fruit or something?" Josie asked.

"How about some grapes?" said Jean

Josie jogged to the trailer while her mother watched. Picking up the appointment calendar, Jean scanned entries for the last two weeks of Brian Gowen's life. As much as she wanted to know, she dreaded finding confirmation of her suspicions.

Brian had been active in community affairs. Jean noted that Brian was scheduled for a Chamber of Commerce breakfast on Tuesday, lunch with Rotary on Wednesday, Lion's Club on Thursday. But there were other entries as well. He had set Friday nights aside for his wife—"Dinner w/Cathy"; "Movie w/ Cathy." Regular office meetings were held on Monday mornings. Here and there were other appointments—meetings with the county planning commission, architects, even Chad's engineering firm. Nothing seemed unusual about any of them until she looked at the week Brian was scheduled to hunt. Tuesday—just one day after his planned return from hunting, Brian had scheduled a morning meeting with his attorney. Then, two hours later, was the initial "T." For Tom, his brother-in-law?

Relieved that Brian's calendar had been kept on computer, so there was no possibility of mistaking "T" for "S," as in Stan Cline, Jean debated what to do next. Remembering to check the date and time of the call to the Weller's home against Kristi's camp registration, she discovered that Kristi had, in fact, been staying at the camp at that time. But she wasn't anywhere near the campground when the call was made. Kristi had been searching the woods with Marni. Jean was sure because, that morning, she had stumbled across Brian's body. The Gowens had been at Whiskey Creek, all except for Tom and Lonnie, who hadn't camped with their wives.

Jean picked up the phone and dialed the sheriff's office. She used his direct line, but was disappointed when his voice mail picked up the call. She left her name, number, and the time, and told him that she thought she had important information that might help solve the murder. She replaced the phone in its cradle as Josie returned.

"Here, Mom," said Josie. She handed Jean a cluster of grapes. "These are cold, wet, and sweet. Maybe they'll help."

"Thanks, Josie." She plucked a big green Thompson grape from its stem and popped it into her mouth. The coolness felt satisfying, and after downing several of the succulent orbs, she felt better.

"Let's go cool off. It won't be long until tonight's campers start arriving," said Jean. "I'd like to meet a few of them today. I feel like I've been neglecting my duties as campground host."

"I'm ready," said Josie. "I don't think your storm is coming, and I can't wait to cool off in the stream," Josie teased.

"Don't be too sure," said Jean. "Those clouds are getting fatter and darker. And they're not moving very fast."

"Well, let's go," Josie said, leading the way to the stream.

Jean tucked the papers she'd poured over for the past hour into the bottom of the registration drop box, in case someone came into the office. She doubted the sheriff would return her call soon, having gone through a similar exercise once before. And she didn't think it would make much difference if she left the phone for an hour or so because they could take the satellite phone with them.

Jean couldn't have been more wrong.

27

The sun beat down on the grass along the path Jean and Josie took to the stream. Withering in the heat, it lost some of its resilience and lay bent, pointing in the direction they were walking. Here and there they stepped on moist ground, imprinting tread patterns from their canvas hikers. They had not changed into their swimsuits, instead wearing t-shirts and cutoff jeans. The forest around them lay still as wildlife rested in its shadows. Even the birds were quiet.

When they reached the water, Jean set the satellite phone case down next to a rock and started to take off her boots. Then she thought of the sharp, slippery rocks lining the streambed. She remembered how she had always worn old tennis shoes when wading in streams as a child.

"Rats. We should have changed into our old shoes. I don't want to go back now, though. Let's just get these wet," said Jean. "They'll dry out by tomorrow night."

Jean retied her shoelace and took her first step into the icy water. Josie followed close behind. Jean flinched as a splash of cold water hit her back and lower legs, and she turned around to a breathtaking blast of spray. She gasped, then opened her eyes to see her daughter laughing.

"I couldn't resist," said Josie, laughing and pointing at her mother, whose hair coiled close to her neck and face, and t-shirt clung to her body.

Jean leaned down, cupped her hands together, and filled them with stream water, and threw it straight into Josie's face. Josie gasped, wiping her face with her hands. Like Jean, the natural curl in her hair contracted into springlike coils, and her t-shirt was soaked.

"You didn't expect retaliation, did you?" Jean said, giving Josie a sly smile and wiggling her wet eyebrows.

"Well, not at first," said Josie, grinning. "But then I remembered watching you and Dad in the swimming pool when I was a little girl, and I figured I'd better go all out."

"I haven't been in a water fight for a long time," Jean laughed. "Maybe we should do it more often."

"When Matt and Ty and Kelsie come back, we should bring them down here and drench them," said Josie, sounding wistful.

Jean sobered, recalling all that led up to the two of them being alone. She leaned over, picked up a flat stone, and half-heartedly skipped it across the stream. One, two, three skips. Josie wandered downstream a short distance, her head down looking for more skipping stones.

"Mom, there's something I haven't told you. I saw something last..." Josie began, turning around and walking by a willow thicket toward her mother. Jean looked her way when her daughter stopped speaking. She saw, to her horror, that a man had one hand over Josie's mouth and another across her chest, pinning her arms to her sides. In that hand was a gun.

It was Tom Weller.

"Tell your daughter to be still," Tom said.

Tom had a firm hold on Josie. And the gun was so close to her...

"Josie, do what he says," said Jean, her voice calm but pinched, its pitch high. Her heart pounded in her chest and her mouth went dry. Please don't let him hurt her.

Josie couldn't respond to her mom with Tom's hand over her mouth, but Jean saw her blink twice. Josie's whistle code, Jean thought. She's telling me she understands.

"We're all going to cross the stream. You first," Tom told Jean, tossing his head to indicate direction.

Jean turned away from her daughter's panic-stricken eyes with a feat of sheer will. Anguish overwhelmed her as she obeyed. Her mind seemed to detach from the rest of her body as she splashed and stumbled to the far side of the stream. No deep holes swallowed her, but she wasn't thinking about that.

Reaching the opposite creek bank, Tom said, "Stop right there."

Jean turned to see Josie half-stumbling, half-carried through the last few feet of water and up the bank. Tom's gun hand was now free, and he leveled it at Jean.

"Move up the path a couple yards. Now!" Tom commanded.

Jean tore her eyes away from Josie and forced herself to climb the rough incline till she had traveled the required distance—out of reach of her daughter. Trees shaded this side of the stream, and though the temperature hadn't changed much, she shivered in her wet clothes. She could hear Josie gasping for breath after the ordeal of being forced across the stream.

Tom let go of Josie's body, but grabbed a handful of her long, wet hair, deepened to a chestnut color by the water it held.

"My rig is below those trees. Get going!" Tom shoved Josie forward with his hair-filled fist. Face toward the ground, Josie grunted but didn't cry out, stumbled but didn't fall. Jean, horrified by Tom's treatment of her daughter, turned her back to Josie and began climbing toward the stand of pines at the crest of the hill. Fearing for Josie, Jean didn't notice her surroundings. What she saw were the bodies of Brian Gowen and Walter Norby.

Refusing to picture what Tom Weller would do to them, Jean began shaking off the shock and mental turbidity of their capture.

If only she had left a clearer message for the sheriff, Jean thought.

Jean, almost breathless, more from fear than exertion, reached the top of the hill. She glanced back to see that Josie looked more composed, although her eyes were still wide-open and her skin pale. Josie moved more smoothly, too, which meant that her abductor wasn't holding her as tightly. And the gun was still pointed at Jean.

Not at Josie, Jean thought. Please don't point the gun at Josie.

From the hill's crest, the SUV came into view. The sun, shining through the windshield, exploded into daggers of light refracted by the crystal dangling from the rear-view mirror.

Taking a deep breath, Jean moved toward the vehicle. A chipmunk raced up the trunk of a tree and peeked down from a safe vantage point, chattering at the interlopers. Jean heard flies and bees buzzing around, active in the heat. Above the tall tufts of green, she saw thick, billowing clouds, darkened by the moisture they carried. The storm is coming, Jean thought.

"Get behind the wheel," Tom told Jean. "You're driving." He opened the back passenger door and propelled Josie across the seat. Tom climbed in behind Jean, next to Josie. The keys were already in the ignition. Jean started the engine and shifted into first gear.

"Go to the main road, then north," commanded Tom. "I'll tell you where to turn."

Since the forest road's slope was gentle, rutting and erosion from runoff was minimal, leaving it only slightly rough. In the rear-view mirror, Jean could see that Josie was regaining her color. Tom held the gun too low for her to see where it was pointed, but Jean knew that it was directed toward either her or Josie. There was nothing she could do except follow his orders.

They reached the main road and Jean turned left, north, as Tom had demanded.

The Branning women and Tom, in the SUV, met a Winnebago going the opposite direction. Jean didn't recognize it but hoped that the driver would remember seeing them. She drove up the hill away from the campground, wondering where they were going.

"Turn there," said Tom, as they approached a road taking off to the left.

Jean turned, but she spun her wheels trying to ascend the steep slope. Maybe that isn't such a bad thing, she thought. There aren't any recent tire tracks here. If anyone realizes we're missing, maybe they'll see these and look for us, Jean thought, clinging to this fragment of hope.

"Keep going," Tom said.

Tom's quietness bothered Jean. I've got to get him to talk, Jean thought, shifting the transfer case into 4-wheel high range.

"What's this all about, Tom?" asked Jean, knowing full well that it was about murder—theirs and two others. Still, if she could get him to talk about it, maybe she could stall for time.

"Shut up and keep driving," Tom bellowed, his face bloated with rage.

"But I don't understand. Can't you tell us?" said Jean, keeping her voice level and calm.

The silence that followed seemed endless to Jean. Then Tom shattered it with hate-filled venom.

"You just couldn't stay out of this, could you?" said Tom. "You're a nosy, smug, self-satisfied snoop like every woman I've ever known! If you hadn't started asking questions, you wouldn't be here now. You could be in your nice cozy trailer waiting for your husband to come home." Tom sneered, glaring at her as she stared back at him in the mirror. "You know why you're here. You left your calling card!"

"But...I was calling to confirm Jim's and Con's campsite reservations for the weekend," Jean said, sounding unbelievable even to herself and thinking that she might as well have broadcast her suspicion over the noon news.

"Oh, come on! Do you think I'm an idiot?" said Tom. "You already knew they were coming."

Tom turned his face to Josie, narrowing his eyes. "Jim told you that I had an Explorer."

Josie shook her head in denial.

"That was the last piece of the puzzle, wasn't it? And you figured it out this morning," said Tom. "I listened in today on Josie's call to Jim. That's how I knew the hang-up call came from the campground. The numbers matched. I knew it was just a matter of time till you told the sheriff."

"I...I..." Josie stuttered.

Tom yelled, "Shut up!"

Josie cowered in the corner of her seat, shrinking from Tom's glare.

"I'll bet you want to know all the gory details," said Tom, turning forward and again looking at Jean in the mirror. "I think you've earned that information. Especially since you're going to pay dearly for it." Tom's laugh sounded evil, sadistic. He wiped sweat from his forehead onto his pants.

"I covered the trail pretty well, if I must say so myself," Tom said, gloating over his subterfuge. "For a few minutes of *work* every month, I banked over two million dollars. Enough to start a new life."

"But what about Kristi?" asked Jean. "Is she going to be a part of your 'new life'?"

"What a laugh!" said Tom. "She had no shares in Gowen & Cline, no ownership. All she had was a two-bit job and an obnoxious teenaged son." He wrinkled his nose in disgust as if assailed by a foul smell.

Tom smirked and said, "Kristi was good for one thing, though. She had access to the company computer and a key to the office. Brian never accepted me as part of the family. He wouldn't consider any of my ideas. What a jerk!"

"Why did you think you deserved any help from Brian?" asked Jean. "He didn't owe you anything just because you married his sister."

Glowering, Tom said, "Brian had everything. Lots of money, a pretty wife, a business of his own, but he wouldn't give me anything." Tom snorted.

"You were jealous?" Jean asked.

"He should have shared!" said Tom, punching the back of Jean's seat. "I asked Brian for a loan to start my own realty office, or to let me in on a joint venture, but he wasn't interested. I had to begin at the bottom with a small loan from a bank." His face reddening with anger, Tom banged repeatedly on Jean's seat with his fist. "Brian could pay for college for that snotty kid of Kristi's, but he wouldn't even consider giving me a loan! He didn't even work through me when he bought the land for the condo development so I could earn the realtor's fee. What kind of treatment is that?" shouted Tom.

Maybe it was justice, thought Jean. Brian must have had Tom's number pegged.

"But you have your own business. You must have done all right on your own," Josie said.

"Yes, I got it started, built it up. But I was about to lose it. That's when I thought of the backdoor approach to Brian's money." Tom's smirk returned. "He thought he was so smart. But it took him two years to catch on."

"He caught on?" prompted Jean, as she guided the Explorer down a steep grade.

"Yeah, he started trying to put funding together for the condo development. There were already people grumbling about the environment. I thought that if the development could be stopped, or even postponed, he might not raid his other assets." Jean saw the muscles in his face twitch as he clenched and unclenched his jaws. "But he was going to. That was *his* mistake."

You're the one who made the mistake, Jean thought as she held her breath, hoping that someone else was on to Tom.

28

As Jean threaded the SUV through the woods, her daughter and their captor in the back seat, she realized she knew where they were going. They were on the road to the old cabin she had seen so many times on family outings, the one she'd just told Josie about. But why go there? she wondered.

In the mirror, Jean observed Josie, huddled close to the door. The air had cooled quite a bit since towering cumulus clouds had obscured the sun. Jean was beginning to feel chilled and assumed that Josie felt even more so. Their shirts had almost dried, but their heavy denim shorts held more creek water. The sogginess of heavy shoes didn't help. Furtive glances at her daughter, taken as she negotiated the forest road and kept an eye on Tom, confirmed her concern when Josie began shivering. We would be happy now to have some of the heat from an hour or so ago, Jean admitted to herself. But Tom wasn't as wet and she didn't want to provoke him by turning on the heater.

Tom continued talking, seeming oblivious to Jean's and Josie's presence. "After I started opposing Brian's development, he didn't want anything to do with me. He had always fished and hunted with the whole family, except me. I don't even think he ever asked if I liked to hunt." A low, malicious laugh emanated from Tom's throat. "I figured that if Brian's body was ever found, no one would ever suspect me, a non-hunter, of shooting him."

Focused for a moment on Tom's face, Jean saw it grow beet red.

Tom slammed his fist into Jean's seat again. "Not many people drive down these old logging roads now unless they are trying to access a stream for fishing," said Tom, his voice rising again. "It might have been years before Brian's body was found, but you had to go and do it!" Another punch jolted her seat.

Jean jumped but didn't reply, afraid that if she did, his fury would escalate even more.

Tom tapped the right side of Jean's head with the barrel of the revolver. "Take the right fork up there," he commanded.

Jean hesitated then did as he said. She looked in the mirror to see what he was doing with the gun, but it was out of sight again. Looking forward through the windshield and using peripheral vision, she strained to find something—anything—in the front seat that could aid in her and Josie's escape.

"Why did you leave his body under a log?" Jean asked. "Why didn't you bury him?" She needed to keep him talking if only to keep him from thinking about his next plan—killing her and Josie.

"The ground was frozen. I wasn't expecting that," Tom said. "I had to leave—I couldn't risk being snowed in up here. I was supposed to be in Denver." Shaking his head, his eyes again focused.

Jean knew that if she didn't do something soon, Tom would kill her and her daughter and dispose of their bodies, probably more efficiently than with Brian's. But what could she do? Jean asked herself in desperation. Think, she told herself.

"If Brian had been smart," said Tom, "he wouldn't have scheduled an appointment with me after he was supposed to return. He should have turned me in to the police." Tom paused.

"Kristi knew better than to confront me with what Brian had told her," said Tom, sneering, his tone sinister and foreboding. "She knew she'd be sorry," he said.

From this, Jean suspected that Tom had abused Kristi, emotionally if not physically. What kind of life had Kristi and Jim had with him? Jean glanced at Josie again in the mirror; Josie was looking back at her, tears puddling in her eyes.

"Does Kristi know you killed Brian?" Jean asked, sickened at the thought that this woman she knew only slightly might have aided her brother's murderer.

"Are you kidding? She doesn't have the brains to figure it out," retorted Tom.

Jean didn't agree but kept it to herself. Kristi was a lot smarter than her husband gave her credit for.

"What about Walter Norby?" pressed Jean, hoping that he wouldn't become too angry at her questions. She wanted to keep his mind off of what he would do next. Jean's stomach knotted.

"Norby was an idiot," Tom said. "He thought he could just call me, demand money, and collect it. So when I saw Norby snooping around at the dance, I carried out my plan for dealing with him. All I had to do was take Kristi home, return to the lake, and make short work of him."

Jean had been winding around a hill, driving closer to the hidden meadow just beyond. It wouldn't be long till they reached the boggy portion. Did she dare get the SUV stuck?

From the rearview mirror, Tom's eyes looked black, his pupils enlarged, their depth fathomless. She couldn't tell what he was looking at.

"He never knew what hit him," Tom laughed, a macabre chortle. "I could have left Steamboat Springs after a while and no one would have ever suspected me if it hadn't been for this red-headed kid seeing me drive away." He stiffened, seeming to gather strength from his rage.

"But I couldn't identify you," Josie said, her throat raspy and dry. "I didn't know who you were."

Josie was surprisingly calm, Jean thought, giving her hope that Josie might be able to fight Tom, too, if an opportunity arose.

"What are you planning to do with us?" Jean asked, as emotionless as possible.

"What do you think?" Tom replied.

§

Jean stayed on the jeep trail that led into the bog, wondering if Tom knew how difficult it was to get through. The marsh was below. Bright yellow mule's ears sunflowers and blue larkspur were blooming. Jean glanced furtively at Tom in the mirror.

"There's the cabin," he said. "Gun the engine and get this rig over there."

That answered Jean's question. He knew what it took to get through the marsh, and she had no choice but to drive through the muck. From a distance it didn't look wet, but she knew better. She stopped to shift into 4-wheel low. She let out the clutch and stepped on the gas, hoping the tires would dig into the mud and maroon them. At first, they seemed to skim the surface, but they quickly began to sink, slowing down until the SUV stalled.

Tom tapped the side of Jean's head hard, dazing her with the gun.

"Get out and help me get some branches to put under the tires." He yanked his door handle and stuck a foot into the slimy, greasy mud. "No, not you," he said to Josie as she opened her door to comply. "I don't want you trying to run away. Stay put." Josie closed her door again.

Jean stepped into the meadow, sinking to her ankles. She looked at the ominous, darkening sky and saw flashes of electricity dancing through the clouds' midst. Wind had increased on the ground but the clouds moved toward them at a ponderous rate, building upward.

Jean knew that the storm would soon be upon them.

§

The forest's edge was a couple hundred yards away. Jean began walking toward it, mud threatening to suck her shoes from her feet. Tom followed her, gun leveled at her back. He wasn't struggling as much since his high-top boots laced above his ankles, but she heard mud slurping with each step, trying to anchor him, and the smell of rotting vegetation sickened her.

Jean gathered as many fallen branches as she could carry and made her way back to the SUV. Thunder rumbled in the distance, growing louder as the storm approached. She spread the wood behind one tire, then watched as Tom did the same with a smaller bundle, keeping his gun hand free.

On the second trip, Jean looked for a branch that might work as a club. Tom stayed close by, watching her as she gathered the wood. Again, he followed with a lighter load as she delivered dry branches to the SUV.

Only one more trip would be necessary before they could attempt to back the SUV out. Her back to Tom, Jean's eyes darted around, frantic to find a weapon. She spied a rock that she thought she could hide in one hand under the wood, but she couldn't pick it up while Tom watched.

A loud clap of thunder pealed overhead, startling both Jean and Tom. As Tom straightened and looked toward the dangerous storm, Jean grabbed the rock.

"Hurry up! We don't have much time till that storm gets here," Tom yelled. "All we need is rain. I'd be stuck for days."

Jean lifted her burden and tried to hurry back to the stranded vehicle. The impending downpour distracted Tom, but she couldn't risk keeping the rock in her hands for him to discover. She dropped it with the rest of her load and straightened to wait for his instructions.

"What are you standing there for? Get behind the wheel and back this thing out of the mud. And don't get any ideas about leaving me here." Tom pointed the gun at Josie's head.

Jean did as he commanded. As she slammed the door, she whispered, "Josie, we have to get away from him. I'm going to get this Explorer stuck again, and he'll have to go with me to get more wood. Watch us, and when his back is turned, get out and run for the cabin. Remember the trail behind it, the one marked with orange plastic ribbons I told you about? Follow it."

"But, Mom, I can't leave you here with him!" Josie said.

"Yes, you can! You have to. Now do what I said!" Jean demanded, meeting Josie's eyes in the mirror.

Jean started the engine, gunned it, and popped the clutch. The tires slung the branches and buried them in the mud. The SUV moved a few inches, then sank again.

Tom yanked open the front door and grabbed Jean's arm. He yanked hard and threw her face first into the mud.

Josie cried, "Mom! Please, don't hurt her!"

"Get up!" he shrieked. "Get some more wood, bigger stuff this time!"

Jean picked herself up and wiped mud from her face and eyes. "If you have an ax or a hatchet, we can chop down some of those aspens." She pointed at a stand of small trees a little farther from the SUV—and farther from Josie—than they had gone on their previous forays.

Tom shoved Jean around to the back of the SUV and opened the rear gate. He pulled a blanket off a pile of tools. A shovel, hatchet, jack, and toolbox lay below it. There was also a sheathed hunting knife and a rifle.

Josie twisted around in her seat, watching as Tom grabbed the hatchet. Jean met Josie's frantic eyes and gave her a barely perceptible nod before turning toward the edge of the aspen grove.

Thunder bounced off the hills and reverberated through the valleys. The storm marched toward them, spewing sharp bolts of lightning across the sky and to the ground. There was so much electrical activity that hardly had one thunderclap begun to die away before a louder, more frightening boom exploded.

Tom stopped near the aspens, and handed Jean the hatchet, then shoved her toward the trees. "Don't get any ideas. I don't have any compunctions about using this gun on you—or your daughter."

Jean began hacking at the base of a young tree. "You can still get away without hurting us," Jean said. "Just leave us here and you'll have a long head start before we can walk out." She glanced back at him and saw Josie running behind the cabin toward the woods and the marked trail. Keep him occupied, she thought.

"Are you kidding? I have to make a run for it *because of you and your daughter*, and I'm not going to just let you go. You deserve to die." His eyelids narrowed. "In fact, I don't need you now. I can get out of here by myself." He tightened his grip on the gun.

The thunder was so loud now that Jean could almost feel vibrations in her bones. A bolt of lightning shot out of the sky and pierced the mountain less than a mile away. Jean began to fear the capricious ferocity of the storm as much as she did Tom and his gun. She gave the sapling one last chop and severed it from its stump. Grasping the sapling like a baseball bat, she stood upright, twisted her body, and lashed Tom's face and torso with one sudden, vicious motion. Soft green twigs bit into his flesh like a cat-o'-nine-tails.

Tom dropped the gun and screamed, "My eyes!" Cursing, he bent over in pain, and Jean seized the opportunity to run. She had gone about twenty feet when she tripped over a hidden rock and fell. Scrambling to stand up, she looked back to see that Tom had picked up the discarded hatchet. Blood and tears streamed down his face.

Tom raised the hatchet above his head, preparing to throw it at her. At the same time, Jean felt small hairs rise all over her body.

Just as the hatchet reached its apex, lightning split the sky, taking aim at the raised metal wedge in Tom's hand. The air crackled and a gigantic thunderclap deafened her as Tom's body jerked in the grasp of a brilliant electrical arc. Suspended for what Jean would remember as an interminable moment, he fell like a discarded rag doll. Jean's body tingled from the shock of the dissipating current coursing through the earth.

The crisp, clean smell of ozone mingled with the sickening odor of scorched hair and flesh. Wisps of smoke rose from Tom's prone body.

Thunder and lightning continued its slow, relentless march across the sky. Jean tried to stand, intending to run after Josie and catch up with her, but pain shot from her ankle up her leg. I guess that's out, she thought to herself. A long branch lay nearby, and she crawled to it on one knee. After breaking off the brittle end, she had a makeshift walking stick.

Jean looked at Tom and didn't see movement. Hobbling with pain, she made her way over to him, squatted near his head, and pressed two fingers to his carotid. She felt no heartbeat, saw no breathing. Tom was dead. But Jean, fearing she might be wrong, used her stick to knock the gun farther from his body.

Again, Jean hauled herself upright, pulling hand-over-hand up the branch's rough bark. Balancing between her good leg and the improvised walking stick, she staggered and lurched around rocks and sticks as she descended the hill.

Jean needed shelter from the storm.

The SUV was closer than the cabin, and its metal shell would protect her from lightening. There was a blanket there, too, she remembered.

That's where I'll go, thought Jean.

Envisioning Josie racing through the woods, Jean stumbled as fast as she could to safety.

§

Rain fell in sheets, beating on the metal roof of the SUV. At least the lightning has passed, Jean thought. She had managed to get into the rear seat and retrieve the blanket stored in the back. She pulled it around her for warmth. Her ankle throbbed and swelled, but she was unhurt otherwise. A few scratches and bruises; nothing serious.

Jean was worried about Josie. She hoped that her daughter would find shelter. It was less than two hours until dark. Nights in the mountains were cold, and Josie was not dressed for it.

The blanket dried and took the chill off Jean's shivering body. As adrenaline wore off, she fought to stay awake. The sky had begun to clear, but humidity was high. Mosquitoes were a big problem at dusk, so she didn't open the windows, and the SUV grew muggy.

Jean slipped into a restless slumber. She dreamed that she was trying to run, but her ankle was so heavy and painful that she could only drag her foot. A storm was coming. The wind roared; thunder boomed.

§

Jean startled awake as someone opened the door beside her. Her heart pounded with sudden fear, but then she remembered that Tom was dead.

"Jean, are you hurt?" asked Bob Duncan. "We found Tom Weller's body. Thank God you're alive."

Jean sat up, grabbed the back of the seat and the door frame, and lurched to the ground. When she tried to put weight on her injured foot, she began falling, Bob grabbed her arms and lowered her on the seat.

"Josie's out in the woods, Bob," Jean said. Her throat dry, Jean's voice cracked as she pleaded. "She isn't dressed for this storm, and she's trying to follow a stock trail out. We have to find her!" Jean pointed beyond the cabin in the direction of the trail.

"She's fine, Jean," said Bob. "We know where she is. She found a sheepherder's wagon a little over two miles down the trail. He had a satellite phone and called for help. That's how we found you so fast. The search and rescue team is going on ATVs right now to get her. They'll have her out safely tonight."

"That is one level-headed kid," said Bob. "You should be proud of her."

"I am," Jean said softly, tears running down her cheeks.

Jean sobbed with relief.

29

Loose ends concerning the two murders and embezzlement of Gowen and Cline, Inc. were tied up in a matter of days. Sheriff Ramirez and his deputies found the lens from Brian's broken glasses wrapped in a rag underneath the hunting knife in the back of Tom's SUV. Traces of blood at the base of the blade matched samples of Walter Norby's blood. The button Con had found under the downed tree near Brian Gowen's body was identified as belonging to a hunting jacket hanging in Tom Weller's closet. Although the jacket appeared unstained, a forensic examination revealed residual blood in its seams, identified as Brian's. While no records from the embezzled firm were discovered, a careful search of the SUV turned up a sheet of paper revealing several bank accounts where Tom had secreted the stolen funds. Gowen & Cline's attorneys were working to recover the stolen money as soon as possible.

Since that terrifying day in the woods, Con and Josie had gone on a couple dates, first to a movie and then a Saturday night dance, and they talked often on weekends when he pitched his tent at the campground. Con felt that he was partly to blame for the danger Josie had been exposed to, but Josie insisted it wasn't his fault, that her involvement had been accidental at first, then necessary.

Jean learned from Josie about how Kristi and Jim were coping. Con had told Josie that Kristi was struggling with grief over losing her husband, despite their marriage having been difficult. She and Jim were ashamed and humiliated by what Tom had done to Brian, Norby, and Jean and Josie, and their recovery would take time. Con also said that he hoped Jim's return in a few weeks to Laramie for summer football camp would help him work off his anger at his stepfather for killing his uncle and for the many years of pain Jim and his mother had endured at Tom's hands. Strenuous workouts might help begin that process, thought Jean.

Tom's actions had been a terrible blow to Kristi Weller and her son, Jim, which saddened Jean. From Sheriff Ramirez, Jean learned that Kristi had been devastated when she learned she had unwittingly supplied Tom with access to the company computer. She had suspected scurrilous behavior by her husband, but she had no solid evidence to go on before Tom spiraled into his endgame. The sheriff's good news was that the investigation proved that Kristi had nothing to do with the embezzlement or murders. Still, Kristi thought that Tom would not have killed Brian without access to the money as motivation.

Jean wasn't so sure. Tom had been so filled with hatred toward Brian that he might have used embezzlement as an excuse to facilitate the first murder. But once he crossed the boundary into criminal behavior, he lost his reason and killed Norby to silence him. Tom had jeopardized his escape by pursuing Jean and Josie rather than running with the money, and he paid for his mistake with his own life.

Soon after Tom's death, Jean made a coffee date with Cathy at Jivin' Java. As soon as Cathy walked in, Jean could see that the terrible weight Cathy had been shouldering was gone. Her skin glowed from spending time outdoors, and her dark circles and frown lines were fading. She wore a pink, short-sleeved top with white capris and sandals. Her hair shone, and she'd applied a little color to her lips.

"Hi, Jean," said Cathy. "I'm so glad you asked me to meet you."

Jean replied, smiling, "I am, too. Thanks for coming."

Cathy said, "What would you like, Jean? It's my treat."

"Thanks, Cathy!" replied Jean. "How about a blended iced mocha? It's so hot today!

Cathy approached the counter and ordered two mochas. When they were ready, she carried them to the table, the same one she and Jean had shared not so long ago.

"How are you, Jean?" asked Cathy. "I feel so awful about what Tom tried to do to you and Josie."

"We're getting back to normal, I think. We're both still having nightmares and looking over our shoulders, but we're doing less of it than right after..." Jean trailed off.

Cathy said, "You were so brave. I can't imagine how afraid you must have been."

Jean, thinking of Josie, said, "My daughter is the brave one, running from the SUV and through the forest like that. After she got away, I just did what I could." Jean looked at her hands, twisting her wedding ring around her finger.

"Jean," said Cathy, "I owe you my thanks for finding Brian's body and enduring what came afterward. Not only that, but your curiosity helped solve his murder. The life insurance company is satisfied that Brian didn't commit suicide and that I wasn't involved in his death. They're settling my claim and sending me a check this week." Cathy reached across the table to hold Jean's hand. "I'm going to be okay because of what you did," she said, gently squeezing Jean's fingers.

"Thanks for saying "curiosity" and not "snooping," Jean said with a lopsided grin. "What about Stan?" Jean asked. "Are the two of you seeing each other?"

"Yes!" replied Cathy, removing her hand from Jean's. "We're spending every minute we can together." Cathy smiled. "I love him so much. We're beginning to talk about a future together."

"That's great news," said Jean. "You and Stan deserve some happiness in your lives."

"I was very happy with Brian," said Cathy, twirling the straw in her mocha with a thumb and two fingers, "and thought that I'd never love anyone else. But Stan loves me, too. He's a good man, and he's supported me through this nightmare. I think Brian would approve." Cathy looked up, her eyes twinkling with tears, a mixture of sadness and joy.

"I've learned a lot about how the world works through this, though," said Cathy. "Stan agrees that we should maintain joint and separate finances when I inherit Brian's share in Gowen & Cline, Inc. We'll be able to collaborate, and at the same time, I'll be financially independent. I'll also take Brian's position as co-owner and have an active voice in running it." Cathy looked out the window, then at Jean. "We're keeping the firm's name the same in honor of Brian, who we both loved and respected."

"That's a beautiful way to remember him," said Jean. "I hope you'll have many wonderful years together as a couple and as business partners."

When the two women finished their drinks and chatting about ordinary things, getting to know each other better, they planned to meet again. Jean left the coffee shop to pick up her kids at the swimming pool, thinking about her and Cathy's budding friendship.

The best news of all for Jean, Chad, and Josie had been that the younger kids had returned to the campground. For a few days, Jean's mother, Natalie, staked her tent alongside the Brannings camper to reassure herself that Jean and Josie were alright. Then she broke camp, kissed and hugged everyone goodbye, and went on her way.

Jean made the most of each day with the kids by taking them fishing and hiking. Josie went into the meadow to dribble the soccer ball with Ty. She stargazed with Matt and even joined Kelsie in playing with Barbies. Together, Jean and Josie took the kids to the creek and began washing bad memories away from the place they loved by splashing and dunking each other, laughing and shrieking, and fulfilling the desire they'd had to be together with the younger kids on that fateful day.

The Branning family was together again for the remainder of the summer at Columbine Campground. Jean fervently hoped they could find a way to continue that way in the fall, but Chad had been offered the job in Saratoga and would have to make his decision soon.

Josie and Jean shouldered their responsibilities for having pursued a dangerous course by investigating the murders. Jean acknowledged that her curiosity about Brian Gowen's and Walter Norby's murders had put Josie and her family in danger. Still, she couldn't promise Chad that, given this or a similar situation, she wouldn't do it again.

§

Fourth of July was a big day in Steamboat Springs and the surrounding area. A patriotic parade kicked off the celebration with a VFW Color Guard, floats, the local high school band, horseback riders, bicyclists, and clowns winding their way along the route handing out balloons, some twisted into animal shapes. Riders on ATVs zipped around, throwing candy to kids standing at the curbs. Fire engines, old and new, blared deep-voiced horns as they inched along behind slow-moving flatbed trailers loaded with snow machines and farm equipment. Pooper-scoopers trailed the horses, saving those who marched behind them from having to either skirt or step on horse apples.

The city park filled with locals and tourists participating in community picnics, games, and skits. A craft fair lined one edge of the park, and people meandered from booth to booth, admiring workmanship and buying goods, keeping vendors busy with questions and sales. Nearby, a huge half-barrel grill, tended by a sweaty cook, turned out hot dogs and hamburgers. Cold pop, ice cream, and small bags of chips were available, too.

The Brannings spent the entire day enjoying the festivities. By the time they climbed into their van to drive to the fireworks show, everyone was tired and sunburned. A stream of cars flowed up the highway toward Steamboat Lake, where the Lions Club had prepared an elaborate pyrotechnics display. As they approached the entrance by the bandstand, a wave of sadness threatened to dampen Jean's mood, but she shook it off.

"Let's take the chairs over there where it isn't so crowded," suggested Chad, pointing away from where they had discovered Norby's body. They each grabbed a jacket and chair and trudged, as night descended, along the edge of the lake to a flat, vacant spot. Jean still limped a little from her ankle injury on the mountain, but she was recovering.

The small band that had been performing patriotic songs put away their instruments, and the bandstand lights dimmed. Event organizers began piping canned music through loudspeakers, and it floated softly through the evening. Jean recognized *Some Enchanted Evening* from *South Pacific*, a musical she loved watching. With chairs unfolded, the family sat in a small cluster to await the fireworks display's opening salvo.

Matt and Ty talked about the fireworks they had watched over Lake Loveland the year before, doubting that this year's exhibition could match it. Josie saw Jim and Kristi with Con and his parents, and she went to join them a short distance away. Kelsie perched on her dad's lap, secure in his strong, warm arms.

"I'm not scared of fireworks," Kelsie objected, as her brothers teased her. She snuggled back into her father's arms, whispering so only Chad and Jean could hear, "Well, maybe I am. A little bit."

Jean and Chad smiled at each other over the top of their little girl's head. Listening in the darkness to the people surrounding them, Jean could hear other children laughing and babies crying, and the soft rumble of the crowd chatting as they enjoyed the evening. Rising above background noises, an animated conversation nearby drew Jean's attention.

"I never would have believed that something so horrible could happen here! Why, you'd think we live in a metropolis!" said one loud, dramatic older woman.

Another elderly woman remonstrated. "Now, Gertrude, murder can happen anywhere. One never knows what another person is capable of. Why, did you hear about…"

A volley of fireworks exploded like rolling thunder, lighting the purplish sky. Sparkling grains of burning stardust drifted down toward the lake in a dance of independence.

THE END

Coming Next

Thou Shalt Not Prey
Book 2 in Jean Branning Mysteries

For news on future books, follow the author online.

Website: donnajevans.com
Facebook: https://www.facebook.com/donnajevans/
Instagram: donna4111

Acknowledgements

Thank you to my husband, David, and our nine children—Jason, Kelly, Wendy, Garin, Carrie, Lori, Logan, Cameron, and Chelsea—who listened to me talk about *Hunter on the Sly* and Jean Branning for many years. Without their positivity and support, I couldn't have completed the first draft, let alone the last. I treasure you all.

A special thanks to David for editing multiple drafts, and to Garin and Logan for reading and discussing my story as it developed. I am grateful to Kelly for the gift of a long weekend at the coast so I could read and revise my first draft.

Thank you, Cameron and Becca, for having me as your guest while I attended Left Coast Crime 2024 and for feedback on my cover design. In addition, I am grateful to Philippe for assisting me with saving my cover image in the correct file format.

As I began drafting this book, Harney Basin Writers, which met weekly at The Book Parlor in Burns, Oregon, welcomed me into their group and served as my first readers. Special appreciation goes to Katie Wendel, Peg Wallis, and the late Myrla Dean, who believed in me and cheered me on.

The English and writing faculties at Eastern Oregon University (EOU) and Washington State University (WSU), taught me sound writing processes and guided me toward my gratifying academic profession.

I am indebted to my local writing group, Grande Ronde Writers, for reading and responding to my penultimate draft. Thanks to Nancy Knowles, Amelia Ettinger, Ryan Scariano, and Susan Jardaneh, for their helpful suggestions and encouraging me to finish and publish my book.

Thanks to my colleagues and close friends, Sarah Witte, Eva Payne, and Tawnya Lubbes, for reading my final draft and encouraging me to continue writing after retirement.

To the writers and panelists at Left Coast Crime 2003 and 2024, thank you for your warm welcome and encouragement to keep going. Special thanks go to pathologist BJ Magnani, author of the Dr. Lily Robinson series, and to retired English professor, Sharon Dean, author of *Finding Freedom* and other books, who invited me into their conversations and recommended the invaluable support available through memberships in Sisters in Crime and Mystery Writers of America.

For a lifetime of recreation in verdant natural spaces, I extend gratitude to the U.S. Forest Service.

Finally, thank you to the publishers who read but rejected my work, but valued it. I am especially appreciative of one who recommended IngramSpark, which has made my indie book publication a reality.

Author

Donna J. Evans, writer and retired professor, began her adult life as a wife and stay-at-home mother, eventually having nine children, and traveling and camping with her family throughout the United States, Canada, and other countries. She started writing in earnest after moving to Oregon. Looking out her van's window on a long drive home to Colorado, the concept for *Hunter on the Sly* was born. Her love of all writing genres propelled her through bachelor's, master's, and doctoral programs, leading to a tenured university position in rhetoric and writing, and publishing academic essays, creative nonfiction, and poetry. She lives with her husband in eastern Oregon and enjoys performing on tenor sax with local concert and big bands, water and oil painting, jewelry making, and many kinds of crafting.